GETTING LEI'D

THE ESCAPE SERIES

ANN OMASTA

JOIN ANN OMASTA'S READER GROUP

The Escape Series: Aloha, Baby!, Getting Lei'd, and Cruising for Love

Get VIP access. Be the first to know about new releases, sales, freebies, and exclusive giveaways. We value your privacy and will not send spam.

Join Ann Omasta's Reader Group at annomasta.com

ALOHA, Baby!
a novella

USA TODAY BESTSELLING AUTHOR
ANN OMASTA

ALOHA, BABY!

THE ESCAPE SERIES ~ BONUS NOVELLA 0.5

regnant and alone. These are words that I never imagined would apply to me. Like everyone else I know, I had always dreamed of finding true love, getting married, and then (and only then) having a baby, and living happily ever after. That is the natural order of progression. It is the way things are supposed to go.

So, why in the world did I go and get myself into this predicament? What had I been thinking? I hadn't been thinking. That is the only explanation for my reckless behavior. I allowed myself to be swept away by romanticizing what turned out to be a dalliance, and in the process, I managed to ruin any chance I had of enjoying a 'normal' and traditional life.

The most I can hope for now is finding someone who will love not only me, but also my fatherless child. I have severely limited my options and possibly alienated my soul mate. After all, how many men are dreaming of finding their one true love, who also just happens to already be knocked up by another man? My guess is that the answer to that question is a big fat zero.

I have been dreading telling my parents about my 'situation.' They are both very conservative and traditional. They have always warned me about the dangers of falling for someone from the mainland. I'm afraid that my news will shock them immensely. Or worse yet, they'll use the ultimate parent guilt-trip phrase––*I'm disappointed in you.* Those words tend to cut particularly deep for me.

Being their only daughter, I have always tried to live up to their extremely high expectations. I've attempted to appear perfect to them, despite knowing that I am nowhere near that level. In school, I became the straight-A student, the cheerleader, the Homecoming Queen, and the lead in all of our high school drama club plays. I did all of this in the hopes of making it up to my parents for being a girl.

My brother never had to work so hard (or at all) for their love. He was praised just for being alive and male. I, however, consistently felt like they wished I had been their second son. Having heard my father speak of "an heir and a spare" more times than I care to remember, I was well aware that I wasn't the 'spare' he had dreamed of. So, I became the consummate overachiever in a desperate attempt to compensate for being born without a penis.

Not going to college had been my first overt act of rebellion. Turning down my full-ride scholarship is something for which my parents will probably never forgive me. I hadn't felt ready to leave behind everything and everyone I had ever known, especially my two lifelong best friends, Kai and Honi, to go to the mainland.

I was afraid to leave and risk losing an important part of myself in the process. Our island's culture and traditions are ingrained into my soul, but I was concerned that my distinct sense of self might become blurred if I were to leave. I didn't want to become part of the melting pot. My parents should have been proud of me for that. Unfortunately, all they focused on were the unredeemed possibilities.

Whenever the opportunity arose, they liked to point out the fact that I was still just working at 'that little hotel.' The disparaging words they used to describe the fabulously authentic resort where I worked made my blood boil. Even the fact that I have become a profit-sharing owner in the successful seaside escape didn't sway their opinions of my career choice.

Rather than admitting that I am already building a sizable nest egg through a career that fulfills me, my parents choose to point out at frequent intervals that I am a glorified maid. In some respects they are right. I do fill in for housekeeping. I also fill in for bartending, reception, grounds, and whatever else needs to be done at the time. All of the employees jump in and help out wherever we are needed. The direct result of the employees being shareholders in the resort is that we all love it as our own (because it is our own) and will do whatever it takes to make it a smashing success. After all, it's in our own best interest.

Even Kai, whose family built the resort from the ground up, isn't afraid to plunge a toilet or launder the sheets and towels. Though he runs the resort, he quickly volunteers to work in the trenches when the need arises. In return, he expects the same from the rest of our close-knit crew. We all gladly comply with anything he requests of us because he respects us and rewards us generously for our loyalty and hard work.

Honestly, it doesn't even feel like work at the resort. We all have fun and love our jobs. It's like getting to hang out with a second family that you like better than your real family. Plus, the longer we stay employed there, the more ownership percentage shares we acquire, which leads to earning more money. Talk about a win-win situation. We have yet to have our first employee/owner quit since Kai instituted the employee shareholder plan. It's that terrific of a place to work. My parents fail to see any of that, though.

Speaking of my parents, my phone is jingling with the song "Mother Knows Best" from Rapunzel's movie, *Tangled*. Mom hates the choice I made for my phone's ringtone for her, but the title perfectly describes how she feels. She seems to think that I should just do whatever she says simply because she feels that she knows better than I do. She has always been heavy on the "because I said so" reasoning in lieu of a valid explanation.

Even though she is returning my call, I chicken out and don't answer. I fully intend to tell her and my father about the pregnancy––just not right this second. I have to do it soon, though, because my body is starting to betray my secret. My belly is already protruding like I just scarfed down a jumbo basket of parmesan truffle fries. I smile to myself, realizing that I know exactly what that looks like from first-hand experience.

The supply of brown paper bags tucked away in my purse is the other dead giveaway to my pregnancy. The near-constant nausea and frequent vomiting this pregnancy has 'blessed' me with are becoming difficult to explain away. Fortunately, I've become extremely adept at quietly slipping away to a hidden corner and throwing up with minimal sound into one of my trusty bags. I guess that's fortunate, anyway. It's not exactly a skill that I had ever dreamed of mastering...Leilani, Queen of the Quiet Pukers. *I can't understand why my parents aren't proud.*

Chuckling at my silly, wayward thoughts, I am once again distracted by a song playing from my phone. This time the lyrics to "My Girl" by The Temptations are blaring to indicate an incoming call from my father. It startles me so much that I nearly drop my phone. The song brings back instant, wonderful memories of the time when I was about 10 years old and Dad was in a rare, silly mood. He danced down our hallway one morning, holding my hand and serenading me with this tune. It is one of the most splendid memories of my childhood.

I had made that his ringtone as a whimsical reminder of that day, but I had never heard it actually ringing since the day I selected it. My dad never calls. The fear that something is terribly wrong courses through me, setting off tiny explosions in my nerve endings and making my breath stop involuntarily.

"Makuakane?" I choke out the traditional Hawaiian word for father, which I know that he prefers. I can't keep the panicked edge out of my voice as I answer his call.

"Just a moment," his gruff voice comes over the line, then I hear a shuffling as he hands the phone to my mother.

"You ignored my call, but answer his??" Mother's shrill and offended voice bellows over the line.

"I'm sorry. I thought something must be wrong for him to be calling me. Is everything okay?" I ask her, still worried.

"No, everything is not *okay*," she informs me briskly. "How could everything be okay in a world where a daughter ignores her mother's calls?"

I take a deep breath and sit down, realizing that this might take a while. I let her rant for a bit about how disrespectful I am. When she pauses to take a breath, I decide it's now or never. "I have something to tell you both."

My heart thrums rapidly in my chest as I wait for her to locate and push the speaker button so I can admit my sins to both of them at once. I can hear the pulsing beat in my head as she finally figures it out and I blurt, "I'm pregnant."

Dead silence greets me. It stretches on for so long that I begin to wonder if she truly did put it on speakerphone or if she accidently hung up on me. I don't want to have to make this confession to them again.

"How can this be?" my father finally croaks. I can tell that my news has stunned him.

The question is silly, and I'm not sure how to answer it. I'm quite certain the snarky response about the logistics of the birds and the bees is not the way to go.

My mother saves me from having to answer. "Leilani Mei Kehele," her use of my full name lets me know that she is not pleased. "I thought we raised you to be a *good* girl."

And there it is. With one sharply edged comment, my mother has managed to make me feel like a complete and utter disappointment.

"I'm sorry," I finally whisper. Unable to think of anything to say to make this better, I click the *End Call* button to hang up.

Curling into the fetal position on my bed, I allow myself a long, cleansing cry.

2

*E*xhausted from my sob-fest, I fall into a deep sleep. Without the protective guard that I keep perpetually staked around my heart, I dream of him. The dream is so vivid and feels so real that even once I awaken, I have to convince myself that it hadn't really happened.

Except that it had all happened––just a few weeks prior. It had been real...to me, anyway. I had believed myself to be in love, or else I never would have behaved with such wild abandon. I thought he had loved me too. I had been willing to bet my heart on it.

When Thomas Drake had breezed into our island hotel, my immediate reaction had been distaste. *Maybe I should start trusting my gut.* He had dirty blond hair and a strong jawline. I found him to be incredibly handsome despite the pompous way he carried himself.

I was covering the front desk when he arrived to check in. I can remember every last detail of my first sighting of him. There was a balmy breeze blowing through the open concept lobby, bringing with it the faint scent of hibiscus, suntan lotion, and pineapple. He had an air of arrogance about him that only certain men from the mainland seem to display. The rakish look and suggestive wink he gave me as I worked the computer and handed him his key made me crinkle my nose in distaste.

People have always told me I am physically beautiful. Men are often quick to proposition me, based on looks alone. I have learned over time that this means nothing. True beauty resides on the inside, so someone who wants to be with me based simply on a first impression of my physical attributes (rather than getting to know me) holds no interest.

An immediate turndown of any of these superficial advances usually results in the admirer quickly moving on to the next beautiful woman that crosses his path. Thomas Drake was not so easily dissuaded.

That night at the hotel's luau, I noticed him watching every move I made during my traditional hula dance. I slowly swayed my arms and hips to the music. My movements told a story of fish swimming smoothly and synchronized in the sea as he sat motionless, mesmerized.

I was used to this type of reaction and tried to quietly exit behind the stage after Honi's beautiful ukulele song, but before the show's finale of Kai's dazzling and dangerous fire-throwing routine. Thomas was too smart for that and was waiting for me to emerge.

Attempting to brush past him, I stopped short when he called my name. He butchered it, of course. It came out like 'Laylaynee,' but I couldn't help being slightly impressed that he had remembered it at all. I hadn't mentioned my name to him at the front desk and in the show the announcer had failed to use our names *again*, despite several requests to do so. We were introduced simply as 'the lovely trio.' Thomas must have taken note when he saw it on my nametag at the front desk.

I turned to correct his pronunciation of my name and was more affected than I probably should have been by the pleading look in his eyes when he asked me to join him for a walk on the beach. Trying to hold firm because I knew where this was headed, I said that I should get going and tried to leave again.

"Please." The quietly spoken word surprised me so much that I acquiesced, still fully intending to bolt as soon as he started getting handsy.

He didn't try to grope me, though. He just wanted to talk and ask questions and learn about me. When I answered, he seemed truly interested in everything I had to say. We sat on the white sandy beach listening to the surf roll in for hours, but it felt like only minutes as we laughed and talked, getting to know each other. I kept waiting for him to try to kiss me, but it didn't happen. He was the perfect gentleman.

I felt completely shocked when the sun started to come up over the horizon. Tom had turned out to be sweet, humble, and funny––the complete opposite of the pompous jerk that I had assumed him to be.

It was a little disheartening to realize that I had been so quick to jump to an incorrect snap judgment about him. How many times had people done that to me––assuming that I was a pretty, but empty-headed shell of a person? And now I had done the same thing.

When I admitted to Tom that I had guessed he would be an arrogant jerk, he confirmed that he had believed me to be a beautiful, but bubble-headed bimbo. We both laughed about how wrong our initial conclusions had been and vowed not to be so quick to judge others in the future.

"I have to get going, or I'll be late for work," I finally decided.

"Sorry I kept you up all night," he replied sheepishly.

I informed him that it was well worth it, gave him a swift

peck on the cheek, and ran off beaming from ear to ear because I had just enjoyed the absolute best night of my life.

3

I'm not stupid. I know that flings with tourists don't generally work out. If my parents had warned me once, they had warned me a thousand times...Visitors have *real* lives to get back to on the mainland. They might be looking for a quick bit of fun in the islands of Hawaii, but they don't intend for it to last. I *know* this, yet somehow I managed to forget it.

My days with Tom were filled with laughter and fun. He seemed perfectly content just to hang out close-by while I worked. He had some project that he was working on, but he fit it in around my schedule. He'd set up his laptop at a table by the pool if I was working at the bar, chat on his cell phone in the lobby while I was at the front desk, or text like a maniac if I was acting as the hostess at the hotel buffet.

He always seemed to have time to share a funny comment, toss me a silly face, or blow me a sweet kiss. His presence made my work shifts fly by. Then, we would spend the rest of the evening together laughing, getting to know each other better, and having fun. We had held hands, but hadn't yet taken our relationship to a more physical level.

ANN OMASTA

My main worry was that he would be leaving soon. Apparently, that was everyone else's concern too, because both of my best friends since childhood, Kai and Honi, warned me to take it easy with Tom. I knew they were right, but felt physically and mentally unable to deny my growing attraction to him.

Deciding to broach the topic directly, I asked Tom one afternoon when he would be leaving. I tried to keep my voice casual, even though I was waiting with bated breath for his response.

His answer was simple. "I don't know if I'll ever have the strength to leave you." His words made me feel warm and gooey inside. When he leaned in for our first kiss on the lips, I willingly complied. The urge to push him for a more specific answer was quickly forgotten.

He was a marvelous kisser. His lips were tentative at first. After a few seconds, they grew more confident, but somehow remained soft, pliable. When he parted them to flick his tongue out, I met it with mine, and we quickly became lost in our exploration of each other's mouths. Any coherent thoughts I had about him leaving were long gone.

As luck would have it, that was a luau night, so I had to work later than usual. It pained me to be apart from him, even for a short while, but I knew he would be in the audience watching me. Watching me turned out to be a huge understatement. When I took the stage, I danced solely for Tom. Our eyes were locked together as I moved my body like the flowing wind. His lids were lowered as he gazed at me, unflinchingly enthralled.

I was tempted to look away. His steady stare was so intent that it should have made me uncomfortable. Instead, it gave me a heady feeling. I felt powerful and desirable. I wanted him to look at me like that--like I was the only woman in the world. I wanted him to want me like he had never wanted anyone else. I wanted to be his.

We had spent numerous nights together in my bungalow. He had started out sleeping curled on the hanging chair near my bed, but I had decided after the first night that it was a silly arrangement. He had joined me in my bed each night after that, but he had been an unfailing gentleman. He held me in his arms each night while we slept, but never attempted anything further.

By some unspoken mutual agreement, we both knew that this night would be different. He traced the backside of his finger along my jawline as my shaking hands attempted to work the key in the lock of my door. When he leaned in to nibble on my earlobe, the intensity of his hot breath traveling along my neck made a thrilling chill race tantalizingly down my spine.

He chuckled near my ear when the forgotten keys clattered on the tiled front porch. His laughter ended abruptly when I turned to him, taking his lips with mine in the boldest, most passionate kiss of my life. My hands found their way inside his shirt and I heard his sharp intake of breath as I smoothed them lightly up his back.

"Let's take this inside," he breathed out as he bent to retrieve the keys and made short work of unlocking and opening my door.

For a brief moment as we walked inside, I considered telling him that this would be my first time having sex. I had always considered my virginity as a badge of honor. It was something that I was willingly giving to him, but I didn't want to put any extra pressure on him. I already knew from our glorious time spent together that he would be a considerate and giving lover, but I didn't want him to feel like he had to make it perfect for me. It already felt perfect because I was with the man I was falling in love with.

Once inside, we lunged at each other, and my concerns over telling him about my innocence quickly vanished. I became swept away as we slowly explored each other's bodies with our hands and mouths.

It was my first time seeing a naked man in his fully aroused form. His erection fascinated me. It was so hard and dangerous looking, yet it had the most velvety smooth skin I had ever encountered. He groaned as I explored every inch of it.

"You have to stop doing that if you want me to make it to the main event," he gasped when I tentatively ran my tongue along the length of him.

"Did I do something wrong?" I asked, concerned that what I had done was inappropriate.

"No, Baby. You do everything right," he reassured me, even as he flipped me onto my back to show me how it felt to have my most private parts kissed.

All of my inhibitions seemed to float away in a cloud of more intense pleasure than I would have ever dreamed possible. My body writhed and pulsed as he loved me with his mouth. All conscious thought left me as every fiber of my being became focused on the ecstasy he was causing deep within me. I was completely open and exposed to him, more vulnerable than I had ever been in my life; yet I raised my lower half up higher to him, craving more of what his talented lips and tongue were offering.

I cried out in sweet release just before he kissed his way up my body and achingly slowly entered me. It took me a bit to adjust to the fullness of having him inside me. He tilted his head back to look at me, and I could see the strain on his face from holding back. "You're so tight," he grunted. At my concerned look, he added, "You feel amazing."

"First time," I panted in answer to his unasked question.

The look he gave me then absolutely melted me. He held

himself steady just gazing into my eyes, then he began dropping sweet, soft kisses down on my face. He showered my forehead, eyelids, cheeks, nose and lips with tender, loving kisses. He remained still inside me, allowing me to savor the beautiful moment.

Deciding he had held back long enough, I began to wiggle beneath him. I rubbed my hands down his shoulders and over his bare backside, cupping his firm cheeks in my palms. Slowly and deliberately, he began moving in and out of me. The friction felt amazing, tinged with the slightest bit of pain. When he reached a hand down between us to rub over me, the pain was soon forgotten, and I felt the pressure beginning to build deep inside my belly once more.

We quickly found our rhythm. When I cried out this time, pulsating around him, he let go as well as he plunged deep inside me.

We stayed like that for a long while afterwards––just enjoying the feeling of being intimately connected as one. I watched my white, linen curtains billow out, carrying in the sea breeze. My body felt as relaxed as a pool of warm wax as the delicious weight of him pressed into me. The thirst that I hadn't known lived inside me was completely satiated.

When he finally spoke, his words were wonderfully perfect and reassuring. "Thank you for giving me the unopened gift of your body. I will treasure it always." Apparently, the two of us had differing opinions on exactly what that meant.

$\mathcal{T}$he next few weeks were nothing short of glorious. We spent every moment together. We talked, we laughed, and we voraciously explored every inch of each other's bodies. We were rambunctious in our lovemaking. My fears and insecurities were long gone, and Tom proved to be a willing, knowledgeable, and sensual teacher. I thought we were falling head over heels in love.

I trusted him unconditionally. My unwavering faith in him probably made his betrayal sting even more. The fact that it seemed to come completely out of the blue didn't help matters either.

We'd just had a particularly boisterous and lengthy bout in the bedroom. It had been rowdy enough that I was certain I would blush furiously the next time I saw my neighbors, despite having closed my windows in an attempt to contain the ecstatic, uncontrollable outbursts that consistently accompanied our exuberant lovemaking. When we weren't in the heat of the moment, the thought of anyone hearing our unrestrained sounds of passion embarrassed me immensely, but not enough to tone things down with Tom. I was so enamored with him that I didn't care what anyone else thought.

Foregoing our usual post-coital cuddle session, he kissed me briskly on the forehead before arising and beginning to dress. "I need to head out tomorrow." He said the remark casually, as if he were talking about running to the store for our favorite warm, apple-cinnamon donuts.

"You mean back to the mainland?" I asked cautiously, even though my heart told me that couldn't possibly be what he meant.

"Yep." Again, his response was far too casual.

My mind was racing, seeking an explanation. Maybe he had some loose ends to tie up and he would be back in a few weeks. Or maybe he was looking for a way to ask me to come with him. I didn't want to seem too desperate and clingy, so I tried to sound nonchalant as I asked, "When will you be back?"

"I really like it here. It is a tropical paradise, after all." He swept a hand out to indicate the lush surroundings just outside my bedroom walls. "So, I'll probably make it a point to return sometime in the next few years." He finally turned to look at me, and his cold stare shocked me. This steely gaze was so different from the warm, loving looks I was so accustomed to receiving from him.

I couldn't believe what he was saying, even though his aloof stance and glare confirmed his words. "Years?" I asked, perplexed.

At his curt nod, my head jerked back as if I had been slapped. Some sad part of me was waiting for him to ask me to come with him. I didn't want to give up my life here, but I couldn't bring myself to believe that he didn't want a future with me.

"What?" His voice sounded snarky. "Did you think I would give up my home and move here to live happily ever after with you?"

I'm not sure exactly what I had thought, but yes, it was something along those lines. I couldn't admit that to him now, though. I was at a complete loss for words. My eyelids fluttered quickly as I tried to think of how to stop this nightmare from happening and attempted to keep my impending tears from spilling over.

Just as I was about to pathetically suggest that I could come visit him, he stopped me in my tracks. "It's been a fun ride, Babe, but now it's over." He sounded so casual. *Did he not realize he was crushing my heart with his cruel words?* He continued as if he had no idea the damage he was causing inside me. "It's time to get back to the *real* world."

There it was. I had just been a brief distraction to him. He hadn't had any real feelings for me. He had intended for our relationship to be temporary all along. My parents and everyone else who had warned me about falling for someone from the mainland had all been exactly right, but I had been too blinded by my own lovestruck feelings to see it.

"Bye, Babe." He said the words on his way out, without a backwards glance in my direction. I was so filled with rage that I threw my favorite vase, which had been holding three brightly hued, fragrant hibiscus flowers that Tom had given me, in his direction. He had already made his quick retreat, so the vase smashed into the door and splintered into a thousand tiny shards of glass.

*I*t was only a few weeks later when I found out that I was pregnant. Some silly, relentlessly hopeful side of me thought that when I told Tom about the baby, he would realize what a mistake he had made by leaving me.

I had retrieved his phone number from the hotel's registration computer because he hadn't bothered to give it to me directly. It wasn't technically right for me to go snooping in his file, but I felt justified due to the extenuating circumstances.

My finger shook as I dialed his number. My stomach roiled, not only with my seemingly ever-present morning sickness, but also with nerves about what his reaction to hearing from me after all this time would be. I pushed it out of my mind that he knew exactly how to get ahold of me and could have easily reached out if he'd had a change of heart. *Maybe he was nervous that I wouldn't be willing to take him back after the way he had unceremoniously dumped me?*

The wait for him to answer seemed interminable. When I finally heard his voice, it was all I could do to keep my pent-up tears from bursting out. His cool, "Yes, what do you need?" when I said my name dashed any lingering hopes of an emotional-filled reconciliation.

I matched his cool tone when I told him about the pregnancy. That jerk had the audacity to ask if it was his! He knew he took my virginity. *Did he think I had already jumped into bed with someone else? Unbelievable.*

The line was silent for so long that I was beginning to think he had hung up on me. I wish that he had because the next words out of his mouth contained an offer to pay for an abortion. My mouth literally hung open in shock at his reaction. He clearly didn't know me at all. This predicament hadn't been in my plans for the future, and it isn't how I would have chosen for things to work out, but I hadn't even considered getting an abortion.

When he told me to think about it because it could make this whole 'messy problem' go away, I hung up on him. He clearly wanted nothing to do with the baby or me, so we were better off without him. Forcing him into some sort of arrangement––financial or otherwise––would only give him a say in how the child was raised. After the way he treated me, I don't want him to have any influence in my baby's life. With his appalling reaction, he had effectively given up all rights to our unborn child. This baby will be mine and only mine. I vowed right then and there to love it with all of my heart and give it the best life I possibly can.

I am still in the fetal position on my bed, but my hand is gently rubbing over my swollen tummy. This pregnancy out of wedlock is sure to alienate me from my family. It had already proven to me that the man I loved was not at all worthy of my affection. It would also make my job more challenging. *After all, who wants to see a sexy hula dance by a huge, preggo lady with cankles?* None of that is my unborn child's fault, though, and I have already grown to love my baby unconditionally.

It's not the hand I would have chosen, but it is what I have been dealt. I will make it work, I decide, just before leaning over to throw up in the giant bowl I keep beside my bed for exactly this purpose. "You can let up on the morning, noon, and night sickness." I say the words aloud to my belly once I finish heaving. Whoever had chosen the name *morning sickness* had seriously understated its proliferation.

I get up to brush my teeth and shower, deciding that both might make me feel better. I can't stop thinking about Tom while I get cleaned up. I had neatly tucked those weeks of my life spent with him into a drawer that I had steadfastly refused to open. The dream about him opened the floodgates, and when I awoke, I had allowed myself to remember it all––the good, the bad, and the oh-so-ugly.

As I shower, bits and pieces of my life with Tom replay, dancing unwanted through my mind. I decide to allow myself this shower to ruminate over it, but once I turn off the water, I must close the door on those thoughts and feelings once more.

I can do this. I will do this. I shut off the warm water and try to let Tom go.

4

*T*hank goodness for work. It keeps me busy and distracted from the utter mess I have made of my life. I throw myself into my job, hoping that I will be so exhausted when I hit the bed at night that I won't dream of my time with Tom. I need to keep my heart closed to those memories in order to maintain my sanity.

I want to tell my two best friends, Kai and Honi, about the baby, but the timing never seems to be quite right. If I wait much longer, my protruding belly will be so obvious that they will figure it out on their own. I don't want that, though. They deserve to hear about it directly from me. After all, we are The Three Musketeers––as others have called us since grade school.

Honi prefers to refer to us as Harry, Ron, and Hermione from the Harry Potter book and movie series. His fascination with that story irks me more than a little, which is why I have never bothered to read the books or watch the movies. The fact that a grown man can be so fascinated with a children's story about magic and wizards blows my mind.

Kai used to be on my side about the whole Harry Potter

23

ridiculousness, but one night Honi convinced him to start watching the dumb movies and he became hooked. Now, they speak in some other language whenever the opportunity arises...quidditch, muggles, mudbloods, and polyjuice potion. I don't know what any of it means, nor do I care to learn. It's infuriating!

Sometimes I wish I had chosen female best friends, so we could discuss manicures, purses, shoes, and periods. Then I look at the two big lugs that have been a vital part of my life for as long as I can remember and warmth bubbles deep in my tummy. I love them both dearly, so I guess I can forgive their tendency to occasionally slip into a juvenile wizard language.

I can't seem to ever catch the two of them together to share my news. We are all too busy lately. One evening when Kai is working late, I realize as I'm leaving the resort that Honi has the night off. I make the snap decision to stop by his tiny cottage on the cliff. If he's home, I'll take it as a sign that I should tell him. I'll just make him promise not to tell anyone until I've had a chance to fill in Kai.

Even though his car is in the driveway, I find myself hoping that by some miracle Honi isn't home. I almost chicken out and leave, rationalizing with myself that I should tell both guys at once. Knowing that is a difficult feat to accomplish without other prying ears listening at work, I take a deep, calming breath and slowly trudge to Honi's door.

He is quick to answer my knock. When he realizes it's me, he breaks into one of his signature beaming smiles and engulfs me in a giant bear hug. He's big and warm and soft. His embrace feels incredibly comforting. We stand there in each other's arms for a long while. That's one of the great things about Honi...he is never in a hurry.

Finally, I force myself to pull back. "Hey, big guy," I greet him. "Whatcha up to tonight?"

24

"Just watching a movie," he informs me. One glance at the people in pointed hats and robes on the paused screen tells me he is watching one of the Harry Potter movies *again*. I roll my eyes, but bite my tongue to keep from saying anything sarcastic. It's none of my business what he watches in his free time.

Honi grabs the remote and powers off the television, clearly ready to give me his undivided attention. Suddenly, I'm overwhelmingly nervous. I can feel the sweat arising on my palms as I try to figure out how to share my news with him. I wish Kai would magically appear here. Things always seem easier with the three of us––more natural. Being alone with Honi has always made my stomach feel a little jittery.

Speaking of that, my queasiness is beginning to escalate. It's usually an unsettled feeling that stays for the most part in the background, but I can feel it starting to upheave, letting me know it is quickly going to be front and center. I put a hand over my mouth and bolt for Honi's bathroom.

I barely make it in time, so I am unable to pause to close the door behind me. As I'm hurling, I'm appalled to feel Honi behind me, lifting my long dark hair away from the back of my neck. The cool air on my neck feels delightful, but I do not want Honi to see this. I use one hand to shoo him away, even as the convulsions wrack my body, but he ignores me.

As soon as I finish, Honi retrieves a washcloth from his linen closet and lets cold water run over it. I'm mortified that I have thrown up in front of him, but allow him to help me up. He places his beefy arm around me, and we walk gingerly to the couch together.

Once seated, he gives me a concerned look as he hands me the cool washcloth. "Feeling better?"

"Yeah," I confirm, before adding, "Sorry about that. I didn't mean to walk into your house and vomit." I swipe the wet cloth over my face before setting it down.

"I know I haven't gotten around to cleaning this week, but I didn't think it was that bad in here," he teases me gently. I smile at his lame joke. Turning serious, he asks, "You okay?"

I nod with the intention of saying yes, but I can feel the unwanted tears beginning to surface before I am able to utter the word. I shouldn't have come to see Honi. He is too kind...too loyal...too understanding. I don't want to admit to him the sticky situation I have gotten myself into. Shame and embarrassment flood my system. My fight or flight response kicks in, and I try to bolt out of my seat.

Honi reaches out and grabs my arm before gently pulling me back down to the sofa. "Tell me."

His request is simple enough, but I struggle with a way to say what needs to be said. Finally, I decide to opt for direct and quick. "I'm pregnant and Tom wants nothing to do with me or the baby," I blurt.

"I'll kill him." It is exactly the reaction I had been expecting, although gentle Honi doesn't have a violent bone in his body. He might look like a sumo wrestler, but he is, in actuality, a giant teddy bear. I know that he will do whatever it takes to protect me, though. He is the most loyal person I know.

Not wanting him to do anything he will regret, I shake my head vehemently. "No." I say the word firmly-- adamantly letting him know in no uncertain terms that he is not to go after Tom. "He has made his choice, and he is the one who will be missing out." I lift my chin slightly, adding weight to my words.

Honi nods slightly, seeming to accept my declaration, so I continue. "I will raise this baby alone. I might not have any idea what I am doing, but I already love this child." I place a protective hand on my belly. "I'll figure the rest out." I sound confident, even though I don't feel it at all.

Honi tenderly places his huge hand over mine on my stomach. "You don't have to do this alone," he reassures me.

I had known that he and Kai would be there for me, but hearing his verbal confirmation felt like a soothing balm to my raw nerves. "You and Kai will make terrific uncles." I smile at him.

"If that's what you wish." He is looking at me intently. I sense that there is more that he wants to say, but he remains silent.

"Of course," I confirm. "The baby will need some male influences in its life. I can't think of any better ones than you and Kai," I tell him honestly. "I hope that you will both be a key part of this baby's life."

He nods, but remains silent as though deep in thought. When he finally speaks, his words blow me away. "I will be as involved in your baby's life as you'll allow, Lani." He is one of only two people on earth who are allowed to call me that. Somehow, the shortened moniker has never bothered me coming from Honi or Kai.

His silence stretches on again. He opens his mouth a couple of times to continue, but seems to rethink it each time. Eventually, he speaks. "I'll raise this baby with you, if you'll have me."

His offer is impossibly sweet. He is such a good friend that he is willing to forego his life goals in order to help me with my predicament. I don't know why his quick and unselfish reaction surprises me. It shouldn't. That is the kind of upstanding, thoughtful, giving man that Honi is. His response is the one that I *should* have received from the father of my baby. Apparently, I have spent my entire life surrounded by the right kind of man, yet still somehow managed to choose Mr. Wrong...Mr. Horribly Painfully Wrong.

While Honi's offer is tempting to accept, I can't be that

kind of dead weight on his life. He deserves to be with someone who chooses him and wants to be with him. He should get to raise his own child––not a deadbeat father's.

He is looking at me anxiously...probably in fear that I will take him up on his generous suggestion. I decide to relieve him of any doubt. "No, but thank you. It was incredibly kind of you to volunteer." *Does he look disappointed?* "You're an unbelievably kind man," I add to soften the rejection of his big-hearted proposal.

We sit in silence for a while, each lost in our own thoughts. When he finally speaks, his words astound me again. "If you don't want to be with me, I understand." I shake my head, intending to clarify my meaning, but he continues before I can. "I still want to be an enormous part of this baby's life. I'll even raise it on my own, if that is what you want, and I promise to love it like my own child."

I am stunned into silence. *Why would he be willing to do this? I know he is a wonderful friend, but this is way above and beyond the bonds of friendship.*

Answering my unasked question, Honi continues. "You are meant for greatness, Lani. I don't want anything to get in your way." I wonder what he means by this, but before I can ask, he goes on. "I'm just an average fellow, but I will make a superb father. If you're not ready to be a parent, I am, and I will. I'm fully committed, and I will love this baby with all of my heart."

His big-hearted offer flabbergasts me. I know that he cares deeply for me, as I do him. I also know that one day he will make a fantastic father. Why he would be willing to step in and act as my baby's father is beyond me, though. It is so far above and beyond what I would have expected him to say that I am uncertain of exactly how to respond.

We are silent for a bit before he adds, "We can even tell people I am the baby's biological father if it will help explain my level of involvement." Seeming to rethink this, he quickly says, "If you won't be embarrassed to have people think you were intimate with me."

My eyes dart to him then. *Is that really what he thinks?* I wonder. He gives me a sad smile and indicates his hefty body. Then he mutters, "I'm not exactly your type," letting me know that is exactly what he believes.

Wanting to set him straight immediately, I say, "Honi, any woman would be lucky to have you——including me." I smile shyly and feel my cheeks burning over the last part.

He shakes his head at my reassurance. "I know that I don't have Kai's looks or charm. In fact, me and everyone else we know can't believe that the two of you haven't gotten together. He's a perfect match for you."

Kai is undeniably gorgeous. There is no refuting that. Honi is not as traditionally good-looking, but he is hand- some in his own right. His sweet, big-hearted, gentle soul serves to make him even more attractive. I start to tell him that, but sense that he won't believe me.

"Kai and I are just friends," I utter for what seems like the thousandth time. Everyone seems to make that same misguided assumption, but I hadn't thought Honi would. He knows the two of us too well. He nods, but I'm uncertain if he truly believes me.

"Just like you and I are——the best of friends." I place my hand over his before continuing. "Which is why I could never accept your wonderful and benevolent offer." He starts to object, but I raise my other hand to stop him. "It is an impos- sibly generous suggestion, and I'm beyond tempted to take you up on it, but I can't take away your chance at love and happiness. It wouldn't be fair."

"It's my choice," Honi objects before adding, "besides, I do love you, and I'll love your baby. We could all be happy together."

I realize that I need to leave before he talks me into accepting his offer. It seems like the best possible outcome from the situation I have created, but I can't do that to Honi. I won't. He deserves to follow his destined path for finding love and nurturing a family, instead of fixing up my mess.

"I love you, too," I tell him honestly. His eyes light up at my words. "You are the most amazing friend I could ask for." I have to look away when I see his hurt expression. Hurting Honi is the last thing in the world I would ever want. I quickly continue. "That's why I cannot take you up on your offer. It would be taking advantage of your kindness, and I refuse to do that. I got myself into this mess, and now it's time to pay for my sins. You deserve so much more than I can give you."

With that, I get up and turn to leave. Honi stops me in my tracks by saying, "I'm always here if you need me. I'd do anything for you."

I have no doubt in the sincerity of his words, which is exactly why I can't let him. It is so tempting to stay here and let Honi comfort me. I know that he would take care of me and my baby, but that wouldn't be right or fair to him. I'm glad my back is turned, so he can't see my face crumple to tears as I walk out his door and shut it behind me. It is one of the hardest things I have ever had to do.

Once in my car, I allow the tears to flow freely. I know in my heart that I have done the right thing, but it still feels horribly, wretchedly wrong.

5

The next day, I wake up and realize that I have to tell Kai about the baby before someone else does. I try to push Honi and his wonderful offer out of my head as I shower and get ready for the day. Determined, I decide that I *will* track down Kai and share my news with him today, even if I have to resort to stalking him. Our beachside resort isn't that big...he won't be able to hide for long.

The quest for Kai gives me something to think about, other than the what-could-have-beens that keep flashing in my head regarding Honi. I'm certain that the mental image of the two of us happily caring for a cooing baby is just my mind playing tricks on me. *Honi feels obligated as one of my best friends to offer to help me out of a tough situation. I can't accept his overly generous gift with a clear conscience. It is too much to ask.* I have to keep reminding myself of these facts because I'm tempted to call Honi and tell him that I would love to raise the baby with him.

I search nearly the entire property, but can't seem to locate Kai. I'm fairly certain that he's not in the restaurant, but that is the only place I haven't been. I had been putting off going there because I know Honi is in there waiting tables. Promising myself to remain strong, I take a deep breath and enter the building.

Immediately, I hear Honi's distinctive high-pitched laugh and spot him chatting it up with the three new arrivals who seem to have taken the resort by storm. Rumor has it that the tall, beautiful one showed up here wearing a tattered wedding gown. Kai has been sniffing around her ever since. The cute, bubbly sister and wild, outspoken grandmother who came with the jilted bride have already been managing to stir up trouble everywhere they go.

I shake my head, deciding that I'll have to get the scoop on these three characters later. Right now, I have one more person to tell about my pregnancy before he hears it from someone else. Not seeing any sign of the man in question, I rush over to Honi.

Grabbing his arm to steal his attention from the three troublemakers he is waiting on, I say, "Honi, do you know where Kai is? I need to talk to him." I don't bother explaining what it is about because Honi is already aware, and I don't need any input from the three busybodies that are currently gawking at me with wide-eyed stares.

I can't help but notice the disappointed look that flashes on the face of Kai's rumored infatuation at my mention of his name, but I don't have time right now to clear things up with her. Besides, he really doesn't need to be getting too involved with a tourist––especially not one who was ready to walk down the aisle with another man.

Then again, considering my current situation, who am I to judge when it comes to matters of the heart? It would be difficult for anyone to mess up things more royally than I have somehow managed to.

Honi doesn't have any suggestions for Kai's whereabouts that I haven't already tried, so I give up. Either I will run into him sometime today, or I'll see him tonight at the luau. I just hope no one spills the beans (or baby formula)––I grin at the silly joke that popped into my head––before I have a chance to tell him myself.

The front desk is extremely busy with check-outs, check-ins, questions about the area, and calls for reservations. The steady stream of requests doesn't let up all day, so I am surprised when I hear the announcer start the luau.

The evening shift had arrived earlier, but we had been so overwhelmed with guests that I hadn't left. Not wanting to be late for my dance, I race quickly outside to the grove, yanking off my floral front-desk sweater as I go. An older gentleman stops to watch me run past. He cups his hands to yell, "Feel free to take off the other shirt, too."

I wait until I'm backstage to do that. Having done the show more times than I can count, I have become a quick-change artist. I hide in a corner so I can discreetly slip into my coconut bra and grass skirt. Standing behind the other girls at the mirror, I slick some lip-gloss over my pout, pinch my cheeks, tousle my long raven-colored hair, and am ready to go on stage with fifteen seconds to spare.

Once my dance is over, I stand just offstage watching the other acts. When Kai finishes his dazzling fire-throwing routine, I'll be here to intercept him. *He is not getting away without hearing my news*, I vow to myself. I just hope that someone hasn't beaten me to the punch.

After his death-defying act, Kai returns backstage, immune to the raucous applause from the audience. He smiles warmly at me before moving to slide past. I am certain he intends to go find the disheveled bride––*I really need to find out her name*. I had been watching her from backstage while Kai performed. She had been absolutely captivated by him. She will have to wait her turn, though. I need him now.

Grabbing his arm, I say, "We need to talk."

He follows me unquestioningly. Deciding we need to get away from people, I head out towards the pristine beach, which is now shrouded in darkness. I'm fairly certain that he doesn't already know about the pregnancy, or he would have tracked me down...likely to give me a lecture. Kai thinks of himself as my big brother—much more than my *actual* big brother does. Most of the time, I like his tendency to watch over me. When I'm getting ready to confess that I am pregnant by a man who wants nothing to do with me, or the child, I'd prefer he wasn't quite so protective.

We reach the smooth sand, and I turn to tell him. Suddenly, my throat is as dry as a sauna in the Sahara. Kai lifts his eyebrows, clearly wanting me to get on with it. "Umm," I start. I scratch my forehead nervously. This isn't exactly the eloquent speech I had planned.

"I'm pregnant." For two such simple words, they sure have a way of knocking the wind right out of people. Kai looks like I have just punched him in the gut.

"The tourist?" He spits the word out like it pains his mouth to even utter it.

He already knows the answer to his question, but I nod in confirmation anyway. "I'm going to kill him."

I can't refrain from smiling. Kai's bullheaded initial reaction identically mirrors Honi's. They are two peas in a pod, and I am so lucky to have them in my life.

"That's not the answer," I remind him.

"Does he know? Is he coming back here? Are you moving away?" I can practically see the wheels turning as Kai works to process my news. A panicked look crosses his face at the last question.

"He knows, and he wants nothing to do with me or the baby." The anger is bellowing off of him in waves. I wouldn't be a bit surprised to see steam spout from his ears.

"Don't worry," I tell him. "I'll figure it out and make it work." I sound more confident than I feel.

"Does Honi know?" At my nod, he asks, "Is he okay?"

What an odd question. Shouldn't he be asking if I'm okay? I'm a little taken aback by his concern for Honi. It seems misplaced. *Maybe he isn't thinking quite clearly. He hasn't had a chance to process the bombshell I just dropped on him.*

"Honi is fine." I answer a little more sharply than I intended to. "Except that he's gone a little loopy and offered to raise the baby with me."

Kai's face turns pale. "Did you let him down easy?"

"Let him down? I'm sure he was relieved to be let off the hook." At Kai's serious look, I continue. "He was only offering out of some misguided notion that it's the right thing for a friend to do. I could never let him make that big of a sacrifice for me."

"Maybe he wouldn't consider it a sacrifice," Kai inserts before changing topics. "Are you sure you want to keep the baby? This can't be how you wanted your life to turn out. This is a game-changer. There are other options."

This is so *not* the reaction that I had been expecting from brave, always-do-the-right-thing Kai. I feel as though he has slapped me in the face. I had briefly considered giving the baby up for adoption when I first found out, but since accepting the news, I had grown to love the life that is growing inside me. I'm shocked that Kai would suggest that I not keep it. "This baby is the most important thing in the world to me, Kai." I inform him. "I'm *not* giving it up," I say vehemently before turning away from him and running back towards the resort.

ANN OMASTA

I notice Kai's rumored lady friend squatting behind a bush not far down the path. Wondering if she was within earshot for all or part of our conversation, I briefly consider stopping to explain. Deciding that she is Kai's problem and that she really shouldn't be spying on people anyway, I keep going.

6

*W*ell, I have officially informed everyone with whom I felt the responsibility to personally share my news. My parents will take care of notifying my brother, if they haven't already. He and I aren't exactly close. I wonder sometimes if his lack of concern for my well-being stems from jealousy over my strong bonds with Kai and Honi. They are better 'brothers' to me than he could ever dream of being. Shrugging my shoulders, I decide it's too late to worry about his feelings about my lifelong friends now. It's not like I could give them up if he wanted me to. I wouldn't even consider it.

I thought I would feel enormous relief at having those closest to me know the secret I had been keeping for what seems like forever, but hasn't actually been all that long. Instead, the weight on my chest feels as elephant-like as ever. *Maybe it is just heartburn, and I'm confusing the feeling with anxiety?* Having never before experienced heartburn, I can't be certain, but it sounds like a good description for my current state.

I have the morning off, but I refuse to sit around moping.

ANN OMASTA

Realizing that sometimes a lady just needs her daddy, I decide to pop by to visit mine at the pineapple plantation where he has worked his entire adult life.

My nerves are jittery, and I begin to feel completely frazzled as I drive. I know my father is not pleased with me, but I can't allow my poor judgment to erect a wall in our relationship. It is my responsibility to reach out and make things right with him. The frightening question that keeps floating unwanted to the front of my brain is—*What if he shuns me?* My father is a proud man. If he decides that I have brought shame onto our family, he will not be quick to forgive and he will never forget.

Since I have the windows rolled down on my little Honda to let the unseasonably cool breeze waft over me as I drive, I smell the fresh pineapples long before I see the plantation. The aroma is sweet and familiar. It reminds me of my father and makes me grin, despite my qualms. I inhale deeply and assure myself that this will work out. It has to.

He will forgive me. I make this my mantra as I find a spot to squeeze into in the busy parking lot. My father has always been the undisputed leader in our household. It makes my feminine hackles rise a little, but I try not to be too judgmental of them. If he finds it in his heart to forgive me, my mother will follow suit. It's just the way they operate, and it seems to work well for them.

I don't bother heading out to the fields because I can tell by the large crowd gathered around the tasting booth that my father is working his magic. He has a real knack for entertaining the inquisitive tourists that come to visit the plantation each day.

Scooting into a space towards the back of the crowd, I watch my father perform his shtick. Even though I've seen him do this same routine dozens of times, I never tire of watching. His dark eyes gleam as he chooses an unsuspecting tourist to razz a little. He finds his prey––a tall man whose wife and kids clap excitedly. The man looks thrilled that he has been selected.

The man waves to his family as he joins my father at the counter and faces the crowd. Rather stiffly, he states his name and declares himself to be from Kansas City before my father asks him to help prepare some pineapples for the gathered crowd to sample. The unsuspecting man quickly agrees. My father hands him a sharp knife with an appropriate warning not to chop off any appendages. This earns him a horrified look from the man's wife and a few chuckles that murmur through the audience.

I sense when my father spots me in the crowd. I can feel his eyes bore into me for a moment before he jumps back into his routine, without missing a beat. I don't know what to make of his initial reaction to my being there. He hadn't graced me with the loving smile that usually accompanies my visits. I swallow the lump in my throat while willing myself not to throw up and ruin the pineapple tasting.

The counter has been set up in advance. Each man has a cutting board and five pineapples. "Would you be so kind as to slice these five juicy and delicious pineapples for our guests to enjoy?"

The man nods agreeably, so my father sets about the business of showing him how it's done. After slicing the top off his first pineapple, my dad cuts through the thick rind and fruit so quickly his knife almost blurs. He places his perfectly proportioned pieces on a serving tray and gestures to the crowd as if to say 'ta-da,' without actually saying a word. The onlookers clap appropriately at his adept handiwork.

Having made the feat look utterly effortless, my father indicates the man standing beside him, letting him know it's his turn. Looking overly confident, the man attempts to slice his first pineapple. Of course, it isn't nearly as easy as my father has made it look--with his thirty years of experience on his side.

The crowd giggles as expected as my father slices two additional pineapples, while the good-natured tourist continues to struggle with his first. Pretending to have figured out the problem, my father over exaggerates his motions as he makes a production of trading knives with the man. Naturally, this doesn't help a bit.

My father now has all of his pineapples perfectly sliced, while the tourist only has a few unevenly cut pieces from his first. Jovially taking over, my father makes short work of the rest of the pineapples and suggests that the man 'stick with his day job.'

To prove that his heckling has all been in good fun, Dad has the crowd cheer for the man as he sheepishly returns to the audience. He then makes a point to let everyone know that this man and his family will be awarded the first samples of the freshly cut fruit. Everyone laughs again when the family comes forward, and he hands them the awkwardly cut slices the man had managed to finish.

Slices are passed all around, as well as napkins to catch the juice now sliding down several people's chins. I hear several murmurs about the delicious fruit. Most are along the lines of it being the sweetest, most flavorful fruit they have ever tasted. I smile, knowing exactly how they feel. Even with as much fresh pineapple as I've eaten over my lifetime, I'm still awed by its wonderful flavor.

Once the crowd disperses to tour the plantation by trolley or peruse the gift shop, I am left alone with my father. I watch him methodically wipe the counter clean of sticky pineapple juice. Since I know that he will want to have his say first--after the bombshell news I dropped on him--I wait for him to talk.

He finally speaks, without looking up. "I'm glad you came, Keiki."

Relief courses through me at his words. Even if he is still angry, it is clear that I will eventually be forgiven. The fear that he wouldn't be able or willing to ever let my perceived betrayal go had been weighing heavily on me since finding out about my pregnancy. I hadn't realized how much I had been worried about it, until he released me of that burden.

Smiling, I wait for him to close the tasting booth and join me. He opens his arms wide and engulfs me in a wonderful hug. Tears of gratitude spring unwanted into my eyes at his loving reaction. He is being much more understanding than I would have ever imagined possible. I manage to keep my tears from spilling over, but it takes all of my concentration.

When he pulls back, he says, "I'm not old enough to be a tutu kane, am I?" His eyes are twinkling, letting me know that he is teasing. He is, of course, plenty old enough to be a grandfather, but I decide that right now might not be the best time to point that fact out to him.

He suggests that I find us a seat outside, while he goes to the snack bar to get us ice cream cones. When I mention that it's a little early for the frozen treat, he waves off my concern by saying, "It's always a good time for ice cream." I can't argue with that logic, so I go save us a spot at an umbrella table.

He brings me what has been one of my favorite treats since childhood––pineapple soft-serve with coconut shavings on top. It is just as delicious as I remember, and it brings back a flood of wonderful memories of visiting my Dad at work. I hope that my child will one day be able to do the same.

Interrupting my thoughts, Dad asks, "So, are you hoping for a boy or a girl?"

The question catches me off guard because I haven't really thought about it. Usually, when I think about the baby, it is as just that––a baby. Gender hasn't made its way into my daydreams yet. I pause to allow myself to ponder his question. I'm fairly certain my father would prefer a boy. I visualize a dirty, gap-toothed, adorable little boy climbing onto my lap for sweet snuggles before running off to his next adventure. The mental image makes me smile. Next, I ponder getting a pedicure next to a ruffly, sparkly pint-sized princess. Having my own mini-me would be so much fun.

"I...I don't know." I answer my father's question honestly. "Either would be fine, I guess." As an afterthought, I add, "As long as it's healthy." My dad says the tired phrase along with me.

"Well, no matter what sex the baby is," he continues, his voice sounding much more stern, "it needs a father." I had known this was coming, but I wasn't sure what I could say or do about the lack-of-a-father situation at this point. He saves me from having to answer by continuing with his own train of thought. Shaking a finger at me, he adds, "Not that shaka-tossing douchebag, either."

I can't help bursting into laughter at my father's out-of-character proclamation. Never in my wildest dreams would I have ever believed that I would hear my dad utter the word 'douchebag.' Tom had been fond of greeting people with the hang-loose hand symbol––thumb and pinkie up. I should have realized that my father wouldn't appreciate a mainlander coming here and thinking he knew our culture or heritage well enough to even understand what the shaka means, let alone having the audacity to flash it to everyone he meets. I guess love, or rather what I had mistaken as love, really did make me blind.

Once my giggles subside, I nod at my dad, who seems to be waiting for an answer regarding the baby-needs-a-father issue. The vague gesture must have appeased him because he stands and pulls me up for another hug. "Mahalo, Makuakane," I tell him, and I mean it.

"You're welcome, sweet girl. Now let me get back to work before I get fired for visiting with my ohana all day." With that, he is gone.

I watch him put on his visor hat and walk out to the field. I am surprised by how easily he has forgiven me. I also know that my mother will follow his lead. Since he has pardoned my indiscretion, she will too. My brother is probably too busy catching the next wave to care either way, but it is wonderful to know that my ohana supports me. Family is everything to me––both the one I was born into and the two men who are my lifelong friends and chosen family.

Feeling abundantly blessed, I drive back to the resort. If I had known what the next twenty-four hours would bring, I would have stayed with my dad.

7

*I*t is still only mid-morning when I return to the resort. Kai's reaction to my pregnancy news keeps swirling through my mind. *Why had he asked if Honi was okay? When I told him about Honi's crazy idea to raise the baby with me, what made him ask if I had let him down easy? Hadn't Honi just made the offer to be a good friend? He couldn't possibly really want to do this, could he?* I have far more burning questions than answers.

Having thought about my situation the entire drive back, I decide to take advantage of the mid-day lull between breakfast and lunch when guests are getting cleaned up and making their plans for the day. I track down Honi and Kai to let them know we need a trio powwow.

They both follow me unquestioningly out to the beach. Seizing the opportunity to indulge in the best loofa in the world, I remove my shoes and let my toes sink into the fine, pale sand. It feels luxurious, so I attempt to focus on that, rather than the potentially life-altering discussion I am about to have.

Even though they both probably have a million other

things they could be doing, neither man attempts to rush me into talking. We all gaze out at the crystal-clear turquoise water, watching the foamy waves crash into shore. A dark cloud is making its way to our island, likely bringing with it a twenty-minute shower of cooling, life-sustaining rain. To look at the three of us, a bystander would think we have all the time in the world. Knowing that we don't, I take a deep breath and dive in.

"You're probably wondering why I called you out here." It had been a while since any of us had called an official meeting. They nod, but patiently wait for me to continue. "I've been doing a lot of thinking." This fact was probably already painfully obvious to them, especially considering my current condition, but they refrain from saying so.

"I've been thinking about Honi's generous offer to help raise my baby." I can feel Honi's eyes intently boring into me, but I am not looking at him. I am watching Kai, trying to gauge his reaction. Kai's face will let me know if I am overstepping my bounds. I don't want to take advantage of Honi's kindness, and it is hard to tell if my desperate situation is clouding my judgment. Unfortunately, Kai is hard to read as he watches Honi. We probably look like a ridiculous triangle––each of us looking at another, desperate to know what the person is thinking––no one returning the gaze.

Swallowing the lump in my throat, I forge on. "If you are still willing, I would love for us to raise this baby together." My heart is hammering in my chest as I turn to Honi. The hope-filled look in his deep brown eyes melts me as I silently pray that I am doing the right thing for all of us.

I can see tears glistening as Honi nods at me in silent affirmation of our agreement. Deciding to give him one last chance to back out, I rush on. "I don't want to take advantage of you or our friendship." Taking his hand, I plead with him.

"If you are just doing this for me, please don't. I only want to accept your offer, if it's what *you* want."

"It's what I want," Honi confirms. His voice sounds croaky, filled with emotion.

Deciding to point out the major flaw with our plan, in case he hasn't fully considered it, I ask, "What about your future wife? What will she think about you having so much baggage––a child and best friend who also happens to be the mother of your child?"

For the first time since we started this discussion, Honi breaks his gaze from me. Looking down, he seems to be pondering what his response should be. I wait anxiously, desperately hoping that I hadn't just talked him out of joining me in this adventure. I turn to Kai, but he is still staring intently at Honi, so I do the same.

"Well," Honi arcs his sandaled foot back and forth in the sand before raising his eyes to me, "I guess she'll just have to deal with it because you and this baby are an enormous and important part of my life, and you always will be."

I feel like bursting with joy when Honi blesses me with one of his trademark ear-to-ear beaming smiles. He looks so happy that Kai and I can't help but join him. We stand there for a bit, grinning goofily at one another.

Being the ever-practical one, Kai breaks up our giddy revelry. "Okay, we need to hatch a plan." Unsure what he means, Honi and I both turn to him for clarification. "We need to decide on the backstory. What is our party line? Everyone saw Lani with Thomas. Do we want to admit he is the father? Or should we say the baby is Honi's? People will wonder why Honi is so involved in the baby's life. Should we say that you two dated for a bit and broke things off? What are we going to tell the baby when it is old enough to start asking questions about its father? We need to try to keep the damage to Lani's reputation to a minimum." He pauses to look at me then, knowing that I wouldn't appreciate the fact that our community judges women so harshly. Knowing that it is just a fact of life in our social circle, I nod at him sadly and he continues. "It is essential that we decide what we want people to believe and that we all stick with the story we agree upon."

Clearly Kai had already given this a lot of thought. He had raised some excellent points. "Shouldn't we just stick with the truth?" I ask them.

Honi turns to me. "Are you certain that Thomas won't decide later that he wants to be a part of the baby's life?" He spat Tom's name like it physically pained him to utter the word.

"I'm positive." I nod sadly to add even more emphasis to my affirmation.

The three of us remain lost in our own thoughts until Honi weighs in with his opinion. "I think, if it's okay with you," he turns to look directly at me, our hands still inter-locked, "that the baby should be mine. Otherwise, everyone will wonder why I am so involved. It also saves you the embarrassment of having people speculate about the baby's 'real' father."

I am surprised by his answer. He is obviously fully committed to his decision. There won't be any backing out of it once people think he is the baby's father.

"Lots of people know she was with Tom," Kai points out. "Do we really want them thinking she was fooling around with him, then quickly jumped into your bed?"

They are talking about me and my situation like I am not even here. I don't like it. "No one knows for sure that I was with Tom physically, other than my parents." Thinking about their reaction, I decide, "They would be thrilled to not have to admit their daughter is knocked up and has been dumped by a mainlander."

"The optics are better if we say Honi is the father," Kai weighs in. "People will forget all about Tom soon enough. The story can be that you guys went on a couple of dates, things went too far one night, you mutually decided you are better off as just friends, but Lani was already pregnant. Honi is stepping up to do the right thing. Lani just had a momentary lapse in judgment with a lifelong friend. The baby ends up with a doting father who is a major part of its life. I think it's the best case scenario for everyone involved."

I am not fond of the way Kai is talking about this like a tactical military operation. I had wanted him here for his unbiased opinion, but now that he is giving his thoughts, it feels like he is overstepping his bounds. Ignoring him, I focus on Honi. "What if you change your mind down the road? What if you want a family of your own, and we hold you back?"

"I won't change my mind," Honi reassures me vehemently. "I want to be the father to your baby." He seems so sincere. I want to believe him, but it seems too good to be true. *Why would he want to do this? Is he giving up too much?*

"There's only one problem with this plan," Honi decides. I'm sure that he is rethinking his willingness to tie himself so permanently to me, and my child, but instead he says, "Who would believe that Lani would be intimate with me?" He indicates his large frame.

His words break my heart. Honi has always been overly self-conscious about his size and his high-pitched voice, but I hadn't realized that he felt undesirable. We all have aspects of ourselves that we judge too harshly and find to be inferior, but most people manage to believe that someone will love them, flaws and all. *Are Honi's insecurities so deeply ingrained that he finds himself to be unlovable? Does he really believe I wouldn't want to be with him because of his physical characteristics?*

Wanting to immediately tamp down his self-loathing, I say honestly, "Honi, any woman would be lucky to be with you––including me." He is looking down, so I squeeze his hand with mine to relay the sincerity of my words. "You are the most kind, generous, loving, hilarious, talented, dorky," his head pops up at the last one, but I finish my sentence, "man I know."

"You were doing great, until you got to the 'dorky' part," Kai informs me.

"Well, you're right there with him on the high end of the dorkiness scale now that he has converted you into a wizarding-world fiend."

They both chuckle at my ribbing, and it lightens the mood considerably. We are on more familiar territory now. They are used to me making fun of their Harry Potter obsession. "You don't know what you are missing," Kai informs me, taking my other hand. The three of us turn to walk slowly back to the resort. Flanked on either side by my two best friends, I feel safe and loved. I am confident that I am giving my baby the best possible version of the future.

When we reach the resort's pool area, it is time to part ways. By some unspoken agreement, we do the secret Three Musketeers handshake, which we haven't done since elementary school. With that gesture, our agreement on our version of the truth is sealed.

8

I feel great about our plan. We all have my baby's best interests at heart, and it feels like we are giving him or her the best possible outcome from an unfortunate situation. I silently amend my thought. I am so used to thinking of the baby as mine, but now I need to start referring to it as ours——mine and Honi's. It is almost too good to be true.

Honi will make an excellent father. He has an almost childlike exuberance for life that will be wonderful to share with our little one. He is patient, kind, honest, giving, and fun. Our baby is lucky to have him in its life, and so am I.

Things would be as perfect as could be under the circumstances, except for the constant, niggling fear in my brain. *Is Honi giving up too much? Am I taking advantage of him? Should I have resisted the temptation to accept his offer?*

The odd sight I encounter as I travel the sand-covered path to the resort's front desk distracts me from my worry-filled train of thought. I encounter one eye warily peering around the corner of the water sports cabana. Pausing to see what is going on, I see a hand slowly rise into the air, with its thumb and pointer finger extended into a mock handgun.

Deciding whatever is happening isn't a true threat, I take a few steps forward. Just as I reach the corner of the building, the woman attached to the finger gun jumps out at me shouting, "Gotcha!"

I had been expecting a youth, due to the diminutive height of the peering eyeball and the childish antics. The tiny, silver-haired lady squints at me suspiciously, her air gun pointing in my direction. I recognize her as Kai's love interest's crazy grandma. The woman's reputation precedes her because I have already heard from several people about her wild behavior around the resort.

"You're not the Big Fettuccine," she announces, seeming perplexed. Then she cocks her head to the side, her wheels obviously turning. "Or are you?" She makes a big, sweeping motion to grab at my hair, trying to yank it off as if it is a wig.

"Ow!" I screech at her. "Stop that." I have to forcibly restrain her, but she maintains her hold on my hair. She seems stunned that it isn't a wig.

I try to be gentle as she struggles against me. Her arm feels thin and brittle in my grasp. I am distracted from holding her back when a lanky man comes running to her aid. "Did you get him?" He pants from the exertion of his brief jog.

Recognizing him as the old codger who suggested that I take off all of my clothes as I was removing my sweater on the way to the luau the other night, I am not surprised that these two oddballs have managed to find each other. "Let her go." He furrows his bushy eyebrows at me.

"Tell her to stop trying to pull out my hair," I fire back.

"This isn't the Big Fettuccine," he confirms, and for some

reason the tiny spitfire believes him and releases her hold on my hair.

I reciprocate by letting go of her arm. I hope that my grip won't leave a bruise on her thin, age-spot covered skin, but she really hadn't left me any choice. Even though she didn't seem to believe it, my hair is attached to my head.

Now that the physical roughness has died down, I get a good look at the two of them. Their scantily clad bodies both have loose, bronze skin that appears to be the texture of leather, and they reek of coconuts. The smell is so strong, I wonder if they've been rolling in coconut oil. At this point, nothing would surprise me with these two.

The man pulls the woman into his arms and assures her that she'll get the Big Fettuccine next time. He leans down to give her a sweet kiss on the cheek. I try not to notice that his hands slide down to cup her rear end as I attempt to slip around them and continue my trek to the front desk.

Shaking my head, I wonder if these two truly believe they are spies. They must have fallen from the same variety of crazy tree. Maybe the strong coconut odor emanating from them went to their heads and made them nutty. Whatever the case, I'm glad they have each other. I guess there really is someone out there for everyone.

Just when I begin to hope I have escaped any further interaction with them this morning, I hear the woman chasing after me. "Hold up," she pants as her sandals click-clack quickly behind me.

Her words make me think she might be playing with her finger gun again. Exasperated, I stop and turn around to see what she wants now. I really just want to go to work and not have to deal with any more of her shenanigans, but she is a guest at the resort, so I need to treat her respectfully.

"I have a bone to pick with you," she informs me sternly as soon as she catches up with me. Although she is nearly a foot shorter than me, she has the audacity to poke her pointer finger into my sternum as she closes in on my personal space.

She has a bone to pick with *me*?? It is all I can do to keep from losing my patience with the tiny she-devil. Instead, I raise my eyebrows in question, wondering what her problem is now.

"Are you blind?" she asks me cryptically.

"Umm, no." I have no idea what she is trying to imply, and I really don't have time for this.

"If you're not blind, why can't you see how wonderful that big hunk of man meat is?" She squints her eyes, inspecting me carefully.

I shift my stance, incredibly uncomfortable with her scrutiny and confused by her question. "What are you talking about?"

"Honi. Don't you see it?" She rolls her eyes skyward as if I am completely clueless. "That giant beefcake looks at you like you are an extra large pepperoni pizza with a hot fudge sundae on top," she informs me. "If he looked at me like that, I'd be happy to give him a taste, if you know what I'm saying." She uses her elbow to nudge my side as she waggles her eyebrows.

I am pretty sure that I do know what she is suggesting, and I prefer not to think about her and Honi together. The mental image that pops unwanted into my head is enough to make my morning sickness flare up, and I don't want to vomit pineapple ice cream on this crazy woman's feet.

She continues on as if she hasn't just made a completely inappropriate comment. She seems to be mulling over something as she taps a finger on her lips. Evidently coming to a conclusion, she informs me, "You know, he might have a little bit of dickie-do disease." At my confused frown, she continues. "That's okay, though. My first husband had a bad case of it, but we were creative and managed to work around it."

I have absolutely no idea what she is talking about. I'm not completely sure that I even *want* to know. My stomach drops at the thought that Honi might be sick, but how would this crazy bat know about it? Deciding I need clarification on what she means, I ask, "He might have what?"

"You know, dickie-do disease." She is looking at me again like I am totally dense. Leaning in, she stage whispers, "It's when their belly sticks out farther than their dickie do!"

Beyond annoyed with this utterly ridiculous and wildly outrageous woman, I turn on my heel to walk quickly away from her. I can hear her cackling loudly behind me as she yells, "Don't let that stop you, though. He's still a great catch!"

9

*T*hroughout my shift, I cannot stop thinking about my interaction with that absurd woman. My curiosity piqued, I get the scoop on her from one of my co-workers, Kalea, when she comes to visit me at the front desk while on a break from whipping up tasty delights in the restaurant's kitchen.

Kalea informs me that the crazy lady's name is Baggy. The odd moniker stands for 'Bad Grandma.' We both have a good laugh over how perfectly the name fits the person. Roxy, Kai's love interest and Baggy's granddaughter, evidently came up with the mangled name when she was just a toddler, and it was so fitting that it stuck. *Maybe this Roxy person isn't so bad,* I decide, smiling. At least she seems to see her grandmother for the troublemaker that she is.

Kalea's eyes light up as she tells me about some of the funny antics the older woman has pulled in her short time here––everything from unabashedly hitting on men a quarter her age, to shaking her coconut-bra covered tatas on the dance floor, to asking the concierge if a man's tallywacker has ever been bit off when he was skinny-dipping in the ocean. For that last one, Kalea jiggles her pointer finger in an impression of Baggy telling the shocked attendant that men's wiggly little bits look like shark bait underwater. It's obvious by her expression that Kalea is already very fond of the crazy lady. I don't get it. Baggy is obnoxious, delusional, and on the verge of being downright rude. *Why does everyone seem to like her so much?*

Shaking my head as Kalea heads back to the kitchen, I can't help but wonder what the appeal of this woman is. Deciding to find something positive to focus on, I admit that things will never be boring with her around to keep us all on our toes.

Even though the vast majority of what Baggy said annoys me, I can't stop thinking about one of her comments. She seems to be under the impression that Honi thinks of me as more than just a friend. *Could she be right, or is that just more of her crazy showing?*

All day, I attempt to tamp down my curiosity, but it just won't go away. Both Baggy and Kai have now insinuated that Honi might want a romantic relationship with me. I have never before thought about the concept of us being a couple. I keep telling myself that it's a crazy idea because taking that chance could ruin the amazing friendship we have spent so many years building, but the notion keeps popping back into my mind.

I'm sure I only keep thinking about it because of the pregnancy and Honi's generous offer to raise the baby with me. A romance between the two of us would tie things up with a nice pretty bow, but it would be for the wrong reasons. I can't be with Honi just because he is convenient and kind. I won't use him like that.

Every time I remember that woman's comments about

Honi's penis size in relationship to his belly, I become infuriated. It was so wrong of her to insinuate. Besides, what does she know about the size of his manhood? I've never before allowed myself to picture what he would look like naked, but I'd be willing to bet he doesn't have dickie-do disease. I smile at the naughty turn my thoughts have taken. It's not at all like me to think about such things at work...especially not about Honi.

Attempting to reign in my curiosity, I think about the rest of his body. Honi is big. There is no denying that. But he's not really what anyone would call fat, either. Maybe he is what would be referred to as 'big-boned.' His hands and fingers are large, he has a beefy chest as well as strong shoulders and arms. He doesn't have rock-hard abs, but his belly isn't *that* big. He also has enormous feet, which are an indicator that he most definitely does *not* suffer from that dickie-do problem. And there it is again...so much for distracting myself from thinking about his penis at work.

I'm not sure how I'll face Honi again after having spent the afternoon visualizing what he looks like naked. At least he won't know about the wayward, sensual thoughts I've been having about him. *Will he??* I'm pretty sure the guilt will creep up my face like a crimson red sign the next time I see him.

I *have* to stop thinking about this. It's like that awful woman has poisoned my brain, and now all I can think about is Honi. The same questions keep floating through my mind...*Does Honi have romantic feelings for me? Do I want him in that way? Would we make a good couple? Would a romance end up ruining our friendship? Or would it make us even better parents?*

And the unanswered questions that embarrass me the most, but keep raising their ugly heads...*His penis sticks out farther than his belly, right?? If it doesn't, what sort of 'creative' solutions was Baggy talking about? Should I get some ideas and tips from her?*

Blast that woman for making me think this way. Her crass inappropriateness has already rubbed off on me. I shake my head vigorously, trying to remove her and her unfounded musings from my brain.

It works for the rest of my shift, but I have the evening off from work, and I can't seem to stop thinking about the possibility of a relationship with Honi that goes beyond friendship. It feels like the perfect answer, but I want to be certain that I'm not overstepping or taking advantage of him in any way. *Am I just convincing myself that I have real feelings for him because it is the best possible outcome for the baby and me? Or is this real?*

The flutters in my belly feel real, but it's so sudden that I can't be certain. It could also be the first noticeable movements of our unborn child. If I'm totally honest with myself, considering the giant chicken and cheese burrito I had for dinner, it could also just be gas. I cringe a little at that unpleasant but accurate thought.

Unable to fall asleep, I decide to watch some television. On a whim, I pull up my On-Demand library and scroll through the movie selection. I find the one I want, and even while I'm whispering to myself that it's silly, I push the button to start it.

I feel stupid at first and almost stop the movie, but before I know it, I am sucked into the magical story and am shocked that so much time has passed when the credits begin rolling. "That wasn't nearly as bad as I expected," I say to no one in particular while I'm paging through the menu in search of the second installment of the series.

Excited to find it, I jump up to microwave a bag of buttery popcorn and take a quick bathroom break. Grabbing the hot popped corn bag and uncharacteristically not even bothering to pour it into a bowl, I jump back into bed, anxious to start the second flick.

Losing myself in those stupid movies, I can barely believe that I'm bawling at the end of *The Half-Blood Prince*. The first color beams of daybreak are already shining through the tiny gap between my curtains. Appalled that I stayed up all night to binge-watch the majority of the Harry Potter movies, I get up to take a shower. Crumbs from the snack-fest I partook in during the brief break between each movie fall from my pajamas as I stand.

While in the shower, I briefly consider calling in sick to work so I can stay home and watch the final two movies in the series. The idea is incredibly tempting, despite the fact that I have never done anything like that in my life. I finally manage to convince myself not to gorge my newly discovered need any further. The main reason for my self-control is because I realize that once I tell Honi I have watched the first six movies, he will likely want to watch the last two with me.

I am so anxious to share with Honi that I am now on board with the Potter series, which I have been mistakenly calling 'juvenile' for years. I can't wait to see his face––he is going to be beyond excited. I wonder if he'll want to watch the last two movies tonight. I need to sleep at some point, but I'm dying to know how everything works out. I bet he'll let me borrow his copies of the books, too. They are probably even better than the movies––as books usually are.

I'm racing around my house as I get ready, even though I should have low energy from a lack of sleep. I will probably hit a wall later in the day, but right now I am just jazzed to see Honi and share this news with him. Maybe I should figure out a way to let him know without directly telling him. I'll have to think on that one on the way to work.

Another bonus about having watched most of the movies is that I am now privy to the peculiar lingo that only people familiar with Harry Potter understand. Sometimes when the guys slip into using those words, it feels like they are speaking a completely different language. *Well no more, boys! I speak it now, too.*

On my short drive to work, I shake my head and marvel at how long it took me to come around and give the series a try. I should have taken Honi's word for it and given it a chance like Kai had, but I was simply too stubborn. Now I'm behind the curve on it, but I'm quickly catching up.

Suddenly, a thought flashes into my mind that has me super excited. I'm pretty sure that Universal has a Harry Potter branded amusement park in California. I picture Honi, our little one, and me reading the books and watching the movies together in preparation for a family trip to check out that theme park. This will be something we can all three share our enjoyment in as a family. The idea thrills me. I cannot wait to tell Honi.

I'm a little early for my shift, so I go straight to the restaurant, knowing that Honi will already be there serving breakfast. He's wearing his aquamarine uniform today, and the color suits him. The shirt features large hibiscus flowers, making it look like what tourists consider a traditional, gaudy Hawaiian shirt. He somehow makes it work though, and I pause to admire him before edging into the room.

He smiles and heads in my direction as soon as he sees me. Once he's close enough, I greet him, before saying, "I think we should start serving butterbeer here."

He nods in agreement, before what I said fully sinks in and he turns to give me a questioning look. In answer to his unasked question, I smile and add, "That slimy Professor Snape is as evil as a slithering snake."

"He's not as bad as you think," Honi advises me.

"What?!?" I screech at him, not caring that a few heads turn in our direction. "He is a horrendous person, and nothing will ever change my opinion of that," I tell him firmly.

"What number are you on?" Honi clearly thinks that my opinion of Snape might still be swayed.

"I just finished the sixth movie, and I *hate* Snape." Admittedly, I had done an about-face on my opinion of Sirius Black mid-series, but I just don't see how that could ever happen with Snape.

Honi nods at my pronouncement. "We'll see," he tells me cryptically, evidently opting not to spill any secrets about what in the world could make me change my feelings regarding that snake.

We stand there in companionable silence for a while. Deciding to tease him a bit, I say, "Why didn't you ever tell me how good they are?"

His face registers shock at first, but he quickly realizes I'm joking. "What made you finally decide to give them a try?" he asks me before blessing me with a huge grin.

"I have no idea," I answer him honestly. "I guess I pictured you reading the books and watching the movies with Little Bit, and I didn't want to be left out."

"Little Bit?" he asks, smiling. I shrug my shoulders before nodding. "I like it," his eyes are barely visible as his smile stretches nearly from one ear to the other.

I ask him about borrowing his copies of the books, and he quickly agrees, telling me that the books are far more descriptive and magical than the movies. I had been trying to restrain myself, but before I know what I'm doing, I ask the burning question that had been bothering me all morning. "Does it end okay?" Before he can answer, I blurt, "Wait. Don't tell me." Half a second later, I say, "Don't give me any spoilers, but it has a good ending, right?"

I'm afraid to hear his answer, but I don't want to wait until I'm able to watch the other two movies to see if Harry and his friends get a happy ending. Honi considers his answer carefully. I tap my foot impatiently. When he finally speaks, I wish that he hadn't. "More people die," is his cryptic answer.

"Who?" I can feel my eyes bulging as if we are talking about real people. "Wait, don't tell me." I change my mind. My thoughts are reeling through all of the possibilities. "Who dies?" I ask again. I'm completely torn between wanting to know and not wanting to ruin the surprise. The giddy antici- pation feels remarkably like Christmas morning.

Honi looks completely uncertain on how to respond. I'm sure he's wondering if I really want to know, or if it's better to make me wait. I make the decision for him. "We have to watch the last two movies tonight after work," I inform him.

"Oh, umm, tonight?" Honi uncharacteristically stammers.

With impeccable timing, Kalea sidles up behind Honi. "Did Honi tell you I'm making him some of my famous homemade lasagna tonight for dinner?" Her round face breaks into a friendly smile. She is clearly completely unaware of anything beyond friendship between Honi and me.

I feel the color drain from my face and the nausea that had stayed at bay throughout my Harry Potter marathon makes a quick reappearance. "No, he didn't mention it," I finally croak.

Honi's face is beet red, apparently all of the color I lost went to him. He looks uncertain what to say. This is obvi- ously why he had hesitated about watching the last two movies with me tonight. He has a date. I've been picturing us going on family vacations together, and he has a date with a sweet and lovely woman. *How stupid can I be?*

Seeming completely unaware of the bubbling tension, Kalea gently pats Honi's slightly protruding belly. "You know,

Leilani, they always say that the best way to a man's heart is through his tummy."

I make a feeble attempt at a smile, mumble something about needing to get to work, and hightail it out of there. At least I make it outside before my churning stomach completely revolts.

10

*H*oni tracks me down at the front desk during his mid-morning lull in the restaurant. I have been doing nothing but thinking about him and short, pretty Kalea. I keep seeing her round face in my mind's eye everywhere I look. I don't want to be jealous of her. She and Honi make a great couple. I am the one who doesn't fit into this picture. That doesn't stop me from practically turning a putrid shade of green with seething envy, though.

I'm ashamed of myself. I want Honi to be happy. I truly do. It's just that I had started picturing him being happy with me and the baby. I hadn't envisioned him going out on dates, although I probably should have.

When I see him nervously messing with his hands as he approaches the desk, I feel even worse. Honi is never anxious about anything. He is normally the epitome of the stereotypical laid-back islander. I'm appalled that I've made him uncomfortable. He has bent over backwards to help me out of a tough situation, and I have somehow managed to make him feel guilty in the process.

"Hi," he gives me a sweet smile, but his Adam's apple bobs

when he swallows, betraying his nervousness. He's silent for a while, but I'm at a loss for what to say, so I remain quiet. Finally, looking down, he says, "I won't go out with Kalea, if it bothers you."

I am aware that my reaction is important, so I frantically but silently summon any acting skills that four years of high school drama club bestowed on me before answering. "No, pfffft." I'm not sure where that odd, disbelieving sound came from, but I try to go on like it was what I had intended. "Why would it bother me?" My voice is much too high, so I attempt to tone it down as I babble. "I mean we were never a real couple, and even our fake relationship status is broken up, right?" I know that I need to stop yammering, but I have one more thing on my mind.

This part is the truth. Accordingly, my voice sounds much more sincere when I say, "I just don't want me or the baby to get in the way of your happiness."

"You could never do that." He reaches over the desk to engulf my hand in his. His large hands feel warm and comfortable. His touch feels safe...like home.

I nod, not trusting myself to speak without crying. He squeezes my hand tenderly before releasing it. I immediately miss the connection with him.

"We're good?" he asks me, tilting his head to check my reaction. I nod again and manage a smile this time.

"Rain-check on the movies," he offers as he's walking away. After giving him my most convincingly cheerful finger wave, I burst into tears as soon as he is out of sight and earshot.

I spend the rest of the day ruminating about what in the world is wrong with me...*How could I be friends with Honi for all of this time and suddenly develop romantic feelings for him when he finds someone else? Is this just a rebound attraction, since I so recently lost a relationship that I had believed to be real? Am I taking advantage of Honi's kindness by allowing him to help raise the baby? Will I be able to handle seeing him with other women? What if he and Kalea get serious? I don't really care about him romantically, do I? Isn't it probably just a reaction to his willingness to be a father to my unborn child? Should I allow him to do that, or will I be limiting his future?*

That last one is my main concern. The selfish side of me wants Honi to be the baby's father. I know that is what would be best for my unborn child. *Is that what is best for Honi, though? Or is he offering too much?* I'm afraid the answers to those two burning questions are the reason my stomach feels so unsettled. This uneasiness is a different kind of queasy than my morning sickness. It's actually much worse because it feels bleak and unending.

My distracted thoughts make me practically useless at work. I normally pride myself on being über professional and helpful at the front desk, but today I managed to hang up on an overseas call...twice, give someone a key to a room that hadn't yet been cleaned, snap at a guest who asked me for the fourth time if we have an all-you-can-eat buffet, and trip over a child's princess suitcase in the entry. As a finale to that last one, I kept from falling down by catching myself on the bellhop's full trolley cart, which proceeded to roll over and spew luggage throughout the lobby.

It might have been funny had I not been in such a dreadful mood. The honked off look I gave the concierge who snickered at the toppling luggage cart kept anyone else from chuckling at my mishap. Deciding that I am doing more harm than good and thankful that it isn't a luau night, I opt to leave fifteen minutes before my shift is over. There is plenty of coverage, and they don't need my sour attitude rubbing off on anyone.

Driving home, I decide to take a bath to help ease some of my tension. Perhaps a soak and a sulk are exactly what I need. It can't hurt, and the relaxation in the tub might help me keep my mind off Honi and Kalea. Even as I'm thinking it, I know that it won't work. I haven't been able to think of anything else all day.

As predicted, the bath doesn't work. I do, however, come up with an ingenious plan to distract myself by zoning out with the last two Harry Potter movies. While heating up my frozen cheese pizza, I try not to think about Kalea's home-made lasagna. If it's anything like her famous cherry cobbler, Honi's tummy will be in love. *Is that really the way to a man's heart? I can make lasagna, too.* I snort at my errant thought. I have no idea where it came from because I haven't ever even tried to make lasagna. *Maybe this baby is messing with my brain.* I suppose that I *could* make lasagna, if I had a recipe to follow. *It probably wouldn't be as good as Kalea's, though,* I decide sadly.

It's difficult to drum up much excitement for the movies, even though I was so anxious to see how it all turns out. With each scene, I wonder what Honi thinks or what he would say if he were here. I know that I need to stop torturing myself with these thoughts, but I can't seem to curb them. More than anything, I want to know if I am just being a jealous and ridiculous beast, or if I have true feelings for Honi. Honestly, I don't know which I hope for, because either way isn't likely to turn out great for me.

Despite my grumpiness, I do get sucked into the movies. When the story takes an unexpected twist, and I do actually start to think Snape isn't completely evil, I say the word "Dammit" aloud. I absently pat my tummy as if some subconscious part of me is afraid the baby might have heard my curse word. Honi was right. I never would have believed my opinion could be swayed about that snake, but it has been––somewhat.

I want to talk to Honi about it. I can't, though, because he's on a date...not with me. I try to shove that distressing thought out of my head, but it just won't go away. I want Honi to be with me.

Making myself focus on the television screen, I finish watching the movies. When the last one ends, I click off the television and quickly fall asleep. For once, having stayed up all night binge-watching something the night before pays off for me.

I sleep like the dead and wake up feeling grouchy, hungry, mopey, and still tired. *That's three or four of Snow White's dwarfs*, I decide, smiling to myself and thinking that this parenting thing will be a piece of cake. *Okay, probably not, but at least it made me smile. Smiley isn't a dwarf, right?*

Pushing Smiley (the dwarf or non-dwarf...I'm not at all certain, but don't have the energy to Google it) to the forefront, I vow to not let my personal problems interfere with my work today. I'm filling in as the hostess at the restaurant, which is not ideal, because that is were Honi and Kalea are both working. At least Kalea will be busy back in the kitchen. I plan to put on my game face and not let anyone know the turmoil I'm feeling inside.

The early morning rush is a breeze, and I'm thinking that I have this shift under control until Kai's love interest, Roxy, arrives. I take her to what has already become her family's 'usual' table. Her sister and grandmother must be sleeping in this morning because she is eating breakfast alone.

When Honi takes Roxy her pot of tea, she asks him to sit down with her. This is a rather unconventional request, but I busy myself with seating the next guests. Despite trying to distract myself, I can't help but notice when she flirtatiously places her hand on his arm. When she bursts out in hysterical laughter over something Honi has said, I feel like walking straight over there and scratching her eyes out. *My extra-long pregnancy fingernails will help with that mission*, I decide before becoming appalled by the gruesome twist my thoughts have taken. I can't seem to stop glaring at her back.

What is it with this woman? As if having Kai completely enamored with her isn't enough, now she has to go after Honi, too? I hate this jealous streak that has been rearing its ugly head within me, but I don't seem to be able to control it. Luckily, a young couple comes in to make dinner reservations, which draws my attention from Roxy hanging all over Honi. I do still notice when she gently pats his arm, and it makes me push way too hard on the pen as I write down the honeymooners' reservation in the book. The entry ends up looking like an angry child has written it.

I'm still fuming, even after Honi has gotten up to take care of his other tables. I know that I have no right to be so angry, but it doesn't stop me. Perhaps I'm especially sensitive to this woman because she is a tourist, and I know that she is about ready to break Kai's heart. Maybe she is an easy target for my anger because I know what a sweet and wonderful person Kalea is, and I can't justify being mad at her for dating Honi. Whatever the case, Roxy is bringing out in me the worst dwarfs I've been yet...Irritated, Insecure, and Hostile. They do not look good on me, but even though I know this, I can't seem to help it.

When she leaves the restaurant, I follow her. I'm uncertain what I'll say when I catch up to her, but I feel compelled to have a chat with her. I tell myself it's for Kai's sake.

When I get close enough, I speak to her back, making her pause mid-step. "Is it not enough that you have Kai panting after you like a Great Dane in heat? Now you have to sink your claws into Honi, too?"

Roxy turns, clearly angry and ready to let me have it, but something stops her. Her expression softens, and then she floors me by saying, "Actually, Honi and I were talking about you."

"Really?" I'm stunned by her revelation and embarrass myself by bursting into tears. I silently curse my spiking pregnancy hormones, even as Roxy puts a comforting arm around me. When she kindly asks if there is anything she can do to help, I tell her that she wouldn't understand.

Proving that I'm right, she says, "I understand that Honi is a kind, loving, gentle giant of a man and that any woman would be lucky to have him." I nod in agreement through my tears before she adds, "I also understand that you have won his heart."

If only she could be right about that, but I am certain that I waited too long to let Honi know how I feel. He has moved on. I missed my shot with him––if I ever had one.

When Roxy suggests that I go talk to him, I turn to head back to the restaurant. I don't have the heart to tell her it's too late. Besides, I've already cried enough for one work shift. I'll save the rest of my tears for when I get home.

11

*O*pting to take advantage of the unbelievably gorgeous scenery that surrounds the resort, I take a leisurely stroll along the beach after work. Too often, I get busy and take my lush surroundings for granted. Removing my shoes, I dip my feet into the warm, salty ocean. Something about the ebb and flow of it is soothing to me. It always has been. It reminds me that while things are not going well for me right now, they will eventually shift in my favor. After all, not that long ago, I had been giddy with happiness and thinking I was in love with a man who turned out to be a total pig. It's amazing how much things have already changed since then.

I walk for a while before plopping my butt down right in the sand, not worrying a bit about the gritty mess I'll have to deal with later. I've been sandy before, and I'm sure I will be again. Besides, getting to relax and enjoy the beach is well worth the extra hassle.

Since I'm so distracted by the steady whirl of thoughts running through my brain, I don't hear Baggy walk up behind me. Surprisingly, she does not have her finger gun at the ready. In fact, she seems almost normal as she sits down right beside me and asks if I am okay.

I nod in answer, but when she kindly starts rubbing my back, the dam bursts on my 'I'm just fine' facade. "No, I'm not okay," I blurt. "I'm pregnant by a man who abandoned me; I'm totally jealous of one of the sweetest women I've ever known because she went on a date with Honi; I'm utterly confused about my feelings for Honi; I'm growing to hate myself for my uncharacteristic indecision and selfishness; and I'm starting to get cankles." The last word is drawn out as I finally let the tears that have been building begin to flow. I lift my foot as evidence that the lower portion of my leg looks remarkably similar to a log because it no longer has any taper.

Baggy shakes her head. "Ugh. Cankles are the worst."

In hindsight, I realize that I should have anticipated this type of reaction from her. I spill my heart out to her, and she chooses to focus on the least important part of my admission. It's nothing less than I would have expected from the batty old woman, had I paused to think this through.

"I'm afraid you're stuck with them until after the baby is born, though." She's still rubbing my back, and it feels divine. The gentle back and forth motion is soothing, and it is the only reason why I don't devise an excuse and make a quick getaway.

We're quiet for a bit, both of us staring out to sea, lost in our own thoughts. It surprises me when Baggy casually says, "I can fix all of that other stuff for you, though."

I'm almost scared to hear what she has to say. Considering the wild antics she is known for pulling, she's liable to offer to make Kalea 'swim with the fishes' to put me out of my misery. Deciding that I will probably be implicated in whatever harebrained scheme she is plotting, I ask her how she can 'fix' it.

"Oh, that's easy," she tells me. "You need to go find that huge and hunky beefcake, Honi." I roll my eyes at her description, but let her continue without interruption. "Once you find him, sit him down in a chair and do a sexy little striptease for him." She leans closer then, as if telling me a great secret. "No man can resist a pregnant, voluptuous woman––especially when she's undressing for him." I'm shaking my head, but she keeps right on talking. "Here's a free tip," she tells me seriously, "dangle your clothes from your fingertips, then toss them at his face. He'll love it!" she hoots with laughter as she shares her plan.

"I don't think––" I start, but she continues talking as if I haven't uttered a word.

"The rest is simple. Once you are totally nude, climb up on him and ride him like a stallion until he forgets any other woman exists." She gives me a proud smile then, like she believes that she has just solved all of my problems.

"Sex isn't the answer," I tell her firmly.

"Ask any man," she responds. "It doesn't even matter what the question is, a man will tell you sex is *always* the answer."

"Sex is what got me into this mess in the first place," I remind her, placing my hand on my somewhat swollen belly.

"You aren't in a mess, Dear," she informs me, and I wonder if she has even been listening to me at all. "I've seen the way Honi looks at you, and I've seen the way you look back at him." She stops rubbing my back and turns to look at me. "You two are in love with each other."

"We're just really great friends." I shake my head, letting her know she has misunderstood. "We always have been."

"If you two are just friends, then I'm an eighty-year-old virgin!" She cackles with laughter at her own slapstick, elbowing me sharply in the side when I don't join her. She looks down at her lap and sticks her lower lip out as she talks. "This poor, wrinkly old vag has never known a man."

Having no desire to talk about, or even think about, this woman's lady parts, I make a move to get up. She takes ahold of my arm to stop me. Suddenly serious, she says, "I may be a crazy old broad, but I know when two people should be together, and you two belong with each other."

With that, she lets go of my arm. I bid her goodnight and scurry quickly away. *Is she right? Do I belong with Honi? Or is she just a loony old bat?*

Deciding that she's definitely a nut, I wonder if I can believe any of what she said. My brain tells me that I should not trust her instincts, but my heart desperately wants her to be right. There's only one way to find out, I guess. Tonight, I'll talk to Honi.

12

I wonder if I should chat about this with Kai first to get his take on Honi's feelings. After a feeble, unsuccessful attempt to track down Kai, I give up and decide it's better to address this type of important discussion directly and first-hand. After all, we're not in middle school any longer. Smiling, I decide that it would be great to be able to give Kai a note to pass to Honi so he could circle 'yes' or 'no' indicating whether or not he likes me in *that* way. Things were so much simpler in adolescence.

During my short commute home, I arrive at the realization that my true reluctance to find Kai most likely had to do with a fear that he would convince me that a romance between Honi and me would be an enormous mistake. It would risk ruining our friendship, as well as our plan to raise the baby as a team. If I spill my guts about my newly awakened feelings to Honi and he doesn't reciprocate, awkwardness will reign whenever the two of us are together.

I can't stop thinking about Kalea either. She's perky, pretty, and perfect for Honi. What if they really hit it off on their date? I'm not at all sure that I can stand to be around the two of them giving each other googly eyes and act like nothing is amiss. What would a serious relationship between the two of them mean for the baby? Will Kalea become the baby's stepmom if they end up getting married?

I'm extremely concerned about what will happen with Little Bit if Honi has children of his own someday. Will he regret his promise to be a father to my child? I would rather my baby not have a father at all than to have one and lose him, or to be treated like a nuisance. That would be unbearably sad.

Determining that honesty is the best policy, I decide to share my jumbled thoughts and feelings with Honi. He deserves to know what is going on in my mind and heart, and I need to know how he feels––even if it's bad news. Before I can chicken out, I shoot him a text. *"Please stop by my house when you get off work."*

He responds immediately with the dreaded and oversimplified, *"K,"* and I flop down on my bed wondering if I'm about to make the biggest mistake of my life.

Feeling exceptionally nervous, I get up and pace my small bedroom while waiting for Honi to arrive. Numerous times, I imagine the possible outcomes of this confrontation I am forcing upon us. The vast majority of them end with me broken hearted and raising Little Bit on my own. There is really only one scenario that ends well. Scratch that...it would end divinely, but only if Honi is interested in me too.

The more likely end result is an overwhelming uneasiness that leaves the two of us unwilling to share the same space for the foreseeable future. Imaginary Kai was probably right when I pictured him telling me that I would end up messing up a relationship that I cherish by moving into the unchartered territory of romance.

It takes Honi longer than I would have thought to get here. By the time his knock at the door startles me, I am certain I have paced ruts into my carpet. I have been unsuc-cessfully trying to stop the mental images of him having to break a date with Kalea to respond to my texted request to come over. *Surely he wouldn't do that. Would he?*

When I fling open the door, he beams at me, obviously unaware that I might be about to ruin our easy camaraderie. He lifts both arms proudly, making me realize what took him so long to get here. One hand holds the last two Harry Potter movies. The other holds a sleeve of microwavable popcorn and my favorite brand of caffeine-free root beer.

I grin back at him, touched that he thought to grab preg-nancy-appropriate snacks. "I already watched them," I inform him, pointing at the DVD's his giant hands are clutching. "I couldn't wait."

His eyes sparkle at this news. "What'd'ya' think?" he asks, sounding like an over-excited schoolboy.

"I loved them, just like you knew I would," I admit, looking down and shaking my head.

Having geared myself up to receive a giant 'I told you so,' I was pleasantly surprised when Honi merely wants my opin-ions. We sit down on my couch as he proceeds to ask me which movie was my favorite, which was my least favorite, if my opinion of Snape had been swayed, what I thought of the music and costumes, and so on.

He mentions that Hermione has always reminded him of me, which I find flattering, since she is incredibly smart and a hero in her own right. I had already suspected he relates to the dynamic of the three main characters, since it centers around three friends—two boys and a girl.

"The books are even better than the movies," he informs me. "They have so much more detail in them. You *have* to read them," he adds excitedly.

"Okay," I smile at him. "Do you know anyone who has them for me to borrow?" I tease.

He lights up. "You can borrow my copies. I'll go get them," he offers.

He's already moving to stand when I say, "I don't need them right this second." I pause for a bit, uncertain how to transition the conversation to where I want it to go. Opting to indirectly mention the elephant in the room, I try to keep the shakiness out of my voice as I ask him, "So, how was Kalea's lasagna?"

"It was delicious," he responds without offering anything further.

"Are you two going out again?" The smile I have plastered on my face feels brittle and fake. I hope it doesn't look as horrid as it feels.

He answers so quietly that I barely hear him. "I don't think so."

He's looking down, so he can't see that my heart is about ready to beat out of my chest. I wonder if he can hear it. The loud pounding is echoing throughout my head.

"She's cute and sweet and a phenomenal cook." I'm glad he is still looking down as he's speaking because I wouldn't want him to see the spurt of jealousy flaring in my eyes before I can cover it. Everything he has said about her is absolutely true, and I don't have any right to be envious, but these facts don't negate my bitter feelings.

"She's also kind," he adds before looking up at me, "really kind."

I nod because I know this to be accurate as well. It doesn't make it an easier pill to swallow, though. I hate the negative emotions I am feeling, but I don't seem to be able to control them. It doesn't feel like me, but I guess it must be. I don't want to be a hateful, envious person.

"I hated to hurt her, but I didn't know what else to do," he says sadly, looking back down now.

My head is still nodding because his words haven't yet

sunk in. "Wait...hurt her?" I ask when what he has said finally dawns on me.

He isn't looking at me, so I have a hard time reading his expression as he speaks. "I didn't want to string her along because it seems like she really cares about me."

I struggle with myself to remain neutral. Honi is coming to me as a trusted confidant. I'm certain it would be wrong to tell him he did the right thing by letting Kalea down. I would only be saying that for selfish reasons. I need to find out the whole story, but he doesn't seem to be dying to spill it.

Deciding to tread lightly and reaching out to lift his chin, I ask, "Would you like some herbal tea?"

He nods, giving me a sad smile before following me to my tiny kitchen. He seems to fill up the entire space, and I like having him in such close quarters. When he reaches around me to pull mugs from the cabinet, his nearness makes my heart skip a beat. Attempting to distract myself from our close proximity, I busy myself with heating the teapot and finding the tea accoutrements.

Once the mango green tea is steeping, I turn to him and catch a whiff of his scent. It's piney and masculine, with a hint of coconut. I want to close my eyes and breathe it in, but I manage to stop myself from going that far.

"Let's chat in the living room where it's more comfort-able," I suggest. My ulterior motive being that on the couch, I won't be as tempted to sidle up to him and see what the warmth of his front feels like against mine.

Curling my legs up underneath me on the sofa, I wrap my hands around the heated tea mug. The action itself is comforting, and it keeps my hands too busy to reach out to Honi. "Kalea seems like she is perfect for you." I force myself to voice my fear.

"I know," he answers, and I try not to let the disappoint-ment show on my face. He's quiet for a bit, then he adds, "My brain knows that she would be ideal for me, but my heart belongs to another. It always has," he admits, sounding sad.

My heart is beating double-time as I try to tamp down the hope that is springing up in my chest. *Is he talking about me? What if he is? What if he isn't?*

He takes a sip of his tea before setting down his mug and turning to me. "I've had feelings for the wrong person for almost my entire life," he admits.

"Why the wrong person?" I ask, almost scared to hear the answer.

Seeming like he is ignoring my question, Honi starts in. "She is beautiful, kind, funny, giving, sweet, talented, smart, and darn-near perfect. What would she ever see in someone like me?"

"Well, if she's so smart, she should see that you are all of those things, as well," I tell him honestly.

"We've been the best of friends our whole lives, and I don't want to risk messing that up." He turns to look at me then and most of the doubts I am having about whether he is talking about me melt away in the warmth of his chocolate hued eyes. "I'll take whatever you can give me, Lani," he rushes on before I have a chance to speak. "I know that I'm not the man of your dreams, but I'll do everything in my power to make you and our baby happy. Maybe someday you'll be able to grow to love me?"

The mixture of humility, fear, and pain in his voice breaks my heart. "Honi, you don't need to settle," I tell him firmly. "You are a remarkable human being, and you deserve to be with someone who appreciates you for who you are-- someone who loves you for you."

He nods, even as he says, "Tell my stupid heart that. It has been pining away for someone who is completely out of my league for over a decade."

Deciding to go all in, I say. "You're in love with me?" I'm ninety-nine percent sure that he is, but I need to be positive.

He is looking down at the carpet, but I can still see that his face turns so red it's almost purple as he nods quickly in affirmation of my question. Leaning close, I take his hand in mine and whisper near his ear. "All of these years, I've been searching for the perfect man, and he has been right in front of me all along. I've been blind, but now I see." I press my lips to his burning cheek.

When he turns to face me, I can see the welling tears glistening in his eyes. "You feel sorry for me." It's part question, part accusation, but before I can respond, he adds, "You should be with someone handsome like Kai or successful like Tom."

"First off, *you* are handsome and successful," I remind him. "Secondly, I should be with who I *want* to be with, and that someone is you." I can tell that he wants to believe me, but his ingrained fears and inferiority complex won't allow it. Delving deeper, I say, "I made an enormous mistake with Tom. I was looking for all of the wrong things when I was with him...shallow things. When I think about what is truly important––like who the first person I think of in the morning or who the last person on my mind at night is, who I want to share big news with, who I feel like I can truly be myself with, who I can laugh and cry with, and who I want to raise my child with––it's all you, Honi."

His eyes are sparkling, and I can tell that he is opening himself up to believing what I am saying. Nudging him gently with my elbow, I say, "You are the Ron to my Hermione." This pronouncement makes him break into one of his signature beaming smiles.

Lifting our joined hands, I place my palm over his on my belly. "This isn't how I would have thought things would work out, but I'm certain it's exactly how they are meant to be."

"I'm pretty sure I'm the happiest man on earth, and I know I'm the luckiest," he gushes, making me feel all warm and melty inside.

I feel overwhelmed with emotion––both deep friendship and a simmering love that I hadn't realized had been there. "Our keiki is so blessed to have you for a father," I tell him warmly.

"And you for a mother," he reminds me.

The happiness is bubbling around us like the frothing sea. We might not have all of the answers right now, and this may not be exactly how we pictured our future, but it feels right.

I lean towards my best friend, the father of my child, and the love of my life. "Shall we seal it with a kiss?" I ask him.

He answers me by tenderly touching his lips to mine. I'm thrilled to discover that I feel his sweet kiss all the way to the tips of my toes. If I had been harboring any lingering doubts about if this was the right decision for us, his lips erase them. My worries dissipate as my mind goes blank and the sparks fly!

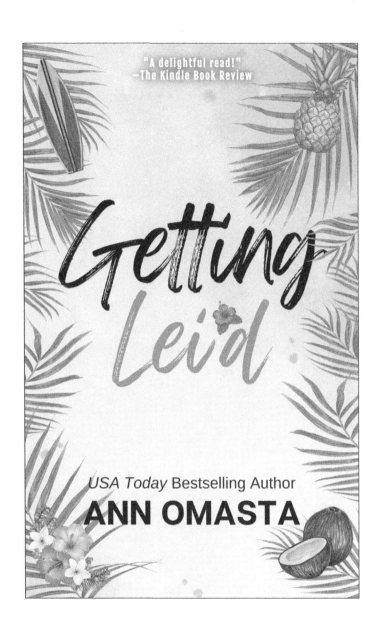

"A delightful read!"
—The Kindle Book Review

Getting Leid

USA *Today* Bestselling Author

ANN OMASTA

GETTING LEI'D

THE ESCAPE SERIES ~ BOOK 1

1

*J*ilted at the altar. These are words that I never in ten trillion years would have thought could apply to me. Okay, technically, I'm not at the altar yet, but I'm already in the white dress. Besides, getting jilted by text message should count for double or triple points, right?

I keep looking from my cell phone to the full-length mirror in the coatroom-turned-bridal party–prep-area in the quaint, white steepled church, which my fiancé and I had recently started attending because I envisioned it as the perfect place to exchange marital vows. The reflection staring back at me from the mirror with big brown eyes is beautiful, and I'm not one to say that (or even think that) about myself. Well, my likeness would be beautiful, if it weren't for the mouth hanging wide open in shock.

The ladies in the room with me are bustling around excitedly. My eyes blink quickly as I work to process the sterile text message and attempt to devise a way to share the bombshell news.

Time seems to slog slowly past. I stare at the mirror and a

bride gazes back at me. I tilt my head to the side, wanting one last glimpse of her in all her Swarovski-crystaled glory. What I am about to say will ruin her big day.

When I finally speak, my voice sounds croaky and muffled, almost like I am underwater. "The wedding is off."

The room goes silent. Everyone is completely still for a moment. I guess they were able to hear my life-altering, shocking mumble.

My practical, ever-rational mother is the first to speak. "Don't be silly, dear. Everyone gets wedding day jitters. Just smile and say your vows. It will all be over in a jiffy."

I cringe slightly at her attempt to comfort me. The fact that she views a wedding day as something to quickly move through, rather than a blessing to cherish as one of the most wonderful gifts that life has to offer, speaks volumes about her relationship with my dad. I can't focus on that right now, though.

Mother begins moving about the room as if her dismissive words negated my previous statement. I guess she thinks telling me to "get over it" will make everything fine. In my mind, I picture her checking "soothe high-strung daughter" off her list of things to do today.

The other women in the room remain motionless. Their eyes roam around uncertainly while their bodies remain frozen in whatever position they were in when I made the announcement. I feel hysterical laughter beginning to bubble up inside me. They look like they are playing a grown-up version of the game "freeze dance" and the music has just stopped.

Mother just doesn't get it. I watch her fluff the deep purple ribbons on my bouquet of daisies as she shuffles about, business as usual. *She's going to lose the game*, I think, and I'm horrified to hear the impending giggles burst out of me.

Since we aren't playing the musical game, my maniacal chortling serves as the catalyst for resumed activity. Suddenly, I am surrounded by five of the ladies I love most on this earth. There are only five because my best friend, Lizzie, is conspicuously absent, and now I know why.

I turn my phone so the group can see the text from my now-former husband-to-be, Gary. I watch as they each read the words, some of them moving their lips as they do so. The shock, pity, and outrage move in waves throughout the group.

"What in tarnation?" This outraged question comes from my wildly irreverent grandma, Baggy. Although she looks like a sweet (although slightly shriveled) little old lady with her freshly set silver curls, bright pink lipstick, and lemon-yellow sweater, she is anything but. "He can't do this. I'm going to give that snot-nosed little wiener a piece of my mind." With that, she whirls around, shaking her white leather Aigner handbag in the air like a battle weapon.

If I weren't hysterical, I would be amused by her typical show of spunk. Baggy has never been the typical grandmother who sits quietly in her rocking chair knitting red mittens. Even as a child, I had known my grandma was different. In fact, her nickname, Baggy, was my toddler version of "Bad Grandma." The moniker is so appropriate that it has stuck to the point that everyone now calls her Baggy.

"Mother, no." My mother grabs Baggy's arm as she smoothly slides into her usual role as the voice of reason. She relishes this responsibility, even with her own parent. She glares down at Baggy through her half-glasses, which are precariously perched on the end of her nose. I decide that one of my mother's odd talents is having glasses that always look like they might fall off at any moment, yet somehow managing to keep them on. It is a trick that works great for intimidation—that and her five-foot-nine height, which she uses to full advantage.

Looking at the two of them, I wonder—not for the first time—how Baggy survived my mother's birth. Baggy has shriveled slightly with age, but she was always diminutive, and my mother is not what anyone would describe as a small woman. She can't possibly have been a tiny baby.

Baggy tries to yank her arm free as she lets out a rallying cry for the group. "We won't let that good-for-nothing, low-life bag of worms get away with this." She continues to hold her purse with her free fist in the air.

Realizing she can't break away from her daughter's firm grip, Baggy tries to start a chant. "Get Gary. Get Gary." The women in the room look around seeming uncertain of what to do. A few of them join in before the chant peters out.

Once the chant fizzles, Mother decides Baggy is not as much of a flight risk and loosens her hold on her forearm. Baggy seizes the opportunity and tries to make a break for it. As Mother realizes what is happening, she whirls around to try to stop Baggy.

In her haste, Baggy trips over my sister's heels, which she has left in the middle of the room (in typical Ruthie fashion). Baggy agilely tucks and rolls her tiny body—just like she always claims she'll do when falling—in order to avoid breaking a hip.

My formidable mother fails to let go of Baggy and falls much less gracefully than her elderly, spry mother.

The rest of us stand there looking at Mother and Baggy for a moment, uncertain if either has been injured. When Baggy shakes her head, her pin curls don't budge. She proceeds to spring up like the Energizer bunny before saying to her daughter, "Get up, you big weenie. I have almost twenty-five years on you, and I'm fine."

I hold my hand out to help Mother stand. She is much

larger and less agile than Baggy, and it takes both of my hands to help heft her up. She groans once she is upright and puts a hand on her back, wincing a little.

"You just need to learn how to fall," Baggy tells her, putting her hand on Mother's shoulder. "You've never been a good faller," she adds seriously.

Suddenly, the ridiculousness of the entire situation sinks in with me, and I begin to giggle again. The whole group turns their attention back to me as the laughter turns to tears.

"Well, let's go then." Baggy pulls me out of the room. This time no one tries to stop her, and I silently pray that she isn't dragging me off to "Get Gary."

With Baggy, it's hard to tell what "get" means. He might not survive it. Although I'm completely humiliated and furious, I don't wish the man dead, but with my wild grandma, you just never know.

2

*B*aggy drags me to the silver convertible classic Mercedes that was meant to be our post-cere-mony ride. The top is down on the pristine car and there are a myriad of cans tied to the back. I can't help thinking that Gary will not be at all pleased when he comes out and finds that someone has been messing with his precious car. That's not my problem anymore, though, I guess. I had been exceedingly close to making his quick-to-anger testiness my problem for a lifetime.

Baggy jumps in the driver's seat as if she plans to take the car. I have let her lead me out here, but now I decide to speak up. "We can't take this car, Baggy. It's Gary's pride and joy."

"He owes you. Come on," she orders me. I hold my ground, so she acquiesces a little. "We'll bring it back. Eventually." She adds the last word under her breath. I can tell by her tone that she is exasperated by my lack of adventure. She seems to think I should agree that grand theft auto is no big deal.

I stay rooted in my spot, so Baggy decides to play dirty.

She shakes her head sadly, saying, "You get more like your mother every day."

That does it. She knows exactly how to push my buttons. Even though I know what she's up to, I can't ignore it. I huffily get in the passenger's seat as she searches for the keys.

"I know they're here somewhere." She checks under the floor mat and in the console. "Jackpot!" she yells excitedly when she lowers the sun visor and the keys fall into her lap. "What kind of dipwad leaves the keys to such a beautiful car out where anyone can find them? He deserves to have his car taken," she informs me with a wink and a huge smile.

She adjusts her seat forward as far as it will go and turns the engine over. When it rumbles to life, she yells out gleefully, "Yee-haw! Purrs like a pussycat." She delves into her white purse and draws out a turquoise scarf to tie over her curls. I shake my head to decline her offer of the orange scarf she draws out from deeper in her pocketbook.

We both look up when we hear my sister running, full-tilt, toward us. She has her violet bridesmaid's gown hiked up and she is making good time, considering the heeled pumps she is wearing, evidently having retrieved them from the middle of the floor where she had left them as a tripping hazard. Billowing behind her are several clear plastic dry-cleaning bags.

Ruthie hurls herself toward the backseat of the car while yelling, "Go, go, go!"

Baggy doesn't hesitate. While Ruthie is still in midair, she slams the car into gear and presses the gas pedal to the floor, lurching the car forward. Amazingly, Ruthie lands in the backseat and isn't injured.

Baggy has two modes when driving (and in life): all-out and stopped. She is so vertically challenged that she peers out the windshield by looking through the space between the top of the steering wheel and the dashboard. I say a silent prayer and buckle my seatbelt as we race through town at nearly three times the speed limit.

The wind is whipping through my hair when I turn to ask Ruthie, "What's that?" I use my head to indicate the bags she stole from the church.

"It's the tuxes." She beams, obviously proud of her theft.

I'm not sure what the point of taking them was. "Umm, I don't think they'll be needing them now that the wedding is off."

Ruthie pouts a little, as if I've just rained on her princess parade. "Well, Gary will have to pay late fees because we aren't taking them back on time."

"Yeah, stick it to him!" Baggy is obviously on board with the thievery.

I can't help but think that the only people we are really hurting are the rental company and anyone who has the tuxes rented next, but I decide to hold my tongue. In some strange way, I suppose it's sweet that Ruthie was willing to do this to avenge my wedding day dumping. Besides, I don't need to be told again that my voice of reason sounds just like my mother's.

"Where are we going?" I ask Baggy in an attempt to change the subject.

"Away" is her simple response, and I decide that for once in my life, I'm just going to go with the flow and see what happens. If anyone deserves to get away right now, it's me.

"We're just like those crazy broads Thelma and Louise," Baggy shouts over the hum of the speeding car.

Her proclamation makes me hope she doesn't intend to drive us off a cliff, like the characters do in the movie. Nothing would surprise me with Baggy. The problem is, she and Ruthie would come out of the crash completely unscathed. Even though I'm the only one in a seatbelt, the best-case scenario for me would probably be a full-body cast.

I'd tense up all over, while the other two would just enjoy the ride down.

I shake my head to try to clear it. I don't want to be negative. I love my grandmother and sister, but they do seem to live charmed lives. If I tried half the crazy, irresponsible stunts they pull, I'd be dead or in prison. Today is the perfect example. Being dumped on her wedding day is something that wouldn't dare happen to Baggy or Ruthie. They simply wouldn't allow it.

I catch a glimpse of my reflection in the side mirror. I'm still in the white gown, but my hair has now been whipped into a snarled beehive of rats. I glance back at my sister, who looks windblown but wild and free. Baggy's hair remains perfectly coifed under her scarf.

Looking at these two reminds me that even though I'd like to be as carefree as them, I'm just not. I seem to be built differently than they are. Maybe I'm more like my mother than I thought. Ugh.

Mother didn't get dumped on her wedding day, though. Double ugh. The more in control of my life I try to be, the more of a hot mess I become.

3

*W*e drive and drive. I try to relax and just enjoy the high-speed ride, but I can't keep my mind from returning to the fear that Baggy's driving is going to kill us all. The fact that the woman has never been in an automobile accident (a detail that she loves to remind us of whenever the opportunity arises) is simply shocking. I'm guessing that she has caused an enormous number of fender benders in her wake. She just careens on too quickly to notice.

"Jive Talkin'" by the Bee Gees comes on the radio, and Baggy cranks up the volume. She and Ruthie are singing and bebopping to the catchy tune as if they don't have a care in the world. I try singing a little and nodding my head to the beat, but I feel silly, so I stop.

A new song starts and Baggy turns the blaring radio down slightly. I use the decreased volume as an excuse to ask again where we are headed, since I don't know how much longer I can endure the near-constant fear of riding in a car with Baggy at the wheel. If we go too much longer, I'll probably develop a killer migraine.

"What? I can't hear you over the banging tunes!" Baggy

yells over the still-loud music. I adjust the volume down further and repeat my question.

"We're cruising," Baggy answers cryptically.

I consider asking her to pull over so I can get a sweet tea. Even though I don't really want one, since my stomach is kind of churning, it seems like it would be a good opportunity to change drivers.

In the end, I decide to continue taking my life in my hands. I don't really feel like taking the wheel, and my sister's driving isn't much of an improvement over Baggy's.

I clear my mind as much as I can under the circumstances, close my eyes, and let the whipping wind wash over me.

4

When I wake up, we are in Atlanta. I can't believe we have driven for more than four hours. Baggy has slowed down somewhat for the exit ramp off the highway, but still takes the curve way too fast. I squeeze my eyes shut, certain that we are going to drift into the retaining wall. Miraculously, we stay on the road, even somewhat in the lane.

Once my heart rate begins to return to a more normal pace, I regain my wits enough to realize we are heading toward the airport. "Are we flying somewhere?" I inquire jokingly, but almost afraid to hear what their answer will be.

"Tell her." Baggy makes eye contact with Ruthie in the rearview mirror, practically bouncing with anticipation.

I turn around to find Ruthie's eyes glistening with excitement. I raise my eyebrows letting her know to spill it. "We're going on your honeymoon," she announces.

I have about forty-seven questions about this odd declaration, but can't seem to formulate one, so I just sit there staring until their harebrained idea gushes out of her.

"While you were asleep, we decided that you shouldn't

miss out on a fab vacay to Hawaii just because that dillweed dumped you." I cringe a little at her harsh word choice, so she throws in a haphazard "Sorry" before continuing. "By the time we thought of it, we had driven too far to get you back to the airport in time to catch your first flight."

She pauses to take a breath, but I decide to wait for her to continue rather than attempt to ask the right questions. "We do have plenty of time to catch your connecting flight, though."

I furrow my brow a little, so she adds, "I borrowed your phone and saw that your connection is in Atlanta. It works out perfectly because we were already practically at the ATL."

"That sounds reasonable," I acquiesce before adding, "But I don't want to go on my honeymoon by myself."

"That's why we're coming with you," Baggy jumps in. "Won't this be a hoot?" She's obviously proud of herself.

Not wanting to dampen their spirits but unable to avoid stating the obvious, I say, "You two don't have tickets."

"Oh fiddle-faddle." Baggy waves off my valid point as if it has no merit. "It will all work out." If it were anyone else, I would doubt it being possible, but I have learned from experience that once Baggy sets her mind to something, nothing gets in her way.

5

*S*ure enough, even with the more stringent security measures in place, Baggy manages to secure two tickets on the same flight Gary and I were supposed to be on. I can't imagine how much two last-minute tickets to Hawaii must cost, but Baggy always seems to have an unending supply of crisp hundred-dollar bills in her billfold. I'm sure she whipped a sizable stack of them out and handed them over to the surprised ticket agent.

We stop to use the assembly-line airport restroom, and I realize that I was too quick to check my suitcase that had been in the trunk of Gary's car. I have no clothes to wear on the airplane, other than my wedding gown. This is less than ideal.

If I hadn't been in such a state of shock, I'm sure I would have thought of this sooner. I'm not overly surprised that Baggy and Ruthie both stood silently by as I checked a bag of casual clothes rather than mentioning that we might want to change out of our formalwear first. I'm sure they consider the trip even more of an adventure in our fancy bridal attire.

I attempt, unsuccessfully, to tame my wild rat's nest of

hair after we wash our hands in the giant metal trough. Giving up my hair as a lost cause, I point out another seemingly obvious fact that they probably haven't bothered to consider. "You two don't have any luggage."

"Oh, barnacles," Baggy sort of curses. "I guess we'll have to buy some grass skirts when we get there." Her eyes light up with a new thought. "Do you suppose I can find one of them coconut bras that will show off my bodacious tatas?"

I can't help but smile at her as I glance at her flat, droopy chest. Anyone else her age would be joking, but with Baggy, I'm guessing I should prepare myself for the sight that I'll never be able to unsee of her dancing around in a coconut bra in public.

One thing this little getaway is sure to be is unforgettable. Adventures with Baggy always are.

As we sit at the gate waiting to board the aircraft, I have a panic attack. What if Gary and Lizzie are on the flight? If Baggy and Ruthie were able to secure tickets, maybe Lizzie did, too.

The image of the pre-wedding breakup text from Gary flashes into my head, unwanted. *"I can't do this. Lizzie and I r in love. Sorry."*

The fact that he deemed it appropriate to relay this information by text is inexplicable. His word choice infuriates me the most, though. First off, when sending a text of this magnitude, is it really too much trouble to spell out the word *are*?

The "Sorry" at the end really irks me, too. He couldn't even be bothered to insert an "I'm" in the half-assed apology? Yes, you are sorry, you ridiculous jerk. Unbelievable. At least it didn't say, "We're sorry."

I know this isn't how it should be when two people are getting ready to promise to spend the rest of their lives with each other, but the betrayal by my lifelong best friend hurts more than that of my almost husband. I wish the text had said that he is in love with her, not that *they* are in love. It hurts so much more knowing that my best friend since the first day of kindergarten would do this to me. I guess my feelings about this whole fiasco prove that it is probably a good thing that today did not turn out to be my wedding day. I was evidently about to marry the wrong man.

Apparently I dodged a bullet. That doesn't excuse the manner in which Gary chose to dump me, though. Inconceivable. That's all I have to say about that right now.

6

*W*hen they call for the boarding of first-class passengers on our flight, Baggy and Ruthie hop up and head to the gate. They are halfway there when Baggy realizes I'm still in my seat.

She turns, perplexed, in my direction. I can see the moment realization dawns on her. I try to get up and close the gap between us because as I watch Baggy's facial expression evolve from confusion to understanding to anger, I know that she is about ready to unleash a flurry of annoyance. At least if I am in closer proximity to her, less of the crowd will hear her rant.

The long, white dress slows me, so I make it only two steps in Baggy's direction before she starts. "You mean to tell me"—she is shaking her bent pointer finger at me. I stop in my tracks because everyone within hearing distance is already looking at us anyway. Baggy continues, completely undaunted by the attention drawn by our spectacle—"that cheap-assed bastard didn't even spring for first-class tickets for your *honeymoon*?" She emphasizes the last word with righteous indignation. "He has shitloads of money. What is he saving it for, a special occasion??"

After a few quiet chuckles, the crowd turns toward me in unison, awaiting my response. The innocent bystanders look like they are watching some ridiculous train wreck of a tennis match that they can't tear their eyes away from.

I feel like an absolutely ridiculous mess, standing here with my unruly hair, wearing my now-rumpled wedding gown. People have even looked up from their cell phones to see how this will unfold. If there's one thing I am uncomfortable with, it's being the center of attention.

Ruthie can't stand it when all eyes are on me, either, so she quickly jumps in. "My sister would appreciate some privacy in this time of great embarrassment and shame," she says to the crowd at large.

I feel like kicking her in the shin. I know there isn't any malicious intention behind her words, but she has somehow managed to make this mortifying situation a thousand times worse. At least everyone is now looking at her. That is the way she and I both prefer things to be.

I close the gap between us so Baggy, Ruthie, and I can talk to one another without including the entire room. People are still staring at us, but normal hushed conversations and cell phone usage begin to resume. "You two are causing a scene," I hiss.

Both of them look surprised and taken aback by my reproach, so I soften my tone. "Go ahead and get on the plane." They seem uncertain, so I fib, "I like sitting in coach. It's a great opportunity to people watch."

"I could trade tickets with you," Ruthie offers. I appreciate the gesture, but also know she would be devastated if I took her up on it.

I refuse, as she had likely known I would, but the relief is still evident on her face. "If you're sure." Ruthie smiles, already grabbing Baggy's hand and dragging her toward the burly female ticket agent.

Nodding in answer, I grin as I listen to them giggling and skipping toward the airplane door. Looking down at my pearly white dress, I vow to be more like them on this adventure. I will have fun and enjoy the moment. That is my new mantra—easy, breezy Roxy. That's me. Well, the Hawaiian me, anyway.

*T*hankfully, Gary and Lizzie are not on the airplane, so I decide to use the quiet time to meditate on my new carefree attitude. Despite my best efforts to stay positive, the flight is interminably long, and my seat is very cramped. My height is definitely not an advantage when it comes to airline seating accommodations. My knees are already touching the seat in front of me, so when the shortish lady in front of me leans her seat back, I nearly come unglued. Instead, I take a deep breath and attempt to refocus my mind. When that doesn't work, I purchase a rum and Coke from the flight attendant and start a slapstick comedy movie on my seat's personal TV.

I only make it a few minutes into the silly movie before the reality of the day's events sets in and overwhelms me. Yanking out my earphones and turning to the grandmotherly lady sitting in the window seat next to me, I splutter, "Today was supposed to be my wedding day." She nods, giving me a sad look that is a mixture of pity and understanding.

I feel like curling up in a ball and hiding for a while, but that isn't an option on the plane. The best I can do is swivel my legs onto the empty aisle seat beside me. Looking at the vacant seat, which should have been Gary's, serves as another reminder of my fiasco of a wedding.

When my seatmate gently pats my arm, I erupt into an odd hiccupping-sobbing combination and lean my head on her shoulder. I spend the rest of the flight alternating between crying and sleeping on this kind stranger.

After landing, I give a goodbye hug to the caring woman who had comforted me during most of the flight. If she thinks I'm a crazy person, she hides it well as she promises me that it will all work out for the best.

It doesn't take long to realize that the mai tais must have been free-flowing in first class because when I deplane and rejoin Baggy and Ruthie, they are both pretty snockered. They valiantly attempt to hide their tipsiness, but they are even more silly and giggly than normal. Baggy wavers unsteadily as we walk to claim my checked bag.

Once we get my suitcase, we turn in unison for the door. Suddenly, I realize the fatal flaw in Baggy and Ruthie's plan: Gary made all of the arrangements for our trip. I don't even know where we have reservations. I gaze at the plethora of chauffeurs holding name signs, along with the taxis and hotel shuttles outside, and realize we have no idea which hotel is ours.

By the wide-eyed looks Baggy and Ruthie give me, I can tell they have figured out our predicament. Baggy is the first to come up with the obvious solution. "We could . . ."

"I'm NOT calling Gary," I interrupt her, speaking with vehemence.

"Well, I'm sure there are some hotels that aren't fully booked." Ruthie tries to take the edge off our situation, even as we all look around the packed baggage claim area and wonder how we'll find a decent hotel with vacancy.

"That hot hunk of beefcake might be the answer to our prayers." Baggy lifts her gnarled pointer finger.

I want to chastise her that it's no time to be on the prowl for a man, but I look in the direction she indicated and realize why she is hopeful. The large Hawaiian man, whom Baggy has accurately described, is holding a sign that reads KNOX.

Inwardly, I cringe a little at the sight of it. Had I really been willing to change my name to Roxy Knox? It sounds like a children's cartoon character. I should have never considered giving up a fab name like Roxy Rose to become Roxy Knox. What in the world had I been thinking?

The three of us head in the direction of the sign-bearing, handsome Hawaiian. He looks even bigger and sexier up close. His jet-black hair, soft chocolate eyes, and dark mocha skin make for an intriguing combination. He has thick dark lashes, but his large, straight nose gives his face some character and keeps him from being too pretty.

Baggy and Ruthie openly stare at him in silence, so I attempt to speak. "We're the Knoxes . . . I mean, our name isn't Knox . . . Our name is Rose . . . well, mine is . . . and hers." I indicate Ruthie. "I think we are the people you are looking for," I stammer.

He gazes down at me and says, "I was expecting honeymooners." He is more than a head taller than me, which forces me to crane my neck upward to make eye contact with him. Having been well above average height my entire life, I am not used to having to look so far up to see anyone. I don't think I like it. This must be how my diminutive sister and grandma feel all the time.

"Oh, we're on our honeymoon," tipsy Baggy responds. At his perplexed look, she clarifies, "Well, her honeymoon." She angles her head in my direction.

I don't want to get into the drawn-out explanation of

today's embarrassing fiasco, so I inform him a little more brusquely than I intend, "We're the people you're looking for, and we are ready to go to our hotel. Can you please take us?"

"Certainly," he responds before placing brightly colored hibiscus leis around Baggy's and Ruthie's necks, who titter in response to his attention. "I was only expecting two people," he explains before turning to me, lowering his lids and adding, "I'll make it up to you later." He tweaks the end of my nose before picking up my suitcase and heading toward the automatic doors.

My nose still tingles from his touch. Baggy and Ruthie sniff their beautiful flower necklaces, and we all watch his tight, perfectly grabbable backside as he saunters out of the airport. Somehow, he has managed to dazzle us all in a matter of moments.

Suddenly, we realize that we are being left behind, so we scurry after him. The heat of the intense Hawaiian sunshine hits us the moment we step outside, but we barely even notice as we watch our gorgeous driver open the door to a dated limousine and give us a grand welcoming gesture by clicking his heels together and holding a hand out to help us. To our credit, we stand there mesmerized for only a moment before practically knocking one another down in an attempt to be the first to accept his outstretched hand.

Proving that she's as spry and full-of-life as ever, even when she has overindulged on alcohol, Baggy gets to our handsome limo driver first and accepts his helping hand. Ruthie shows us that she is wilier than she looks by lunging around us to grab the front passenger-side door. She grins at me slyly, saying, "I think I'll sit up front with the driver. We don't want my motion sickness to kick in." She pats her tummy for added emphasis.

I roll my eyes because I know that, unlike me, she has never suffered from any kind of movement-related nausea, but I refrain from pointing it out. Besides, my attention is diverted when our studly driver takes my hand to help me climb into the backseat of the limo beside Baggy.

I don't know if it's my imagination, but it seems like he gives my hand a tender squeeze and allows his hand to linger on mine longer than necessary, or even socially acceptable. When I make eye contact with him, wondering why he hasn't let go of my hand, I think he winks at me. It happens so fast I can't be certain, though.

In any case, my palm is still tingling from his touch, my heart is racing, and I feel more alive than I have in years. I don't think this is the appropriate reaction to a handsome stranger for a woman who was meant to marry someone else only a few short hours ago.

Maybe I should send Gary a text to thank him for stopping me from making a colossal mistake—likely the biggest of my life. Nah, I'm not ready to let him off the hook just yet.

Speaking of texts, my phone and Baggy's both buzz at the same time with an incoming text. The message is from Ruthie in the front seat of the car and it reads, *"He looks like Jason Momoa!!"* Our phones buzz again. *"Without the scary eyebrows, of course."*

I have figured out that she is talking about our driver, since she feels she can't share her thoughts aloud, but I have no idea who Jason Momoa is. *"Who?"* is my simple response.

Ruthie shakes her head in disbelief as if I am the most sheltered person on the planet before responding. *"Google him."*

Before I can get the Internet browser pulled up on my phone, Ruthie sends us several pictures of our driver's gorgeous, apparently famous doppelganger.

"Ooh-we, he is a handsome devil," Baggy blurts out upon receiving the text with the photos.

Baggy's words are the first that have been spoken aloud

since we left the airport. I make eye contact in the rearview mirror with our chauffeur, and I can feel my cheeks blushing pink. He has to know from the buzzing of our phones that we are talking about him. Why else wouldn't we just speak like normal people? His bemused expression hints that he's not offended, but I still feel ashamed to have been caught in the act of admiring him (and his lookalike) by text.

Rather than calling us out on it, he takes the high road and begins pointing out various attractions and little-known, tucked-away gems along our drive to the hotel.

As we pull into the parking lot of our resort, I realize that it is not at all what I had expected. It is so much more me than Gary. Gary probably would have been sorely disappointed and referred to it as a shabby dump, but I am completely enchanted from the moment I set foot on the property.

Our rustic thatch-roofed hutlike villa is romantic and has an island feel that a standard hotel room couldn't accomplish, no matter how much Hawaiian-themed artwork is displayed. The hut is warm, but a breeze blows in the open windows from the ocean. The scent of bougainvillea or hibiscus or some other beautiful, exotic flower fills the air in our room as the rhythmic sound of waves crashing into shore lulls me into relaxation.

This place is truly paradise. It is the Hawaii of a childhood dream, so perfect that it can't possibly be real, yet here I am.

Baggy and Ruthie head down to the gift shop to see about getting some clothes. I unpack, change into a sundress, and scoot the small desk over by the sliding glass door before inspecting and setting out my art supplies. They all seem to have survived the trip unscathed.

As I inhale a deep breath of salty, fragrant air, I look out at the unfathomable beauty surrounding me. If I can't create a terrific piece of art in this stunning location, then my mother is right, and I really should stay a responsible (if slightly boring) accountant.

Before long Baggy and Ruthie return to the room wearing brightly colored, slightly skimpy island attire. They are carrying several bags, so I can only hope that some of their purchases provide a little more skin coverage.

Even though our bodies tell us it is late at night, the bright sunshine indicates otherwise, so we decide to head outside and check out the pool, beach, and (perhaps most importantly) the bar. It's time for me to relax a little and release some of the stress of this incredibly long, unexpectedly horrible day.

8

$\mathcal{O}$ur resort is on the small side, but it is stunningly beautiful. As my eyes scan around, they land on either huge bushes bursting with enormous, colorful blooms or crystal-clear water in every direction. I have traveled to Florida and several islands in the Caribbean, but this place takes the cake for both natural and man-made visual delights.

The tropical bar, which features both a swim-up section for service from the infinity pool as well as a more traditional land-based side with comfy-looking bar stools, catches the attention of all three of us. I am surprised to find as we belly-up to the bar that our chauffeur is now playing the role of bartender.

He hands each of us a tall glass garnished with pineapple and filled with a fruity, frozen beverage that smells of rum before giving us an enthusiastic "Aloha!" and a dashing, white smile. I am pleasantly surprised to see a tiny gap between his two front teeth. Somehow, it makes him even more attractive. I consider mentioning that we didn't order these drinks, but after taking a sip, decide to just twirl the tiny umbrella and smile back at him.

"Mmm, delicious." Ruthie licks her lips, thrusts her small but perky boobs onto the bar, and gives him her best flirtatious 'come hither' look. Most men would jump the bar to be at her beck and call, but our driver/bartender doesn't seem to take notice.

Giving a slight pout, but clearly undeterred, Ruthie twirls her hair and says to him, "You have been driving us around and now you are plying us with drinks, and we don't even know your name."

He looks directly at me when he answers her question. "My name is Kai." His name sounds Hawaiian and exotic. It suits him perfectly, and I try not to make it obvious that I am repeating it silently in my mind, practicing to say it sexily. *Kai. Kai. Oh yes, Kai . . . Nope, I just don't have it in me—not even in my imagination.*

Kai has already fixed drinks for two other patrons and is now focusing on something below the bar. He apparently doesn't share the island-time attitude that allows many workers in tropical locales to move in extra-slow motion.

Baggy, Ruthie, and I sit in silence, which is a rarity with these two. Our breathtaking surroundings, along with lengthy flight and six-hour time zone change, seem to be finally catching up with us.

Kai finishes what he has been working on and comes to stand in front of me. He gently places the most gorgeous, brightly hued flower necklace I have ever seen around my neck. He leans over the bar to kiss my cheek before saying, "You can't arrive in Hawaii without getting properly lei'd."

Ruthie snorts at the double entendre; and call me crazy, but I could swear that Kai blushes a little. He has such a dark complexion that it's hard to tell, but I'm pretty sure I see a pink flush rise on his cheeks before he turns away to take another patron's drink order.

The blushing must have been my imagination. I'm sure he uses that tired line multiple times every day. It sure felt good when his lips pressed gently against my cheek though, and my skin still feels tingly where his fingers brushed against my neck when he was adjusting the lei.

Ruthie looks a little perplexed by the attention he is giving me, but she doesn't comment on it. Baggy's eyes are glassy as she stares off in the distance. I mention what a long day it has been and suggest returning to our room. Surprisingly, neither of them pose an argument.

As we shuffle back to our room, Kai dominates my thoughts. I don't care if he makes a habit of flirting with guests at the resort. I like it, and I want more of it. I gingerly touch my kissed cheek, not wanting to rub off any of the lingering effects. I feel enveloped by the tantalizing aroma of the fresh flowers that Kai has hand-strung for my lei. Even though this has been one hell of a day, I can't seem to stop smiling.

he three of us sleep like the dead. When I finally open the light-blocking curtains, it's obvious that the sun is high in the sky. Baggy and Ruthie screech at me and squint like moles coming out of a cave, but I feel fantastic and insist to them that it is time to rise and shine. They both eventually rise, but are too grouchy to shine before having an infusion of caffeine.

We head down to the resort's restaurant in search of bacon. I scan the large open-air-concept room, attempting to look casual, so it won't be obvious that I'm looking for Kai. "I don't think he's here." Ruthie whispers the words near my ear, proving that I wasn't nearly as stealthy with my search as I had thought.

"Who?" I ask, trying rather unsuccessfully to keep a straight face. She gives me a knowing smile, but doesn't directly call me out on my bluff.

As the hostess leads us to a table, Ruthie informs her that we would like coffee and hot tea to drink. "Just bring us a whole pot of each, please." I start to interject that this is not the hostess' job, but Ruthie beams a sweet smile at the young

Hawaiian woman and circumvents the table, heading straight for the buffet line before I have the chance.

My first instinct is to follow normal restaurant protocol by sitting at the table to wait for the waiter or waitress to give us permission to go fill our plates with food. My tummy grumbles as I start to pull out my chair, so I throw caution to the wind and follow Baggy directly to the delicious-smelling custom-order omelet station.

Once our plates are filled to the point of having food nearly topple off, the three of us head to our table to find two large pots of steaming liquid, exactly as Ruthie had demanded. I shake my head slightly as I riffle through the wide selection of tea bags. Ruthie wouldn't know how to react if something ever didn't go her way. She is just one of those people who expects everyone and everything to accommodate her wishes, and somehow it always works out for her.

I try not to be bitter about my sister's charmed life, but sometimes it just gets to me. Just as I'm telling myself to be happy for her and not let it bother me, I look up to find Baggy giving me a shockingly silly smile. She has taken a piece of the sweet, juicy pineapple and stuffed it in her mouth, leaving the rind side out so it looks like frightening teeth. She looks ridiculous, and I have to hold my hand over my mouth to keep from spewing papaya-infused pancakes everywhere.

Just as Ruthie is looking at me to see what is so funny, we all hear a sound that makes us freeze. It is the loudest, most high-pitched, joyful giggle that I have ever heard. When I turn to discover the source of the laughter, I almost fall out of my chair from shock. The bellowing, gleeful cackle is coming from an enormous giant of a Hawaiian man. He is pointing a sausage-size finger at Baggy's pineapple wedge smile and doubling over with laughter.

Even bent over, it is obvious that he is a huge man. He looks to be the size of a successful Sumo wrestler. The girlish tone of his laughter doesn't match his stature at all, and the pure joy escaping from his lips makes all of us join in with him. Before long, we all have tears streaming down our cheeks and Ruthie has to make a break for the restroom to avoid wetting her pants.

The large laugher plops down in Ruthie's vacated seat to try to calm down. He finally wipes his forehead with the back of his hand before saying, "Phew, that's the best laugh I've had all day." His speaking voice is almost as shrill as his laughter. He continues as if Baggy and I aren't gawking at him in wide-eyed shock. "I am your waiter, Honi. Please let me know if there is anything I can get for you."

Baggy and I nod and watch as he braces his arms on the table to heft himself upright. Just then, the most gorgeous, exotic woman I have ever seen rushes up, grabbing him by the arm. "Honi, do you know where Kai is? I need to talk to him."

I try to hide my disappointment. Honi excuses himself and walks away, talking in hushed tones with the beautiful woman. I feel tears welling in my eyes and silently curse myself for being so irrational and flighty. *Of course Kai is involved with a beautiful woman. With his drop-dead gorgeous looks, how could he not be?*

When Ruthie returns, she and Baggy talk animatedly. I barely listen to their conversation because I am so annoyed with myself for allowing any kind of hope to creep in about having a fling with Kai. *What had I been thinking? Maybe this is just some kind of rebound daydream that is a result of being left almost at the altar. I need to focus on me (and my happiness) during this trip. I do not need a man to be happy.*

As we walk to our room to change into our beachwear, I promise myself that I will not give Kai another thought. Even as the oath is fresh in my mind, I can feel my misbehaving eyes peeking over to the not-yet-open bar to see if he is there.

He's nowhere to be found. *I really don't care about his whereabouts anyway. I was just curious what time the bar opens.* I try to convince myself of that, but even I don't believe it.

10

*B*aggy and Ruthie decide to head down to nab some poolside lounge chairs, but I opt to take advantage of being so near the sea and tell them I'm going for a swim in the ocean. They both seem a little surprised at this newly discovered, somewhat adventurous streak in me, but they refrain from commenting on it.

The pale, large-grain sand tickles my toes as I walk along the shoreline. I stop and gaze out over the water, letting the wind and fresh air sweep over me. I stand there wondering if it's possible to actually smell sunshine. Inhaling the faint scents of salty water, marine life, fresh pineapple, coconut tanning oil, and some tropical flower, I decide that this must be exactly what sunshine smells like—and happiness. I am breathing in the aroma of pure happiness.

I peel my black cover-up over my head, toss it on the sand, and jog into the water. I had been braced for it to be chilly, so am pleasantly surprised to find the undulating water to be warm and inviting. *Of course it's warm*, I tell myself, smiling as I lower my body farther into the foamy ocean. *This place is truly paradise. How does anyone ever leave?*

I don't want to think about ever having to go home, so I clear my head by diving into the next big wave. The water swirls around me while I swim out to where the water is calmer, past where the waves are breaking. I decide that this is a great opportunity to get some exercise that is actually enjoyable, so I start swimming parallel with the shore.

I swim and swim. Periodically, I check to make sure the current isn't pulling me farther away from the beach. When my out-of-shape legs get tired of kicking, I take a break and float for a while, but soon I get back to swimming. I think I could swim miles here. Speaking of that, I pop my head out of the water to gauge how far I have gone. There are beautiful houses along the shoreline. I spend some time swimming on my side, looking at the understated but amazing beachside residences.

For a moment, I consider turning back. After all, I should swim only half as far as I intend to go, so that I have enough energy to swim back. I almost have a panic attack when it pops into my mind that I might be swimming with the current and it might be a lot harder to swim back, until it dawns on me that returning to shore and walking back is an option, if needed. Considering that, I decide to keep swimming in the direction I've been heading.

The sun is warm and feels wonderful on my shoulders. I swim a good while longer before heading toward shore to walk back to the resort. The walk is almost as enjoyable as my swim had been. The homes, resorts, and restaurants along the shore are all lovely.

I am shocked to pass numerous chapels along my path. They all seem to have huge windows overlooking the ocean, and weddings in progress. I try to figure out if this is a special date, which would explain the large number of ceremonies, but I can't come up with anything. Weddings must be big business on this island. Each time I see a bridal party and photographer outside, I scurry quickly past, in an attempt not to photo-bomb the pictures of their happy day. Just because my almost-wedding wasn't picture-perfect doesn't mean I should ruin someone else's photos, although some shameful and sinister side of me is tempted to do just that. Luckily, the urge is not a strong one, and I am able to quickly tamp it down.

By the time I get back to our resort, I am mostly dry but beginning to sweat from the heat and my exertion. I retrieve my cover-up from the sand and don it after showering off inside the gate at our resort. Before returning to the pool area, I scrunch my hair in an attempt to make it presentable. I wonder why I am suddenly concerned with my appearance and tell myself that it is *not* because of Kai.

Even as I'm trying to convince myself of that, my eyes wander over to the bar. Kai has his back turned, but I can tell by the shirt stretched taut over his broad shoulders that it is him. I hide my smile as I rejoin Baggy and Ruthie.

"We were about ready to send out a search party," Ruthie informs me, shading her eyes with a hand to look up at me, even though she has on oversized sunglasses.

"Your concern is touching." I roll my eyes after making the snarky comment. They are both sunning themselves on lounge chairs and sipping frozen concoctions from split-top coconuts. They couldn't have been too worried.

I plop down on the empty lounge chair beside them and peel off my cover-up. When I see Kai looking my way, I decide to stretch my arms, arching my back. When I peek back in his direction, he is still looking and rewards me with a huge grin. I smile back before looking away and wondering what has come over me. *Had I actually been flirting with this visually stunning man?*

I decide that maybe this new, braver, Hawaiian version of me will have way more fun than the old Roxy did. I get up and try to saunter sexily over to the bar. Since I still have my long, awkward limbs, I fear that the reality of my gait is more gawky than sexy, but I'm in too far to turn back now.

"Roxy." Kai flashes a dimple at me as he finishes a drink for another patron and hands it over to her. I decide that I love the sound of my name when it comes from his lips. The woman breathily thanks Kai and tucks a bill into the tip jar. He gives her a quick, almost curt nod and starts dumping ingredients into a blender for his next concoction. The woman pouts for a moment, but hops off the barstool and heads back to her lounger.

Kai pours the contents of the blender into a hollowed-out coconut, adds a tiny umbrella with a pineapple wedge and cherry, and sets it in front of me. I turn my head from side to side, wondering if he has accidentally given me someone else's drink. "I didn't order this," I inform him, unintentionally furrowing my brow.

He reaches out to run a finger down the line on my forehead. "Trust me, it's exactly what you need. There is no frowning allowed in paradise."

I had always been a firm believer that you can't trust anyone who says "trust me," but somehow it didn't sound like a used car salesman's pitch when Kai uttered the words. I sit there for a moment, uncertain why my gut is telling me that I should, in fact, trust this man.

Kai must have taken my silence for annoyance at his presumptiveness because his next words are, "Just give it a try. If you don't like it, I'll make you something else—whatever you want. On the house," he adds when my silence continues.

My brain is fluttering with potential responses, but not any that I wish to utter aloud, so I lift the coconut and try to look sexy as I seek the straw with my tongue to take a sip. My attempt at flirtation must not have been a total fail because Kai is gazing at me like he wants to jump over the bar and have his way with me. Normally, that thought would scare the crap out of me, but for some reason, I find the idea oddly intriguing.

When the fruity, rum beverage hits my taste buds, I can't hide my delighted reaction. I close my eyes, tip my head back, and release a deep "Mmmmm" as the delicious coolness slides down my throat.

Upon opening my eyes, I find that Kai is watching me intently. The look on his face is priceless. We stare at each other in silence for a long moment before he breaks the tension. "Well, now that I have no blood left in the upper half of my body . . . I take it you like the drink?"

I nod at the rhetorical question and manage to wink at him before sliding off my barstool and taking my drink back to my seat. I can feel him watching me go, and I have never in my life felt so sexy and wanted. I don't care if this is his game and he flirts with everyone, I like how having his attention makes me feel.

When I maneuver the shady umbrella to cover my lounge chair, Ruthie almost jumps out of her seat. "You're blocking my sunshine," she screeches at me before turning to smile prettily at the handsome lifeguard. I wonder at her ability to turn her feelings on and off so quickly and with such vehemence.

Once we get the shade situated to everyone's liking, the rest of the day is spent basking by the pool. I pretend like I'm not watching Kai. I hate to admit it to myself, but there is something about him that is disturbing to me. I decide to bring it up as we are eating lunch at the resort's café, which is situated across from the pool, still in Kai-viewing proximity.

"So, what do you guys think that bartender is up to?" I broach the subject with Baggy and Ruthie, trying to sound vague and casual.

Baggy jumps on the opening. "Do you think he's selling drugs or firearms or something behind that bar?" I had been hoping they hadn't noticed the brown paper bags that Kai periodically exchanged for money. I had wanted to believe that I was imagining it or that there was a logical explanation for the seemingly seedy transfers that Kai was conducting. Hearing that Baggy noticed and was suspicious completely dashes that hope.

"No, I'm sure it's nothing like that," I inform them, trying to convince myself as well.

Even though I had brought the topic up, I suddenly want to dismiss the subject from our conversation (and my mind), but Baggy latches on to it and won't let it go. She holds her pointer finger and thumb up *Charlie's Angels* style into a pretend gun. "We'll get to the bottom of this," she assures us before jumping up from the table and peering around the corner of the restaurant, finger gun at the ready. She peeks around to make sure it's safe, before waving Ruthie and I over. Ruthie immediately jumps into the fun, raising her imaginary gun to follow Baggy.

"What have I started?" I wonder aloud, shaking my head at my own stupidity before getting up to follow them.

$\mathcal{W}$e decide to attend the resort's weekly luau that evening. I am able to successfully convince Baggy and Ruthie that they will be less conspicuous spies if they keep their finger guns put away. They don't want to oblige, but finally agree that the weapons might blow their cover.

Being with the two of them is almost like having two young children to monitor. I'm not sure why I always end up playing the part of the responsible parent. In any case, getting them to sit down and behave is easy once the show starts. The performers are incredibly talented, and I recognize several of them from around the resort. Employees here must have to be flexible and capable enough to fill numerous positions.

When Honi comes out on the stage, he dominates the ukulele. His high-pitched voice accompanies the instrument, creating a beautiful song with a haunting melody. The lilting sound is both sad and mesmerizing. When he finishes, the crowd sits in stunned silence for a moment before erupting into loud applause.

Three lovely Hawaiian women take the spotlight to perform a traditional hula. I recognize the middle one, who has been introduced as Leilani, as the lady who was looking for Kai at breakfast. The ladies smile and relay the story of the song with their swaying hips and graceful hand movements. I can't take my eyes off Leilani. She is the embodiment of perfection. She and Kai must look amazing together. I can't imagine the heat of the two of them naked and melding together, nor do I want to.

Speaking of Kai, his death-defying fire-throwing act is the finale of the show. He is scantily clad in a loincloth. His dark skin glistens and his muscles flex as he does seemingly impossible stunts with flames. I am nervous, intrigued, and incredibly turned on all at once. I don't want to see him get burned or hurt in any way, and it seems impossible that he won't, but I can't tear my eyes away from the incomparable beauty of his performance.

When he finishes unscathed, the crowd goes wild. I clap so hard my hands hurt. He bows and brings the others out for a final bow. I feel like he is looking right at me, but I know the stage spotlights make this impossible.

When the noise dies down, Baggy leans over the table to say, "I don't care what he's up to. He's so handsome and talented, I wouldn't kick him out of bed for eating cookies, if you know what I mean." At this, she waggles her eyebrows suggestively. I'm not sure exactly what she means, but I do know that I don't want to hear any more, so I simply nod.

Just then, an older gentleman plops down at the unused fourth chair at our table. He smiles at Baggy with a lemon wedge in his mouth, similar to what she had done to us with her pineapple. The gesture makes Baggy bubble with laughter. He kisses her hand before introducing himself as Jim Bond. *Is that short for James Bond?* I wonder, shaking my head at his ridiculousness.

Mr. Bond tells Baggy that he has been keeping an eye on her since we arrived. "It seems you're quite the spy." He leers at her. "I hope you're not after me, or you just might catch me." Just as I'm about ready to tell this smooth operator to get lost, Baggy titters. Is that even a word? It seems like the only appropriate word for her reaction.

Before I can intervene, Mr. Bond asks Baggy for a dance, and they begin a dramatic tango on the empty dance floor. I look to Ruthie for help, but her attention has been caught by the lifeguard/scuba instructor/general watersports dude who is surrounded by a bevy of females at the bar. Sensing a challenge, she instructs me "not to wait up" before sauntering off in his direction.

I turn my attention back to Baggy just in time to see Mr. Bond produce a red rose for her, seemingly out of thin air. Baggy giggles as he places it behind her ear. Wow, this guy is slick.

"Guess I'll take a walk along the beach." I say the words aloud, even though no one is around to hear them.

As I take the path toward the water, I see Kai and Leilani. They are clearly having a heated discussion. I really don't want to spy on them, but something makes me hunker down behind a bush within earshot. *This is so unlike me*, I think as I'm squatting near the ground. *All of Baggy's crazy antics must be rubbing off on me.*

Then I hear something that makes me cringe. Leilani's voice is shaky as she says, "This baby is the most important thing in the world to me, Kai." With more conviction she adds, "I'm not giving it up."

I am well aware that none of this is any of my business, but I still somehow feel betrayed. I wish he would step up and accept responsibility for his actions. I put my head farther down as Leilani bursts into tears and runs back toward the resort. Kai turns and heads toward the beach, not bothering to chase after her.

Once they are each out of sight and I don't have to worry about being caught eavesdropping, I stand up. Rather than continuing on my planned walk, which would run me the risk of bumping into Kai, I decide just to go back to our villa. I'm feeling a little depressed. After all, if someone as gorgeous as Leilani has man troubles, how much hope is there for the rest of us?

When I get back to the room, I take a nice hot bath in the giant spa tub to relax and try to wash off the minor blues I am experiencing. It doesn't really work, so I go to bed. I don't even wake when Baggy and Ruthie finally straggle in.

12

*T*he next morning I am awake with the sun, and I feel like a new woman. Baggy and Ruthie are both sound asleep. I get ready quietly and leave without disturbing them. It seems we are on completely different waking schedules.

Since I am filled with energy, I decide to take a hike. There is an amazing-looking lush green peak that has been calling my name in the opposite direction of yesterday's swim, so I set off toward it. It is probably much bigger than it looks from a distance, but I decide to give it a shot. Besides, I don't have to go all the way to the top.

I just hope it's not an active volcano. They wouldn't let people near it, if it were, right? Or, do they just assume that people have enough sense not to climb into molten lava? I shake my head at my errant thoughts, unsure why my imagination can turn something as harmless and fun as morning exercise into a life-threatening, panic-inducing experience.

I am relieved to find a well-worn path at the base of the hill and set off on my adventure. Before too long, I discover a faded sign pointing to a scenic overlook. Since I'm already a little out of breath, I decide to take this clearly less-traveled path rather than attempting to head up to the peak.

This path is more overgrown, and I feel adventurous and daring for opting for it when I arrived at the proverbial fork in the road. I move an overhanging branch out of my way and almost gasp at the beauty as I step into the clearing. A huge waterfall is crashing into a deep, clear spring of water. I have never encountered such a naturally perfect spot. I wish I'd had the foresight to tote my painting supplies with me. This place is practically begging to be set to canvas.

A head emerges from the water and I realize I'm not alone. Instinct has me dive behind the shelter of a nearby boulder so I won't be seen. I hold my breath as I crouch in my hiding spot, hoping the swimmer didn't see me.

After waiting a while and not hearing anything, I peek out from behind the rock. The figure in the water is a man. I can tell by the broad shoulders and strong arms that erupt from the surface each time he does a stroke through the water. I watch, mesmerized, as his lean body slices through the water. He is clearly a natural swimmer.

My legs get tired of squatting, so I sit down with my legs crossed. I keep my body hidden behind the boulder, but allow my eyes to peek out and watch him swim. When he stops under the waterfall and raises his head, allowing the water to crash down over him, recognition dawns on me. Kai. Of course, I should have known.

I wonder if he has on swimming trunks or if he is skinny-dipping. I can't stop the fantasy popping into my head of joining him in the water au natural, although I would never actually act upon the naughty impulse. It is intriguing to think about, though. I bet Kai in the buff is a sight to behold.

He deftly swims over to the side, and I notice for the first time that a dark blue towel is folded neatly near the edge of the water. Here comes my chance to get a glimpse of him in all his glory. I strain my neck to peer out from behind the rock without poking my head out too far and risking being seen.

I watch as his shoulders flex to raise him up out of the water. It's as if time has slowed to allow me to fully enjoy this moment. The water runs down his back in great rivers that turn into tiny rivulets, which I imagine chasing with my tongue. *Here comes the moment of truth*, I think to myself as his waist breaks the surface.

Just then, Baggy's voice echoes across the canyon. "What'cha lookin' at?" I jump up and whirl in her direction to pull her down next to me.

My face is burning red with the shame of being caught leering at Kai without his knowledge. Baggy is unfazed. "Oh, we're spying, eh?" she stage-whispers, quickly converting into her role of super sleuth. "Ya think he hides his drugs down there?"

I shake my head, bugging my eyes out at her and holding a finger to my mouth, silently praying that she'll be quiet for once in her life. Some higher power must have been listening to my request because she remains silent as she slowly peeks up over the rock.

I stay below the surface of our hiding spot, not yet daring to look back out. *Had he heard her? What am I thinking . . . of course, he heard her. She was so loud Ruthie probably heard her from the resort. Did he see us?*

I slowly raise myself to peer over the ledge of the giant rock. Kai has wrapped the navy towel around his waist and he is scanning the trees in our direction. He definitely heard something, but the good news is that he would have to swim across the spring or go up and around to get over to us, and either would give us time to get away. I don't think I could face him right now.

Baggy and I watch as he gives up on his perusal and bends

to pick up a water canteen. "Ooh-wee! Look at that tush!" Baggy says—much louder than I would have dared speak. I nudge her with my elbow but keep watching Kai. He proceeds to take a drink from his water container, seeming unfazed by Baggy's loudness.

"You s'pose he's naked under that towel?" Baggy has returned to her loud whisper.

I grit my teeth before whispering near Baggy's ear. "Just because you don't hear anything doesn't mean that others can't. You're being too loud." She huffs out a breath but she doesn't say anything else. Then she plops down on the ground with her back against the rock, pouting.

I wonder if our cover has been blown, but I'm scared to look. Finally, I decide I need to check, if for nothing else than to make sure that he hasn't set off in our direction. When I raise myself to look in Kai's direction, he is looking right back at me. I quickly lower myself, but not before I'm almost positive he winked at me. When I work up the nerve to look again, he is gone.

"Come on, Baggy," I say to my grandmother, taking her hand and pulling her upright. "We need to get out of here before he catches us."

Baggy's sense of adventure kicks in, and she quickly forgets that she is angry with me as we scurry back to the resort.

"You think he saw us?" she questions me quietly, looking around as I use my key card to enter our villa.

Now she decides to be quiet, I think to myself. "I hope not," I answer her honestly, even though I'm almost positive that he did.

I'm surprised to find that Ruthie is up and showered. I join her to sit outside on our balcony enjoying the fresh air while Baggy takes her bath. When Baggy emerges from the bathroom, she informs us that she and Jim are taking a drive to explore the island in his Range Rover today. "You are welcome to come with us," she offers, but we both immediately shake our heads to decline.

Ruthie declares that she plans to sign up for parasailing lessons. I am certain that her newfound interest in watersports has to do with the handsome guy who gives the lessons.

I ponder their plans for the day for a minute, trying not to focus too much on the fact that they have both already found love interests.

They decide to head down to breakfast. When I inform them I am staying in the room for the day, but would love it if they could bring me a croissant with guava jam, they both look concerned.

"I want to paint today," I say breezily in explanation. They still seem uncertain if they should leave me in the room alone, so I add, "Besides, I don't want to get sunburned."

They seem to buy this excuse as plausible and leave. "I'm not hiding from Kai." I say the words aloud, once they are gone. "I'm not," I say again, unsure whom I am fighting with.

I let my inner turmoil go once I make the first swipe of my brush across the canvas. From then on, I am swept into the world my brushstrokes want to create.

13

*J*ust because my painting turned into a waterfall scene, doesn't mean anything. It's a beautiful spot, after all. It practically begs to be recreated on canvas. The fact that my paintbrush decided to add the vague form of a man slicing through the water does *not* mean it is Kai. It could be anyone. I had intended for the piece to be a traditional landscape, but it had seemed incomplete until I added the person.

I stand back to admire my work. The man makes the painting come alive. He makes the entire scene more real—less perfect, yet somehow more perfect at the same time. I'm happy with the final product—really happy with it, and that rarely happens. I almost always feel like my work is missing something, but this time I nailed it.

I have never before painted from memory. The lack of clarity into each leaf and cloud forced me to use a little more impressionism than I normally would have. As I worked on it, I closed my eyes to imagine the scene, then I let my brain and hand work together to do justice to the setting. The resulting artwork is much more stunning than any of the previous pictures I have painted.

This painting captures perfectly the scene I stumbled upon this morning, and I'm certain I could sell it at a gallery. Well, if I could part with it, of course, but I don't think I can. I want to remember this amazing locale and the terrific feeling of being here long after I return home. I will find the perfect spot to hang it in my condo.

The knock at our door startles me out of my reverie. I can't imagine who it could be. Baggy and Ruthie have keys to get in. I had put out the DO NOT DISTURB sign in hopes that housekeeping would just leave fresh towels outside the door, rather than come in for a full cleaning.

Maybe Baggy or Ruthie requested that room service be brought up for me, knowing that I wouldn't stop painting long enough to seek out food? That must be it, I decide, before looking down at my paint-splattered T-shirt. I'm an absolute mess. It was very thoughtful of my family to save me from having to go out in public looking like this, especially since they hadn't bothered to bring the croissant I'd requested earlier.

My naturally cautious personality has me pause to look through the peephole before opening the door. I nearly jump out of my skin when I see a distorted version of Kai looking back at me through the tiny glass. *Geesh, does he deliver room service, too?*

"You can just leave the tray outside the door," I yell, hoping he'll just drop off the food and not see the paint-covered mess I have made of myself.

"It's Kai. What tray?" he asks, sounding genuinely perplexed. "I didn't see you today, so I wanted to make sure you are okay."

"Oh, I'm fine." I am touched by his concern. I guess this really is a full-service resort. "Thanks for checking on me."

"I'd prefer to see for myself." I can hear the grin in his voice.

Shit! I look behind me at the painting. There isn't any place to hide it except the bathroom, and I don't want to risk smudging it while trying to move it. It's still wet, so I can't throw a dropcloth over it.

I make a snap decision and unlock the bolt on the door, leaving the chain hooked. I open the door the chain's width and smile at Kai. "See, healthy as can be."

He beams at me as if I don't look like a paint-covered fool. "Ah, you've been painting. I wasn't sure if you were sick, so I brought chicken noodle soup." He holds up a container as evidence.

"Thanks," I tell him, truly touched that he would think to do that. I reach through the crack in the door to grab the soup container, but it won't fit through the still-chained opening. I squeeze it slightly, but can't pull it through.

"I think you might have to open the door." He states the obvious fact that I have been refusing to accept.

Sighing, I release the container back to him long enough to close and unchain the door. When I reopen the door, I stand in the opening, hoping to block Kai's entry into the room. I grab the soup container once more and try to send him along with a simple, "Thank you very much for bringing this by. Please add the charges to our room bill."

He frowns slightly at that, but his eyes have already been drawn to the easel. I strain to my full height in a futile attempt to block his line of sight, but he is tall enough to look right over my shoulder. "Is that what you've been working on today?" he asks, opening the door wider and strolling inside.

I sense the second he recognizes the scene. He pauses. "Is that . . ." His voice trails off, leaving the rest of the question unasked. When he turns to me his face is bright crimson, and I'm sure mine is a matching shade.

I can't stand the embarrassment, so I start rambling. "Yes, I stumbled upon that waterfall during a hike, and it was so serene and lovely that I wanted to recreate it on canvas." He's looking at me now, and I can tell that he knows I saw him. The tension is unbearable, so I fill the void with more chatter. "The figure there"—I actually point at the man in the water—"is a figment of my imagination," I lie. Unable to stop myself, I add, "The pool was completely empty when I saw it."

He's giving me an odd look, as if he can't decide what to say. I cannot believe I spied on him then lied about it, then to make it even more ridiculous and unbelievable, restated the lie. I wonder if he is going to call me out on it. He has to know that he is the figure in the painting. *Why didn't I just fess up about it?*

We stay silent for a while, just looking at each other. I am beyond embarrassed, but am determined to keep my mouth shut, so I don't dig myself any deeper into this hole. Finally, he gestures at the soup container and plastic spoon. "Enjoy your soup," he says simply, turning to leave.

I feel both relieved that he didn't call me out on my lies and humiliated that I got myself into this situation in the first place. When he stops and turns to look at me, I am convinced that he is going to shame me for my indiscretions. "You know," he starts, and I suck in a deep breath, dreading what I know is coming, "it seems to me that imaginary man in your painting needs a sexy lady to join him in the water." With that, he beams a dazzling, reassuring grin my way and closes the door behind him.

After he's gone, I plop down on the couch. He had to have known that my running of the mouth was all lies, but he had been gentleman enough not to point it out. I test the soup, and it is delicious. Gorgeous, thoughtful, kind-hearted, and a gentleman—Kai is the total package. *I hope Leilani realizes how lucky she and her baby are.*

Baggy interrupts my rumination by bursting into the room and setting down a plethora of bags. "What a day," she announces before joining me on the sofa. She sounds completely enamored as she tells me all about her adventures with Mr. Bond. Jim Bond.

I can't believe she is falling for his hokey fake-spy ploy. Of course, I have no room to talk. I spent the day painting and just got caught daydreaming about a man who has someone else knocked up and spends his time bartending to cover for the drug or other trafficking operation he runs behind the counter.

We sure have chosen some winners, I think to myself while Baggy and I get ready for bed. Maybe there is something in this Hawaiian air that makes otherwise logical women make poor choices when it comes to men. Not that anyone would ever accuse Baggy of being logical, of course.

Ruthie returns to the room much later. She giggles to herself while putting on her jammies and visiting the bathroom. I hear her take a deep, satisfied sigh before rolling over and going to sleep.

I smile at the ceiling, glad that she and Baggy are happy. They both deserve it. This trip is turning out to be anything but boring, I decide, rolling over and wondering what new adventures tomorrow will bring.

14

I wake up early again and decide to go for another ocean swim. The warm, salty water washes over me as I pump my legs and rotate my arms. I had forgotten how much I enjoyed the feeling of sluicing through the water. I need to find a place where I can swim at home. Of course, doing laps in a pool won't be nearly as luxurious as exploring the sea in Hawaii, but it beats not swimming at all.

I put my head down (except for every fourth stroke, when I turn to take a breath), and really stretch my limbs. I am booking at a brisk pace through the water and thinking that I might be in heaven when I feel a sharp sting on my leg. The pain jolts through me, so I stop swimming and switch to an upright position to tread water.

While I rub my fingers over my hurt calf, assessing the damage, I look toward the shore and try to determine the best way to get back to land with my now-gimpy leg. Just then, I feel a sharp pain on my shoulder. I gasp before turning to grab the newly injured area. Floating in the water behind me is a translucent pink blob. I feel a little panicky as

I circle my hands in the water, trying to propel myself away from the stinging bastard.

When I flail out of its range, I feel yet another sting on the back of my neck. My eyes bulge as I turn from side to side, only to realize that I am surrounded by dozens of the gooey creatures and their trailing tentacles. I can barely breathe, but still manage to let out a frightened sound as I try to figure out how to escape this predicament.

A small wave of saltwater splashes into my face as I feel the burn of another sting on my ankle. All I can think about is getting back to land, but each way I turn is blocked. It appears that I have somehow managed to swim into a swarm of jellyfish, and I don't know how to get out. Every direction I attempt to move brings me closer to another sting. My whole body is ringing, so I straighten my body and make myself as still as possible while remaining afloat, in an attempt to let the umbrella-shaped jellies pass me by.

Another tentacle grazes my ear, and I let out a pained cry. Just then a strong arm scoops under my arms. The tangled jellyfish tentacles are surrounding us, so I know my rescuer is being stung as well, but he never flinches as he moves us quickly and efficiently through the water toward the shore. I allow my tired body to go limp in his strong hold while he propels us to safety.

Once we make it to shallow water, I expect him to set me down to walk, but instead, he continues carrying me. I turn to look at his face for the first time and am only nominally surprised to see Kai. Normally, I would insist on walking, but it's nice to feel safe in his arms after the scare I just had in the water. A quick look down confirms that the stings are already forming nasty, red welts. He continues carrying me up the beach toward a beautiful beachside home.

Finally, he sets me down on a bench in the home's lush garden area. "I'll be right back," he tells me before jogging into the house. I cringe when I see the angry, red marks slashing across his back and legs.

While I wait for him to return, I look around. The house is large—almost mansion large—especially for being water-side. It has an open-air concept and is stunningly perfect in every way. I wonder how a hotel employee is able to afford such an amazing place. Even if he does perform numerous jobs at the resort, he can't possibly make enough to pay for a dwelling of this magnitude. His under-the-table brown bag deals at the bar must be quite lucrative, I decide sadly.

When Kai returns, he has a glass jar in his hands. He dips his fingers into the mixture to retrieve a large dollop, which he proceeds to smear on my shoulder. I flinch reactively, thinking that whatever this is might hurt, but quickly discover that the balm is cool and soothing to my hurt flesh. "Ah . . ." I enjoy the immediate relief. Somehow, amazingly, it has taken the pain away where Kai has applied it.

My eyes dart to the jar, and I try to grab it from Kai's hands. I want its quenching relief on all of my stings—NOW. He chuckles, saying, "Just relax, I'll take care of it," before bending down to rub a generous dose on my ankle. Again, the relief is almost instantaneous. "Where else does it hurt?" he asks me, looking deep into my eyes. I point out the spot on my ear, before turning so he can reach the welt on my neck.

Once all of my spots have been covered with the magical goop, Kai sits down beside me and begins applying it to his own spots. A strange mixture of shame and horror course through me when I realize that he was taking care of me before tending to his own wounds. "I'm so sorry," I tell him honestly. "I assumed you had already put some on your spots."

He gives a simple shake of his head, as if it is an everyday occurrence to save someone and treat her stings while ignoring your own significant pain. This time when I reach for the jar, he lets me have it. I dip my hand in before gently dabbing it on Kai's chest and smoothing it in. I coat each of his stings with the same care and gentleness that he has shown me. When he turns to give me access to his broad shoulders and back, I am tempted to place my lips on each of the spots in an attempt to make them better with a kiss, but I refrain.

"What is this miracle salve, anyway?" I ask him once each of his stings is coated.

He smiles then—a truly gorgeous smile, with the slight gap in his teeth adding even more character to his face. "It's my Nana Lana's Super-Secret Magical Jelly." The way his eyes light up when he speaks, I can tell that his Nana Lana is very special to him.

"Well, it's magical, all right. I can vouch for that. It took me from extreme pain to mild discomfort in a matter of moments." I smile back at him, and he looks proud. "I want a gallon of this stuff to take home with me. Does it work on anything else or just stings?"

"Well, Nana Lana thinks it cures everything." He raises his eyebrows, making me wonder if his grandma is as crazy as Baggy. "It is amazing stuff, though, and people swear by it to relieve everything from sunburn to dandruff to acne. We have customers come from all over to get it. We could make a fortune, if she would mass-produce it, but Nana refuses. She makes each batch by hand, saying she instills love into each jar, which is what makes it work so well." Now I'm really wondering if he has a crazy grandma, just like I do, but I don't say anything about it. After all, he obviously loves the woman a great deal, and it's a completely different ball of wax when you insinuate that one of your own family members is loony versus someone else implying you have a nut job in your family.

Kai cocks his head to the side. "I'm surprised you haven't seen me selling it at the resort. I sell it to all of my favorite guests." His words create extremely conflicting emotions inside me as a silent *Ohhhh* sounds in my head. On the one hand, I'm glad to find that he isn't selling drugs or anything else seedy. I am distressed, though to learn that I am not one of his "favorite" customers. If I hadn't been dumb enough to swim through a swarm of jellyfish—is it a swarm?—I probably would have never found out about the magic potion.

Determined not to focus on the negative, I change the subject. "So, what is a group of jellyfish called? A swarm? A pack? A herd?"

Kai laughs at my last suggestion. "Actually, I believe they are called a smack."

"Well, that seems appropriate." I chuckle with him. "I sure felt like I'd been given a few hard smacks before you came along." I turn serious. "Thank you for rescuing me."

"You're quite welcome," he tells me, and something deep inside me wonders if he might kiss me. I think my ears are ringing from the blood rushing through my head, until he tells me he'll be right back and jogs to pick up his cell phone. "Leilani," he answers, after looking at the display screen.

Hearing him utter her name immediately squelches the wayward thoughts. As much as I would like to fantasize that Kai is all mine, it just isn't in the cards. It never was, never will be. End of story. I don't want to overhear his conversation with his pregnant lover, so I decide to explore the gorgeous grounds at his home. I'm surprised to find a circle of outdoor showers that are secluded by dense tropical foliage. I can't stop the mental image of Kai and Leilani, wet and entwined, when I see this outdoor hydrotherapy paradise. Not wanting to think about their beautiful, writhing bodies making love under the warm spray, I quickly move along.

I notice a pathway that has various smooth stones sticking up from the concrete, so I decide to go investigate. "I see you've found my reflexology path." Kai has come up close behind me. "Try it out," he encourages me. I set off down the walkway but quickly find that it hurts, so I jump to the side and off the path.

Kai takes my hand and leads me back to the beginning. "You're going too fast. Slow down and enjoy it. Slowly roll your feet through each step." Not letting my hand go, Kai steps onto the path, leaving me no choice but to join him. This time, I follow his instructions and am amazed to find that slowly pressing my feet into the stones feels like a relaxing foot massage. I close my eyes as we traverse the path in super-slow motion. By the end, my entire body is zinging with energy from the rock massage of the pressure points on my feet—and the hand-to-hand connection I am sharing with Kai.

After we finish enjoying the reflexology path, I circle around to what appears to be a hot tub. "That's an icy plunge." Kai informs me. I stick a finger in and jerk it back, shocked to discover numbingly cold water. "You take a dip in there to rev up your circulation," Kai tells me, and I can't help but think that my circulation is already plenty revved when he is near. "Then you get in the hot tub." He gestures to a large in-ground swirling infinity pool of water. "The fast temperature change gives you pins and needles in your limbs, but it's a good tingling. Go ahead and give it a try. You'll never feel more alive," he promises.

My body already feels more alive than it ever has before just by being near him, but I don't want to embarrass myself by saying it. "I wouldn't want to wash off my magic jelly," I tell him, silently thinking that I can't be so near him in a hot tub, either. My fantasies about him don't need any more fuel added to the fire.

"If you're sure, then I'll take you back to the resort," he tells me before adding, "I'm already late for work, anyway."

I can feel a panic attack starting over his words. "I'm so sorry," I gasp. "Let's get going."

"It was so worth it," he reassures me. "Besides, what are they going to do, fire me?" He chuckles, but I can't help thinking that he is taking this much too lightly. Is this some kind of stereotypical "island attitude" about time and work? I would feel horrible if he lost his job for saving my life, even though from the looks of his house, he evidently doesn't need the money. He clearly wants to work, and I don't want to get in the way of that.

Kai walks me to a white Jeep and opens the passenger-side door before indicating he'll be right back and running into the house. When he returns, he has on shorts and a polo shirt and is carrying a large brown bag. I look down at myself and suddenly feel silly in my dark blue racer-back Speedo swimsuit. As if he had anticipated my discomfort, he tosses me a T-shirt from the bag before placing the bag in the backseat. I catch a whiff of his scent as I lower the T-shirt over my head. *I'll be keeping this*, I think to myself as we take off in the topless Jeep.

Once we park at the resort, he retrieves the bag from the backseat and hands me three jars of magic jelly. "How much do I owe you?" I ask him.

"Don't be ridiculous," he responds.

"No, I pay my own way," I inform him in my no-uncer-tain-terms tone.

"Okay then, I'd like a kiss." He leans toward me, smiling.

There is nothing I'd rather do than press my lips against Kai's, but an image of Leilani flashes into my mind. "I can't," I tell him before turning and running toward my room.

15

*W*hen I return to the room, Baggy and Ruthie are awake and beginning to move. I give them each a jar of the magic jelly with a brief explanation of the morning's events. Baggy is slightly bummed to learn that Kai's brown-bag dealings at the bar are not something seedier, but her eyes light up when she tells Ruthie and I about her latest scheme.

She confides to us that she and Howie are going on a top-secret sting operation to catch a jewelry thief at the Marriott a few hotels down the beach. "Howie?" Ruthie and I ask in unison, looking at each other to see if we had missed something important.

"Oh, Howard is Jim's real name," Baggy tells us, as if that explains everything. When we continue to look perplexed, she adds, "He only uses Jim—his code name—when he is undercover on super-secret spy operations." I am tempted to tell her that the very fact that he has shared all of this information with her proves that he is not a real spy, but I don't want to rain on her parade. She seems almost giddy with

147

happiness, so I suppose a little pretend danger won't hurt anything.

Ruthie tells us that she is going to try snorkeling today. For someone who normally only dips her toes in the water to bathe, she sure is turning into quite a fish. I'm pretty sure it's only because of her latest conquest (whose wardrobe seems to consist solely of shorty wetsuits and long board swim shorts), but I decide not to call her out on it.

I inform them that again I intend to spend the day painting, and they both head out, excited to begin their next adventure in paradise. I pull out my easel, admire my waterfall rendition for a moment before I set it aside, and stare at a blank canvas. I'd like to replicate the emotion of being pulled into Kai's strong embrace as he saved me from the smack of jellyfish, but I can't paint a muscular arm wrapped around a damsel in distress. I had enough trouble attempting to explain away the waterfall scene. If Kai saw a water rescue scene, he would think I am some kind of deranged stalker.

In the end, I decide to create a super close-up impression of a jellyfish. As is usually the case, I lose myself in the pleasure of painting and have no idea how much time has passed, other than the fact that my tummy is growling angrily. I stand back to look at the finished piece and am pleased. I have captured the iridescent essence of the animal and somehow found a way to express the beauty in a creature that I now fully despise. Feeling rather pleased with my emerging talent, I head in to shower off the paint and grime of a long day's work.

Jim, or Howie, or whatever we are supposed to call him, joins us for dinner. He regales us all with tall tales of his spy adventures. I wonder if he is delusional and really believes the stories he shares, or if he is just eccentric and likes to entertain. Either way, he is funny and charming, and Baggy seems to be completely taken with him. When he takes her hand and says, "Let's go cut a rug," Baggy giggles like a schoolgirl before following him to the dance floor.

I sit back in my chair to enjoy watching them for a bit. Their effervescence for life is apparent as they flounce around in each other's arms. We should all be lucky enough to find someone to share that with, even if he is a little crazy. Besides, she's more than a little crazy herself.

Ruthie spots her crush at the bar and saunters off. It's so odd to see her being the chaser, when she is so accustomed to being the chased.

I sit at the table for a few minutes pondering my life and wishing there was a luau tonight. Kai drops into Baggy's vacated chair and asks me if I'd like to take a walk along the beach. I smile and agree to go with him.

As we walk, I can't help but wonder if it is part of the resort employees' jobs to help entertain the lonely, loser guests who don't have anyone special in one of the most romantic spots on Earth. The thought dampens my spirits, and I decide to relieve Kai of his duty. "You don't have to spend time with me," I tell him. "I know it is part of your job to make sure the resort's guests have fun."

He gives me an odd look. "I don't know what you think is in my job description, but it's nothing like that. I'm not a gigolo."

"I thought this might fall under the 'other duties as needed' category," I tell him, only half-joking.

"No, I'm here with you because I want to be."

His words are sweet and perfect—exactly what I want to hear—and it frustrates me beyond reason. I run a hand through my hair before calling him out on it. "I know that Leilani is pregnant." I let that hang in the air for a bit. Kai is silently looking at me, like he needs more of an explanation than that. "Well, don't you think you should be going on a romantic stroll along the beach with her, not me?"

149

"No," he tells me before understanding dawns. "Oh, you think the baby is mine. Leilani and I are just friends—have been since we were kids." Relief floods through me at his explanation, until he bowls me over with a surprising statement. "The baby is Honi's."

You could have knocked me over with a feather. *Huge, sweet, high-voiced Honi is the father of Leilani's baby?*

"Honi has always been in love with her, and I think she feels the same way about him, but she's scared to admit it, even to herself." I nod, trying to absorb what he is telling me. Honi seems like a terrific guy, but he is not at all the type of person I pictured being with someone like Leilani. "He's not exactly who she envisioned herself ending up with, but love sneaks up on us sometimes." Kai's words mimic my thoughts exactly.

"Whoa," is all I can say. Suddenly, it sinks in with me that all of the barriers between Kai and I were figments of my imagination. His shady dealings behind the bar and his gorgeous, pregnant girlfriend were things I had blown out of proportion in my own mind.

I am in paradise with a sweet Hawaiian hunk, and there is no reason why I can't have a hot, sexy fling with him. The realization washes over me. We have stopped walking and are standing very close. The moon isn't quite full, but it's big and shining brightly over the ocean. There is a light breeze tossing my hair back. This is the perfect moment for a kiss. I tip my head back and wait, but nothing happens.

He asks if I'm ready to head back to the resort and the moment is gone. *Maybe I have misread him? Is he just being friendly?* We walk alongside the pool and I torture myself with these thoughts. *Why didn't he kiss me? Should I have kissed him? There must be a reason why he didn't. I wonder what it could be.*

Suddenly, he stops and turns to me. He hesitates as if

undecided about what to do. Finally, he steps closer to me and drops his lips down to mine in a tender, tantalizing kiss. I open my lips seeking more, but he pulls back.

"Goodnight, Roxy." He says the words, and then he is gone. I stand there with my eyes closed, feeling like I am floating for a minute. I bring two fingers up to my lips, savoring the feeling of having just received the best kiss of my life.

"Wow." I say the word aloud since no one else is around. Finally, I return to our cabana, even though I know there is no chance of my heartbeats slowing enough to allow for sleep anytime soon.

*a*pparently, my heart rate did eventually calm down because I sleep like the dead. I awaken with a start and realize someone is knocking on our door. As I stumble to answer it, I'm surprised to see daylight. I am alone in the room, so I must have slept through Baggy and Ruthie getting up and leaving, which can't have been quiet.

I fling the door open and am only moderately surprised to see Kai on the other side. He doesn't seem taken aback by my appearance, which I'm sure is a hot-mess mix of disheveled bedhead and raccoon-eyed smeared makeup.

"The market is open today. Would you like to go with me?"

I have no idea what the market is, but if Kai wants to take me somewhere, I am there. "I should probably shower first." I point in the general direction of my head and smile with closed lips, careful not to show my fuzzy, unbrushed teeth or spew any of my dreadful morning breath in his direction.

"I'll wait by the bar," he tells me and spins on his heel to head that way.

I shut the door and spring into action. I want to get ready quickly so he is not waiting on me for too long, but I also want to look great and be ready for any adventure he wishes to embark upon. I finally decide to wear a bathing suit with a cute sundress over it.

I take my choices to the bathroom and glance in the mirror after starting the shower. My reflection is downright frightening. The fact that he didn't go running from this room at the sight of me is amazing. I take the speediest shower I can without skipping shaving, which isn't an option. I do take the time to rub some magic jelly on my dry knees and elbows. It feels so great on my skin that I decide to douse my entire body in it. Why not? Besides, I smell like a delicious coconut concoction that Kai might blend behind the bar.

I take the time to apply sunscreen on my face. After adding mascara and ChapStick, I pull my hair into a low ponytail and declare myself presentable. Not just presentable, I decide as I catch a glimpse of my swingy skirt in the full-length mirror. I'd give myself a 6.5 today, maybe a 7. I'll just try not to think of the fact that Kai is a 9.5, possibly a 10.

When I join him at the bar, he beams at me like I am the most beautiful woman in the world, and I instantly forget all the one-to-ten rating-scale nonsense. I look around to tell Baggy and Ruthie that we are leaving, but can't find either of them. I decide to just go. That is what they would do. Besides, they can call my cell if they really need me.

Kai leads me to the limo that he picked us up from the airport in. "You're allowed to drive the resort's limo when you're not working?" I ask him.

"Nana Lana needed the Jeep today." I try to picture a grandmotherly type tooling around the island in Kai's Jeep.

His grandma must be even more like Baggy than I had imagined. "Besides, I am working," Kai adds.

I raise my eyebrows in question, so he continues, "I'm picking up fresh fruit and juice at the market."

"Oh, you just invited me along to help tote and carry, eh?" I tease him. Going to a grocery to pick up supplies for the resort isn't something I would have thought I'd want to do on a Hawaiian vacation, but I'd be willing to do about anything with Kai.

"You've figured out my evil plan. Gorgeous and smart—I am a lucky man." I beam at his praise and successfully fight the urge to deny its accuracy.

I get to ride in the front of the limo this time, and I'm thrilled when Kai reaches over to hold my hand in his much larger one. We ride mostly in silence. I enjoy the scenery and the wonderful feeling of connection with Kai. Occasionally he points out something of interest, like the elementary school he attended, but for the most part we are quiet.

When we arrive at the market, I'm surprised and delighted to see that it is an enormous farmer's market, not a grocery, like I had assumed. The vendors sell everything from delicious fresh fruit to souvenirs of every imaginable size, shape, and type. The tables stretch on for what seems like miles, and I am in heaven.

I purchase a cup of pineapple and mango from a smiling man who faintly reminds me of Honi. The fruit is so sweet and juicy that I actually groan in delight at the taste of it. Kai seems to take pleasure in watching me enjoy it. When I bite into a large piece of pineapple and juice runs down my chin, he leans in and flicks his tongue out to catch it. It is an intimate and sweet gesture that sends a thrill of excitement down my spine.

While Kai negotiates with a vendor over the bulk price of

coconuts, I continue shopping. I discover a booth with locally made, adorable magnets. I purchase three for five bucks, which seems like a fantastic bargain anywhere, let alone Hawaii. My selections are a colorful surfboard for Ruthie, a silly googly-eyed turtle for Baggy and a tiny hand-painted waterfall scene for me.

I walk away from the magnet vendor feeling rather pleased with myself. Then it dawns on me that it's a little strange to have bought souvenirs only for the people who are with me on the trip. I stop at the next booth and purchase a bowl made of palm fronds for my parents, just so I have something to give them when I get home. I don't even want to think about going back, though.

Kai catches up with me just as I stop to look at a table of coconut oil-based lotions and creams. "Nana Lana would not approve of you supporting the competition," he teases near my ear.

"Just looking," I tell him.

He continues to nuzzle my neck. "You're wearing magic jelly on your neck." The words vibrate close to my skin, making the tiny hairs on my neck stand at attention. "You smell good enough to eat," he growls.

I wonder if we are making spectacles of ourselves, but his nearness feels so terrific that I almost don't care. He trails soft kisses behind my ear. When his tongue brushes against my skin, my knees almost buckle. Kai steadies me as I lean into his tantalizing mouth. The lotion vendor is discreet enough to busy herself with aligning bottles as if she doesn't notice.

"You drive me absolutely insane, Roxy," he informs me before pulling back. I instantly miss his touch.

I decide that "insane" is the perfect word for how he makes me feel. I lose all of my normal inhibitions when Kai

155

is near, and when he touches me, my body comes alive with a fire inside that I didn't know was there.

Suddenly, we hear a high-pitched wailing voice about twenty feet from where we are standing. Kai springs into action. By the time I realize what is happening and follow him, he has already assessed the situation and taken off in pursuit of a young man. I quickly deduce that the tiny, upset woman has had her purse stolen.

I put my arm around her to try to offer some comfort as she continues to wail. Another bystander pulls out her cell phone to notify the police. A crowd has gathered around, and we all watch helplessly as Kai chases the thief.

They run across a busy street toward a residential area. The boy has a good lead on Kai, but Kai is closing the gap. When the young man climbs over a tall privacy fence, I hear a man from the crowd say, "That big guy isn't going to be able to get over that fence." Kai proves him wrong by hurtling himself over the fence at full speed as if it requires no effort at all.

I smile in secret pride at Kai's athletic ability, although I'm not sure why. "Looks like he made it," I say to the doubter, who now has a surprised, slightly envious look on his face.

Now that the runners are out of sight, the crowd begins to disburse. I still have my arm around the tiny victim. Her wailing has stopped, but tears are streaming down her face. I feel so bad for her, but I'm not sure what to do to help. "It will be okay," I tell her, even though I'm not at all certain that is the case. I don't like not being able to see what is happening with Kai and the pickpocket. What if he pulls a weapon on Kai? The thought makes me shudder, so I try to push it out of my mind.

It seems like we stand there forever. After what feels like an incredibly long time but is probably actually only a few minutes, a policewoman arrives on the scene. She tries to get details from the victim, but the elderly lady is still too upset to be of much help. I step in and share as much information as I know. When I get to the part about Kai taking off after the thief, the officer stops me. "Kai Mauka?" she asks me, smiling.

I nod, even though I'm appalled to realize that I don't know Kai's last name. I'm going to be rather embarrassed when he gets back, if he is not the Kai she is referencing. I wonder how common the name Kai is on the island.

The officer doesn't seem to notice my stress. "Nothing to worry about, then. Kai will bring him in," she reassures us.

Now, I'm pretty certain that we aren't talking about the same person. After all, why would a police officer have faith that a resort chauffeur/bartender/fire thrower would win a foot chase with a criminal and bring him in?

It isn't long until Kai proves her absolutely right. He and the young man approach us. Kai has his large hand around the gangly lad's arm, but other than that, they look like they are on a friendly stroll.

"If I'd have known you were chasing after him, I wouldn't have bothered driving over," the officer says to Kai, beaming a huge smile at him and tossing a familiar arm around his shoulder. I immediately wonder how acquainted Kai is with the lovely lady.

"Happy to help anytime I can." Kai returns the hug with his free arm and gives her a sweet kiss on the cheek, which makes her blush. I can feel jealousy bubbling at the familiarity they share, but I force it down.

Kai turns his attention to the boy. "Don't you have something to say?"

"I'm sorry," he mumbles, handing the stolen handbag back to the distraught lady.

"We didn't hear that." Kai gives him a stern look.

ANN OMASTA

"I'm sorry for taking your purse, ma'am. I won't do anything like that again." This time he looks the woman in the eyes and speaks with purpose. It makes me wonder exactly what went on when Kai and the young man were out of our sight.

"I'll take over from here," the cop informs us as she places handcuffs on the young man. Kai finally releases his grip on the lad's arm and the officer begins reciting the boy his rights and leading him to her patrol car.

The tiny lady is staring at her purse with a huge look of relief evident on her face. She carefully unzips the bag and inspects its contents. Satisfied that her belongings are all present and accounted for, she pulls out her wallet. She reaches in and pulls out a crisp twenty-dollar bill, which she shoves at Kai's chest.

"Oh, no." He backs away as if the money has burned him. "No reward needed. You try to enjoy the rest of your day," he tells her and turns to leave, effectively taking away the option of her insisting that he take the money.

We continue on through the vendors, but I am no longer interested in shopping. "You are an amazing man," I tell Kai honestly.

He grins down at me. "You're pretty amazing yourself, Roxy." He brushes a brief but tender kiss across my lips.

I am so completely and instantly aroused by this simple touch that I would likely go along with anything he suggests. If he asked me to sneak off to a public restroom for a quickie with him, I am quite certain that I would follow him. I try not to touch anything in public restrooms, yet if Kai wanted to, I'd get naked and naughty with him in one. The power he has over me is frightening but exciting at the same time.

We leave the market without visiting the restroom—to my relief and disappointment. I spend the entire drive back to the resort looking for places that we could pull the limo over and climb into the back. Although I see several, I am too chicken to suggest it. Kai is a gentleman and returns me safely and uneventfully to the door of my room.

He gives me a quick peck on the cheek, says he'll see me later, and leaves. Sigh.

17

*I*f I had known what I would find on the other side of the door, I would have never opened it. I did open it though, and what I saw can't be unseen.

I didn't see them at first, which is why I walked all the way in, leaving me no way to gracefully retreat. "Hi!" The word startles me, but not nearly as much as the sight of the man uttering it.

My eyes quickly assess the situation I've walked in on. The only good thing about the entire scene is that I wasn't five minutes later. The scenario I probably would have encountered then would have definitely scarred me for life.

For some reason, I seem to be the only one embarrassed by my walking in to find Baggy and Jim, or Howie, or whatever his name is, in their bikinis and lubed up from head to toe in magic jelly. The air in the room is filled with an odor similar to what I would imagine a coconut processing factory smells like, so that probably should have been my first clue to enter with caution—or better yet, not at all.

Baggy's boyfriend is sporting a bright yellow banana hammock, and his skin is as shiny as an oiled pig. He has both hands raised and is waving in welcome at me as if I should come in and sit down. The full-frontal view of his barely covered junk is almost too much to take in.

Baggy is wearing a red bikini and her skin is glistening as well. "This stuff is magnificent!" she raves, holding up her almost empty jar of magic jelly.

"Yeah, it's good stuff," I respond. I try to avert my eyes but the sight of the two of them is almost like a train wreck—you don't want to look, but for some reason, can't quite tear your eyes away. Finally, I come to my senses enough to start backing out of the room.

"I'm going down to the pool," I inform them.

"Don't leave on our account," Jim/Howard says.

"Nope, that was my plan all along. I just came to the room to grab a towel," I add quickly, snatching one from the bathroom. They are polite enough not to point out there are plenty of towels for guests at the pool. "Enjoy the rest of your day," I yell on my way out.

Once it closes, I lean back on the door. "Wow." It's really the only word that fits the situation. Then a snort of laughter erupts out of me and I giggle all the way to the pool.

As I lay back on a lounge chair to absorb a few minutes of sunshine, I try to decide if I should warn Ruthie or let her discover Baggy and Jim/Howie on her own. I finally decide that if I happen to see her, I'll tell her. Otherwise, she's on her own. I'm not going to seek her out. Besides, *I* had to see it. I snicker to myself, imagining how Ruthie's eyes would nearly pop out of her head as she described the scene. Once she gets over the anger of me not warning her, this will likely strengthen our sisterly bond. No one else could possibly understand.

"You look like you're up to something." Kai smiles down at me as he walks past.

"You have no idea," I tell him mysteriously.

He winks at me but keeps walking, so I enjoy a long, luxurious look at his fabulous backside.

18

I move to a lounge chair in the shade in order to avoid getting sunburned. I didn't have time to grab a book from the room, so I spend a few minutes looking at my cell phone. I have now been e-mail- and social media–free for a few days, and I quickly find that I haven't missed it. The volume of notifications that ding when I sign on to the resort's Wi-Fi feels overwhelming, so I put the phone back to sleep and stow it in my purse.

There is no way I am going back to the room and risking seeing whatever wild activities Baggy and her man are up to in there, so I slide on my blingy sunglasses and tip my chair back to a more relaxing angle. I decide the best use of my time is to daydream about Kai—this pastime has become one of my new favorite activities.

I let steamy Kai fantasies wash over me. Remembering his sweet kisses on my neck and lips is enough to make me smile like a Cheshire cat. When I allow my mind to wander into the territory where our bodies have not yet gone, I can feel a familiar and delightful tension building deep inside me.

I imagine us on a deserted stretch of beach, lying on a

large blanket. He slowly trails kisses down my chest. His tantalizing tongue laps out to caress me. My vivid imagination comes in handy as I picture the two of us slipping out of our clothes and touching each other all over. Of course the sand isn't a problem. This is my daydream, after all.

Even with the magnificence that Kai's body promises when clothed, I am pleasantly surprised to discover it is even more impressive when I envision him in all his glory. I picture myself slowly pulling his swim trunks down. Naturally, in my daydream, I am much sexier and more graceful than I am in real life. Someone walks hastily by me, dribbling pool water along my calf. The chilly water stuns me out of my fantasy.

I open my eyes to look around. No one seems to be staring, so I must not have been moaning in ecstasy. Since I had been enjoying myself, and no one seems to be suspicious of the naughty turn my thoughts had taken, I allow my mind to dip back into the fantasy.

Kai and I are nude, lying together on the beach. Our bodies are touching in all the right places. Our hands rove all over, exploring each other's bodies. Kai rises up and looks down at me with adoring eyes. I have never felt so beautiful and desirable. Just as he begins to lower himself, Ruthie plops down in the lounge chair next to me, announcing that she's hungry.

I consider telling her to go away, but instead, I grudgingly sit up and ask her what sounds good for lunch. As much as I'd like to continue my naked roll in the sand with dreamy Kai, I'd prefer to have the real-life experience—and the memories of it to relive once I get home. The thought of having to go home brings me down, so I immediately push it out of my head.

Deciding to get my mind off that topic completely, I say to Ruthie, "You'll never believe what I just walked in on in our room." This opener allows us to talk and laugh hysterically throughout our seaside cafe lunch of fried clams and parmesan truffle fries. Ruthie physically covers her eyes, as if that will block the mental image I am describing of seeing Baggy's man in his skimpy yellow ensemble.

"O-M-Geeee, please stop talking." She laughs as I tell her about their slick skin shining with magic jelly. "Why do you suppose they were getting all lubed up? Wait, don't answer that!" She rethinks the question before I can answer.

We are both still chuckling at our wild and crazy grandmother when Ruthie turns serious. Holding up a fry, she says sadly, "I'm really going to miss these when we go home."

"They are delicious," I agree, knowing that we are both going to miss a lot more than the tasty French fries we have discovered on the island. The thought of having to leave Kai depresses me. I refuse to think about it anymore.

Ruthie must feel the same way because she abruptly changes from her almost pensive mood. "Whelp, I'm off to take a WaveRunner lesson. See ya later," she calls over her shoulder, having already hopped out of her chair. I shake my head and watch her shaking her fanny on the way to the watersports shack. The fact that we are sisters absolutely blows my mind. I love her to pieces, but we couldn't possibly be more different.

Maybe I should practice my butt-shaking walk the next time I see Kai. If nothing else, it would probably give him a good laugh.

19

$\mathcal{I}$t turns out that I don't have to bother practicing my butt-tastic walk because Kai plops down in Ruthie's recently vacated chair. I quickly forget all about my plans of seduction. All I can feel is the instant magnetic attraction I feel for him. He's beyond handsome.

When he asks if I'm up for a hike, I don't hesitate. As I realized earlier, I would probably follow this man anywhere —a walk on a scenic island trail is a no-brainer.

He takes my hand and we set off together. I am a little distraught when I discover that we are heading along the path that leads to the waterfall where I spied on him earlier. He wouldn't bring me up here just to chastise me for watching him, would he? When we come to the fork in the path, he steers me in the less worn direction, and I realize that we are indeed heading to the waterfall.

I hear the roaring of the water before I can see it. When we step into the clearing, I suck in my breath at the natural beauty. Even though I have been here before, the stunning perfection still surprises me.

"This is one of my favorite spots," he confides near my ear, so I can hear him over the loud water.

I nod in appreciation. I'm still not certain if he saw me here the other day, but I'm sure he recognized his form in my painting. I suppose it really doesn't matter. He doesn't seem to be angry about it, and it's not like I can do anything about it at this point anyway. "It's really beautiful," I gush honestly as he eases himself behind me, wrapping his arms tightly around me. The feeling of having him at my back is divine. I lean my head back into him, savoring the feeling of his firm chest.

"Would you like to go for a swim?" he asks me.

"I'd love to," I answer, and I mean it. As we walk down the path to the water, I am thankful that I had thought to don a swimsuit under my dress this morning. If Kai goes in the water in the buff, I'll be happy to skinny-dip with him, but this way I am prepared for anything.

When we near the bank, he yanks his shirt over his head. I stare at his perfect shoulders for a few moments. Not wanting to get caught, I break out of my trance and begin removing my Keen sandals. Kai gallantly steadies me by my elbow as I balance on each leg to take off my shoes. Since I don't have anything else on, I slide my sundress up over my head. I am pleasantly surprised to find that Kai isn't as bashful as I was about gawking. He is openly looking at my barely covered body, and he seems to like what he sees. When he licks his lips and finally raises his eyes up to meet my gaze, we both chuckle with nervous energy.

I take a couple of steps toward the water, but turn to watch as Kai quickly shucks his board shorts. He has stripped down to a pair of black boxer briefs, and I feel a warm and pleasing sensation in my belly when I notice how they are bulging in all the right places.

He takes my hand and we walk together the rest of the

way to the water's edge. I daintily dip a toe in and am pleasantly surprised to find that the water is warm—luxuriously warm. "That's not how you get in," he teases me. He points out a couple of feet into the dark turquoise swirling water. "Just jump out past this ledge. See it?" When I nod, he starts a countdown. "Three-two-one." We jump in together.

The water feels glorious. Kai is an excellent swimmer, but I already knew that based on his rescue of me from the smack of jellyfish. We glide through the water together—sometimes floating lazily on our backs, sometimes splashing each other playfully. Finally, I can't resist the draw of the falling water any longer. Kai quickly deduces my destination and dives under water. He expels a rush of bubbles, which tickle my underside and make me giggle.

We arrive at the waterfall at the same moment and let the water rush over us. I tip my head back so it washes down my back. It feels cleansing and powerful. Being in this pristine location with the man of my dreams is truly a gift—a gift that I don't want to waste. I boldly declare to myself that I don't want to have any regrets when I go home, and I'm quite certain that not jumping Kai's bones right now would be a huge, lifelong regret.

Kai is a gentleman, so I decide to give him an indisputable sign that I am ready for more. I reach one hand behind me under the water, while using the other to dog paddle to stay afloat. On the sly, I unclip the clasp at the back of my bikini top. Once it is unhooked, I make short work of the tie at the back of my neck, freeing my ample breasts.

I take a moment to enjoy the feeling of the warm water rushing over my bare skin before clearing my throat. Once I have Kai's full attention, I raise my brightly colored bathing suit top up out of the water. His eyes widen in surprise, and then he breaks into a huge grin, which is exactly the reaction I had been hoping for.

I wad the top into a ball and toss it to the embankment. Once I am free of it, Kai and I lunge at each other. We kiss each other hungrily. It is difficult keeping our faces above the water while attempting to grope each other, so Kai says, "Come back here." I follow him behind the fall and am pleased to find a shallow ledge. The wall of water gives us some privacy in case anyone should join us at our scenic, yet somewhat public spot.

Kai sits down on the ledge, and the water laps gently at his chest. I look around our secluded cove and decide this location is absolutely perfect. So rather than sitting beside him on the ledge, I climb onto his lap and straddle him. Our lips and tongues meld together in a delicious kiss. His large hands cup my breasts gently. I tip my head back and enjoy his touch as he kisses his way down my neck and chest. When he suckles a nipple, I cry out with the pleasure of it. My lower half seeks his. I scoot myself along his massive erection, making us both groan.

Deciding that there are too many clothes between us, I reach down to relieve us of the remaining frustrating barrier. I decide to start with Kai's—mostly because I want to get my hands on him. When I slide my fingers under his waistband, he wraps a hand around my wrist—stopping me. We sit there like that for a moment—both of us breathing heavy, but otherwise unmoving. I am uncertain why he has a vise grip on my arm, but he isn't letting go.

Finally, he croaks, "I can't," before diving under the wall of water and swimming away from me. I sit there for a long while, stunned and embarrassed. I have never been half-naked and willing to fool around with a man who turned me down before, and I don't like how it feels.

I chastise myself for being so stupid. He's clearly not attracted to me—why would he be? He is perfection personified and I am lanky and slightly above average at best. There is no denying his body's reaction to me, but that is purely physical. A healthy, virile man would probably become aroused by anyone who brazenly takes off her top and climbs on him behind a majestic waterfall.

I shake my head in exasperation at myself. I can't believe I tossed my top to shore. How can I gracefully retrieve it without making even more of an ass of myself? I know the answer to that question. I can't. What had I been thinking? I guess I could sit back here and hope that he leaves, but the fear of someone else coming along and seeing my shucked top makes heat rise up on my cheeks.

I am ashamed of myself, and I just want to extricate myself from this situation as quickly and quietly as possible. I dive under the falling water and surface as close as I can to the point where I threw my top. I am pleased to find my belongings lying neatly by the edge of the water. Kai must have placed my clothes within reach to minimize my embarrassment. I guess that's the least he could do after shunning my sexual advances.

I put my bathing suit top on under the water, then pull myself out of the water and slip the dress over my wet skin. After sliding my feet into my sandals, I turn toward the path to head back to the hotel. Kai is waiting for me—ever the gentleman, with his back turned to give me as much privacy as he can. I don't want to face him right now, but I don't see another way to leave.

Deciding to just get it over with, I trudge toward the path. When I am even with Kai, he turns to me, "Ready to head back?" he asks me as if everything is normal.

I feel like kicking him in the 'nads. How can he just ignore the fact that I am completely humiliated? How can he act like nothing happened back there? Why did he shun me? Rather than physically harming him or asking him any of the numerous questions that are swirling around my head, I nod and continue walking.

The walk back to the resort seems interminable. When we finally get to the bar at the resort, I mutter a quick "See ya" over my shoulder before speed-walking to the villa's door. When I put the key in the door, I say a silent prayer that Baggy and her man are finished with whatever kinky, slick games they had previously been enjoying.

The island gods are on my side for once because the room is empty. I collapse onto my bed before I start sobbing as a pathetic mixture of sadness, hurt feelings, and humiliation overwhelms me. I cry myself to sleep and don't even hear Baggy and Ruthie return to the room.

hen I wake up the next morning, I have a revelation. I decide to focus on helping others rather than wallowing in my own misery over Kai not wanting me, and I know just whom I am going to assist.

Having a selfless mission brings a bit of a spring to my step. I am in paradise after all. I shouldn't be surprised that Kai isn't sexually interested in me. I was silly to think that I might be sexy enough for him. He can probably take his choice of any woman he wants. I'll just avoid him until the awkwardness passes or it's time for me to go home—whichever comes first.

I go down to the breakfast buffet and am surprised to see Leilani filling in for the normal hostess. It seems like each employee of this resort covers several positions. Leilani seats me at what has now become our usual table. A beaming Honi arrives just as I sit down and delivers my piping-hot tea. It's amazing how quickly these workers have learned the nuances of our likes and dislikes. They all seem to really pay attention and truly enjoy their jobs.

Once Honi sets down the tray—which includes sugar

cubes and cream, just the way I like it—I ask him to sit down for a moment. If he is surprised by my request, he hides it well. He amiably lowers himself into the chair next to me and asks how I am doing. I fib by telling him that I am doing great then I say that I would rather hear how he is doing.

Once I am certain that Leilani has seated her next table and is walking back in our direction, I rest my hand on Honi's beefy arm and lean toward him. I see her eyes resting on us for a moment, but she quickly flits past, so I decide to step up my game a little.

When Honi tells me the old joke about the customer asking the waiter what the fly is doing in his soup, only to have the waiter reply, "The backstroke," I laugh much louder than necessary. My outburst is rewarded with a sharp glare from Leilani, which makes my day. I had been hoping that Kai was right about her feelings for Honi, and the eye daggers she sends me suggest that he was.

Leilani is busy chatting with a young couple about their dinner reservations, so I use the time to talk to Honi. "You should ask Leilani to go out with you." I nudge his arm with my elbow.

I see a wave of sadness pass over his eyes before he masks it with his usual charm. "We've been out on a few dates, but she broke things off," he confides in me. I can't tell if he knows about the pregnancy.

Honi is silent for so long, I start to think that he isn't going to continue; but then he does. "What would someone as beautiful and amazing as Leilani see in someone like me, anyway?" His question mirrors my own about Kai.

Even though his question was rhetorical, I feel compelled to answer him. "You are a great guy, Honi," I tell him honestly. "She would be lucky to have you." Honi shakes his head sadly, clearly not agreeing with my assessment.

I notice Leilani checking us out, so I pat Honi's arm

gently. "I think we've managed to make her jealous," I confide in him when I see her reaction to my hand on Honi.

Honi's features brighten instantly. "Yeah?" he asks me hopefully.

"Definitely." I nod, winking at him.

"Thanks, Roxy!" he says enthusiastically before hefting himself out of his chair.

I spend the rest of my meal only slightly uncomfortable from the unkind looks I can feel Leilani aiming at my back. When I leave the restaurant, she follows me.

"Is it not enough that you have Kai panting after you like a Great Dane in heat? Now you have to sink your claws into Honi, too?"

Turning to face her, I don't bother to point out to her that Kai isn't at all interested in me sexually. Seeing the look on her face takes away any hurt feelings I experience from her comments. It is obvious from her pained expression that she cares deeply for Honi. I decide to put her out of her misery. "Actually, Honi and I were talking about you."

She seems surprised and completely taken aback by this revelation. "Really?" She looks hopeful for a moment, but her face quickly crumples into tears. I put a comforting arm around her and am surprised when she doesn't immediately push me away. "You wouldn't understand," she tells me when I ask if there is anything I can do to help.

"I understand that Honi is a kind, loving, gentle giant of a man and that any woman would be lucky to have him. I also understand that you have won his heart," I tell her. She smiles through her tears at that, but stays rooted to her spot. I gently suggest that she should go talk to him and am happy when she follows my advice.

I watch her walk back into the restaurant with what probably looks like a self-satisfied grin on my face. I head back toward my room feeling quite good about my match-making skills. Hopefully, the two of them can make it work.

21

*K*ai swoops up behind me, placing a casual arm around my shoulders. "Mornin', sunshine." He beams the words at me as if everything is hunky dory, even though it's not—not at all.

Isn't it a prerequisite of being a single, heterosexual man to try to bang any available, willing, moderately attractive female? I wonder, silently fuming.

I had been hoping to avoid the awkwardness of seeing him for the duration of my stay. He seems to be completely unaware of the tension emanating from me. "Aren't you supposed to be working?" I ask in an attempt to let him know that he doesn't need to humor me by flirting with me when he doesn't have any desire to bed me.

"I put the Be Right Back sign up at the bar and left. It's one of the perks of owning the resort." He says the words as if they are no big deal, but his revelation stuns me. This man who works as the chauffeur/bartender/fire dancer owns the resort?

Kai can evidently see the questions in my expression, so he expands. "The hotel has been in my family since my grandfather had it built over fifty years ago. When he passed away, Nana Lana assumed ownership and immediately started grooming me to take it over. Now, she and I share 51 percent ownership of the property and the other 49 percent is in a trust for the employees. Each employee earns a fraction of a percentage of the trust for each year they work here. Our arrangement makes for loyal and happy employees."

He says it simply, as if everyone is this generous. This explanation clarifies why everyone takes on multiple posts and seems so genuinely thrilled to be here. They have an employer who isn't afraid to get down in the trenches and also profit shares with them. Despite myself, I am incredibly impressed with Kai and his grandmother. They are clearly hard-working, giving people. I admire the work ethic of a man who is willing to fill in wherever needed when he could easily hire others to do the more mundane jobs.

I'm not sure why he has shared all of this information with me, and I grudgingly realize that it makes me like him even more. I don't want to like him more. I want to find his flaws—other than not wanting me, of course.

I decide to be direct. "Why are you telling me all of this?" Before he can answer, I continue, "You don't have to explain anything to me. It's okay that you don't want me the way that I want you."

He seems completely taken aback by my words. "You think I don't want you?"

I widen my eyes at him, but don't answer. *What else could I possibly think after yesterday?* I wonder.

Kai pulls me into his arms, but I keep my upper body stiff. "I want you more than I have ever desired anyone," he tells me.

I turn away from him then. His words are exactly what I want to hear, but after he left me willing, topless, and completely aroused in the water, I know they can't possibly be true. I can't take any more of this hot-and-cold treatment.

He moves close behind me, and I can feel the heat of him at my back as we stand near my villa. "Does this feel like a man who doesn't want you?" He presses into me and I can feel his hot, hard erection against my lower spine. He nips at my ear, and I gasp at the pleasure of it.

I glance around to make sure no one is watching us. He puts his hand over mine and pulls it to him, guiding my hand up and down his length over his jeans. "I want you with every inch of my body and soul." He breathes the words out along my neck, and then hisses as my fingers squeeze over him.

Since my hand is rubbing him without his help, he brings his arms around me to pull me tighter back against his front. His hands slide up my belly and under the waistband of my bra. He gently pulls and lifts the undergarment until my breasts spring free underneath it. When he places a hand on each breast and nibbles at my ear, I let out a quiet whimper of delight.

I want this man so much. Right here and right now. Well, inside the room, but as quickly as possible. I turn to face him and press my front into him as I kiss my way along his neck. He has to bend down for me to kiss his lips—a first for me— but he obliges.

Soon our tongues are tangled and our hands are roving over each other's fully clothed bodies as we meld into each other. I boldly decide to throw caution to the wind and reach for the snap of his pants. His hand closes over mine, halting its progress.

"We need to go inside." I quickly realize that things have gotten out of control. Saying a silent prayer that Baggy and Ruthie have vacated the room, I use my free hand to dig in my bag for my room key.

"No, we have to stop," he tells me, backing away slightly. I feel like I have been slapped in the face with icy-cold water. How can we be desperate for each other one moment, and he shuns me the next? I just don't understand it.

"Do you need to get back to the bar?" I ask, almost hopeful but knowing deep down that I am grasping at straws, reaching for a plausible explanation.

"No, I can't do this with you at all." He dashes my slight hope as he backs away from me, running a hand through his shiny black hair.

"I see." I say the words flatly, and I do see. Some part of him wants me. Even though it is a substantial part (as I discovered through his jeans), the logical and rational side of him knows that I am not good enough for him. All sorts of insecure thoughts erupt in my brain while we stand there for what seems to be a very long time, but probably actually isn't long at all. I turn to go into my villa.

"You don't understand." I halt, hoping beyond hope that he can come up with something that will help his sudden change of heart make sense and not hurt so much. "I want to rip your clothes off right here. I want it more than I've ever wanted anything," he informs me.

His words make warmth spread back through me, but I still don't understand what the problem can possibly be. He is silent for a long while, making me wonder if he is going to explain or make me guess.

Finally, he speaks again, but his voice is so soft that I second-guess if I have heard him correctly. I think he said "I can't make love to you."

I stand there waiting, uncertain what to say. His next words, while still quiet, confirm that I heard him right. "I can't have sex with anyone."

My eyes involuntarily travel down to his still enormous penis. It is obviously not a lack of ability to get it up that is causing his hesitation. My next thought is that maybe he has a sexually transmitted disease. If that's the case, I appreciate his concern and caution, but I have a solution for that. "Why don't you wear a condom?" At his perplexed look, I expand, "I know guys don't like wearing them, but sex with a condom is better than no sex at all, right?"

He doesn't seem to be getting what I am saying, so I go on. "Besides, a condom will protect me from an unwanted pregnancy and any issues you have going on down there." I point to his genital region, thinking that he has probably bedded a significant number of women.

"I don't have any STDs." He wrinkles his nose. "It's nothing like that," he tells me. Again, he stops talking for so long that I wonder if he is going to explain more, but he takes a couple of steps away from me. Just when I begin to think that he really might leave me hanging like this, he stops and speaks without turning to face me. His words are so quiet that I instantly become convinced that I have misunderstood him.

"Wait, what?" I ask him.

He speaks only slightly louder this time, but confirms what I thought I had heard him say—some of the most unbelievable words that could possibly come out of his mouth. "I'm a virgin."

"A virgin?" I blurt out, almost sounding angry in my disbelief. His words are incomprehensible. How could this sexy, virile hunk of manhood have not had sex before? The idea is completely preposterous. It would have been easier to believe he had a third testicle or even a polka-dotted penis than to buy this "never been touched" bologna he is trying to feed me. "No way," I finally splutter.

Eventually, he turns to face me, which allows me to better gauge his sincerity. "It's true," he says simply.

My instincts believe that he is telling the truth, but my

mind just can't accept his revelation as fact. I don't know if I can trust my inner voice or if I just want to believe him. "How? . . . Why? . . . What?" I can't seem to formulate a question that asks him what I want to know without sounding rude. I feel like yelling "How in the hell have you existed in that perfect body for this long without someone jumping your bones?" An appropriate version of that question eludes me, though.

Seeing my inner struggle, Kai finally decides to provide a better explanation. He takes my hand, and we both sit down in the rattan chairs outside the villa. "My father was from the mainland. He came to the island to scout some property for his job, and he swept my mother off her feet. She thought they were in love. He apparently was just looking for a good time during his stint in Hawaii. On his final night here, she thought he was planning to propose. She was working out in her mind how she would make arrangements to move to California to be with him. Instead of a marriage proposal, he informed her that he had enjoyed their visit, but he needed to get back to his *real* life."

I can hear the sadness for his mother's heartache in his voice as he continues. "She was devastated and never fully recovered from her broken heart. When she found out she was pregnant with me, she did some research to find him so she could let him know about the pregnancy. She even went so far as to fly to California to tell him in person, only to learn of his engagement to someone else. She left without talking to him and spent the rest of her life turning down offers from every man who approached her. She was a beauty on the outside, but her heart was too damaged to ever fall in love again."

Hearing about his mother's heart-wrenching sadness makes my throat burn in empathy for her. She loved with her entire heart, only to have her feelings stomped on, and it created a lifetime of loneliness for her. I fear that I may be headed down the very same path with Kai. How could I help but fall for this handsome, kindhearted man even more as he shares his mother's story with me? I still lack clarity on what her sad past has to do with Kai's alleged virginity, though.

We sit in silence for a while before he continues. "She raised me to be nothing like my father. She taught me to respect women and to treat them like goddesses." He grins sheepishly at me before going silent, apparently lost in thought.

When he starts speaking again, his voice has taken on a melancholy tone. "When she got sick, I spent every moment with her I could. She was more than my mother. She was my best friend, my rock. Toward the end, she became almost delirious from the pain." I wince at his words. Although he hasn't explicitly said, I assume that she had some form of cancer.

"She became delusional, often mistaking me for my father. She would scream about how I had ripped her heart out, sobbing that she had never gotten over it. In my attempts to soothe her, I told her that I wasn't at all like him and that I would never treat a woman that way. During a lucid moment toward the end, she grabbed both of my hands in hers, looked deep into my eyes, and made me promise never to take advantage of an innocent girl. She asked me to wait to have sex until I loved someone enough to make her my wife, so I swore to her that I would."

I can see the pain in Kai's eyes as he shares this with me, and I realize that as far-fetched as his claim had seemed at first I now believe him.

Kai continues with his story. "After that, a calmness came over her. It wasn't long after that she passed. It was as if my promise allowed her to rest at peace." He sighs deeply before going on. "It hasn't been easy, but I have kept the vow I made to my mother on her deathbed. I take it very seriously."

I feel immensely sad for the heartbroken, dying mother who forced her son to take a vow of chastity and equally sad for the young man who was willing to say anything to ease his mom's suffering—even something that would bring him years of denying himself of one of life's greatest pleasures. I respect his willpower because I am certain that he has faced a great deal of temptation since making that promise. The fact that he never gave in speaks volumes about his character.

"Okay, then." I crane up to press my lips against his cheek. "Sex is off the table," I say matter-of-factly.

"Until we're married," he adds to my statement.

I find his word choice odd, but know that it is just his way of flirting with me. I want to shut it down so no errant daydreams about marrying Kai start wafting through my brain, so I say, "Like I said, off the table."

He grins at me mischievously. "For now," he finally acquiesces before turning to head back toward the bar.

I shake my head as I unlock the door to my room. "Forever." I whisper the word sadly and let the wind carry it out to the sea.

22

*B*aggy and Ruthie both stare at me, mouths agape. "A virgin?" Ruthie finally asks, as if I have somehow offended her just by uttering the word.

"No way," they say in unison.

"I hate to say this," Ruthie starts, making me sure she doesn't hate it at all, "but he is playing you for a fool. I say pretend like you believe his silly story and take that stud muffin's 'virginity.'" She actually does air quotes with her fingers when she says the word *virginity*, as if the mere idea of it is completely inconceivable.

"He doesn't want to have sex until he's married," I tell them, reiterating the fault in her theory. "How is that playing me? What benefit does he get for us not to have sex?"

"That is horse pucky," Baggy decides, finally accepting that Kai might be telling the truth. "His mother had no right to ask that of a virile young man. I say you jump him and ride him like a wild stallion. He must have so much sexual energy built up by now that he won't be able to resist you."

"I can't do that, Baggy. He would feel guilty for breaking

his promise to his mom." I quickly jump into my role as reasonable adult.

"He'd get over it fast enough, once he realizes how much fun he's been missing out on. I bet he can get it up three or four times in one night, and work it like a boss while he's plugged in. I'll have a go at him, if you don't want to."

Ruthie and I both stare at her in wide-eyed shock. Her last statements were outrageous, even for Baggy. She looks back at me, apparently oblivious to the fact that what she said was completely inappropriate and cringe-worthy. "Um, no," I finally answer, stating the obvious—in case she wasn't kidding.

Baggy raises her shoulders in a shrug, as if she has offered to help and can't understand my refusal. Ruthie shakes her head, probably to relieve her mind of the horrifying mental image. Then, in an uncharacteristically selfless move, Ruthie tells Baggy that they should leave me alone to get some painting done.

"Don't wait up," she tells me over her shoulder. "If Curtis plays his cards right, I'll be spending the night in his room." I can only assume that Curtis is the watersports guru who she's been chasing around the resort.

I nod at her before Baggy adds, "Don't wait up for me, either. Howie doesn't even have to play his cards right. I'm planning to rock his world tonight anyway—assuming he can raise his ding-dong again."

Ruthie quickly shuffles her out the door so I don't have to respond. As they are leaving, I can hear her asking Ruthie if she knows where she can find some little blue pills that will bring "Little Howie" to life. Once they shut the door behind them, I heave a sigh of relief. Having a sister to run interference definitely comes in handy sometimes.

23

*S*ince I have the room to myself, I decide to take Ruthie's suggestion and paint. As is usually the case when I start a new piece, I lose myself in the brushstrokes. When I step back to take a look at my creation, I realize that, once again, I have no idea how long I have been at it—nor do I care.

I admire my work. The painting is one of my best ever. It's another view of the waterfall where I spied on Kai and he later shunned my advances. This one uses more muted tones than the one I painted of Kai swimming, but the two pieces complement each other perfectly.

The angle of the viewpoint allows two entwined bodies to be seen on the ledge just beyond the crashing water. I am certain that Kai and I would have been those naked forms, had his mother not forced him to promise away his premarital sexuality.

The knock at the door comes just as I am cleaning my brushes. I am not overly surprised to find Kai standing on the other side of the threshold. "Are you avoiding me?" he asks me in a teasing tone, although I sense some underlying hurt feelings.

Before I have a chance to respond to his question, he spies the just-finished painting over my shoulder. He gasps—yes, actually gasps—as he veers around me to walk over to it. "I love it!" he practically gushes, making my cheeks turn pink.

He takes his time perusing the painting. He inspects it closely initially, before standing back to look at it from various distances and angles. He gazes at it for so long that I start to become slightly self-conscious. I wonder if, despite his previous raving, he might not like it as much after further inspection.

After what seems like an inordinate amount of time, he turns his attention from the painting back to me. "I need this painting," he says matter-of-factly. "How much do you want for it?"

"It's not for sale," I tell him firmly. This painting will serve as the perfect reminder of my time in Hawaii and my almost-affair with Kai. I will display it in a prominent location in my condo so that I am able to gaze at it and daydream about being with Kai anytime I like. There isn't enough money in the world to make me part with it.

After lightly badgering me about it for a while, he finally gives up. "I'll let it go for now, but I will have that painting," he tells me.

Before leaving, he asks if I'd like to go sailing with him tomorrow. I jump at the chance—eager for the opportunity to mark something off my bucket list. "Bring your family," he adds kindly. I wonder if he has any idea what wildness he might be signing up for with that invitation, but I nod, indicating that I will ask them.

He kisses me at the door, and I forget all of my concerns. His soft lips and smooth, warm tongue send me to a wondrous place where worries wouldn't dare exist. I float to bed and dream of Kai's tender, sweet kisses turning insistent with passion and searing over my skin—all of my skin.

We spend a luxurious night ravaging each other's naked bodies in my dreams. When I wake up, I stretch my limbs, longing to do in real life what we had spent the night doing in my subconscious. As fabulous as it had been, I bet having real-life Kai in my bed would be better than anything I could create in my dreams.

I guess we always want what we can't have, but knowing that Kai is physically unavailable to me makes me want him even more. I have never craved a man's body the way I desire Kai. The knowledge that I'll never have him makes it that much worse. As anxious as I am to spend the day with him, the idea of keeping my hands off him is becoming more of a challenge than I could have ever imagined.

I decide to take a cool shower in hopes that it will help stave off the burning desire building in me. As much as I want Kai, I have to think about how he feels. Having never had sex, he is probably practically bursting with need. Stepping out of the shower, I realize that I admire his extreme willpower and the unwavering respect he has for his dying mother's wishes, so I don't want to tempt him into doing something that he will regret.

Do they still make chastity belts? I wonder, chuckling as I head down for breakfast.

$\mathcal{I}$ am pleased to find Baggy and Ruthie at our usual breakfast table. Both of their men have joined them, so I have to scoot over a nearby two-top to be able to sit with them. They all seem to be excited at the prospect of sailing with Kai, so we scarf down our food and agree to meet down at the docks in twenty minutes.

Having never been sailing, I'm not exactly sure what to expect. I had hoped that it would be as carefree, fun, and relaxing as it looks in photos, and I am pleasantly surprised to find that it is even better than I had imagined.

Kai is super-patient as he shows us the ropes. Rather than barking out orders and becoming impatient with my flighty family, like Gary no doubt would have, Kai calmly explains what needs to be done in his good-natured manner. I am slightly embarrassed to realize that this fleeting, unflattering thought of Gary is the first time my almost husband has crossed my mind in days. Clearly, it is a good thing that we didn't get married. *How could I have thought I was in love with him? He didn't make me feel a tenth of the emotion that Kai does.*

I watch Kai's muscular shoulders work the jib or mast or

whatever it is that he called the big triangular doo-hickey. He has shucked his shirt, and he looks tan and delectable. I sit back, relax, and enjoy watching him.

Curtis seems to be the man of all watersports. He has quickly picked up on sailing and is cheerily helping Kai, which takes the pressure off the rest of us. Ruthie seems as happy to sit back and watch Curtis as I am to gaze at Kai.

We get a good chuckle watching Jim/Howie and Baggy on the bow of the boat. At first, Baggy acts like a beautiful mermaid statue leading our boat's charge through the water. Unable to resist, Jim/Howie soon joins her leaning out over the water and declaring, "I'm the king of the world."

"Those two are a match made in heaven." The wind carries Kai's voice in my direction.

I nod in agreement. As uncertain as I was at first about her new man, I have to admit, they really do seem to be perfect for each other. I never would have thought that Baggy would find someone as eccentric and full of life as she is, but I think she might have succeeded in doing just that. They certainly seem to have fun together. I don't recall ever seeing Baggy this happy.

Kai asks if we'd like to stop at a deserted island, and we are all in agreement that this sounds like loads of fun. He drops anchor, and we set off in pairs.

Ruthie and Curtis dive into the water and swim toward shore. I hear them giggling as they jog hand-in-hand into the lush foliage. Kai gives me a shy smile as we make eye contact —both of us know exactly what they're going to do.

Baggy and her man set off in our boat's small dinghy. He gallantly rows while Baggy sits with her back stiff and straight, like she is the homecoming queen riding in a convertible red Corvette. I almost expect her to give us a prim curved palm wave, but she refrains.

Kai and I don snorkel gear and jump off the Catamaran. I am simply stunned by the vibrant colors and variety of marine life that is teeming just under the surface of the water. We hold hands as we glide through the water enjoying the show. It is a whole other world under water, and I feel lucky to be able to get a glimpse of it, even if I am an intruder. We are careful to keep our distance and avoid touching anything, so as not to upset the delicate balance of this undersea utopia.

We snorkel for a long while before heading toward shore. I have lost track of Baggy's boat and Ruthie hasn't emerged from her tryst in the jungle, so it feels like Kai and I are the only people on Earth as we walk along the shore together. He finds a beautiful, unblemished conch shell, which he holds up and blows loudly. The tooting sounds like the dinner bell for a luau, and it makes me laugh.

We walk for what seems like miles along the pink sandy shoreline. When we stumble upon the beached dinghy, but don't see any sign of Baggy, I start to become a little concerned. I say as much to Kai.

"I think they're okay," he tells me, pointing out the pile of clothes farther down the beach.

Quickly realizing they must be skinny-dipping and *so* not wanting to see that, I suggest that we turn back. Kai readily agrees—likely not wanting to risk seeing Baggy frolicking au natural with her man any more than I do.

Once we reach a safe distance from any chance of seeing the elderly bumping of the uglies, we sit down on the sand, our legs touching. Kai addresses the elephant in the room—or rather, on the island. "I think everyone here is having sex, except for us." When I nod, he continues, "I'm sorry that we can't fool around," he tells me earnestly. He is quiet for a while before adding, "You'd probably much rather be here with someone who you could get naked with—someone who can show you the pleasures that I can't. It is supposed to be your honeymoon, after all."

Since we haven't discussed this before, I give him a questioning look. "The wedding gown at the airport gave you away." He smiles, but I still feel slightly guilty for making him draw his own conclusions about my non-wedding, rather than telling him about it sooner. He has shared his secret with me, and I need to be more open with him.

It feels good to talk to Kai about what had happened with Gary—especially when I hear his reaction to what I now refer to as *the dumping text*. "Crazy bastard," he says simply, shaking his head.

We are quiet a while, each lost in our own thoughts, until Kai murmurs, "He might be crazy, but he could have at least had sex with you, unlike me."

I don't want Kai to feel insecure. I long to make him feel better. "I want to be here with *you*," I tell him honestly.

I wonder if I should suggest we play around in ways that don't involve actual intercourse, but I'm not at all sure that we would be able to keep things from going too far. I'm also not crystal-clear on exactly what the acceptable activities boundaries are. Finally, I settle for saying, "If we could get naked, that would be great," he blushes a little at my words, "but you are the one I want to be with, whether we're clothed or not."

"I feel the same way," he murmurs near my ear. "Someday, I'll bring you back here, and we'll spend hours ravaging each other's naked bodies."

I wish that he wouldn't make promises that he has no intention of keeping, but I decide to enjoy the fantasy and not call him out on it. After all, it seems that fantasy is all I'm going to get with Kai. *That sounded bitter*, I think to myself. *I don't blame Kai at all for our circumstances. In fact, I admire him for his incredible restraint. Being on a secluded island where my sister and grandmother are getting down and dirty, while I sit with the man of my dreams holding his hand is for the birds, though. More than that, it just plain sucks. There, I said it—in my mind, anyway. That counts, right?*

By the time the others finally return, I have released my sour mood and am just grateful to be in this amazing place with this wonderful man. I hand the other two ladies gorgeous pink hibiscus flowers, and we each place one behind our ear. Kai tells us we look like Hawaiian beauties, which makes us all preen a little.

He gently switches my flower to my left ear, whispering that a hibiscus worn on the right side of the hair means you are available. "You're taken," he growls in a deep voice before nibbling my ear and sniffing the flower. The sentiment makes a delicious shiver zing up my spine, despite my effort to keep my hopes for a real and lasting relationship with Kai at bay.

The men set about catching fish and building a fire on the beach. I had been uncertain about eating a fish that I had just seen wriggling on the line, but I have to admit, it is really delicious. We sit around the fire eating and laughing, enjoying an utterly carefree, wonderful time.

When Ruthie pulls from her pocket a dark lava rock that she has picked up, Baggy shocks us all by being practical—well, somewhat practical. "You can't take that from the island," she tells Ruthie vehemently. "It's a piece of the island, and it belongs here. Taking it will only serve to anger the land, and it will seek vengeance." We all stare at Baggy. This warning is so out of character for her. She's normally the one getting into mischief, not doling out precautions.

Just when I start to think that she might have a conservative and responsible side, she proves that she's still Baggy by adding in a serious voice, "Didn't you see the Hawaii episodes of *The Brady Bunch*? Bad things happen when people steal from the islands."

We are all laughing as we climb back aboard Kai's boat. "What? It's true!" Baggy declares, not seeing why the Brady Bunch reference makes her statement seem so much less ominous.

"Only you," Ruthie tells her lovingly, shaking her head as she chucks the rock back into the sea.

25

*L*ater that evening, depression over our imminent departure starts to set in. I have been somewhat successful at refusing to think about leaving this lovely island or the fantastic man I met here, but all too quickly our stay is coming to an end. The time has flown by, and now suddenly it's time to start packing. I feel like hurling myself onto the floor like a two-year-old and kicking my feet because I don't want to leave.

The fact that I was able to enjoy today and not spend the entire day thinking about having to leave is a huge improvement over my norm. I have always been this way. I would ruin Sunday by dreading school on Monday. I am always looking forward at what is coming around the bend rather than enjoying the here and now. I'm actually rather proud of myself for not letting the impending end to our trip dampen my spirits until now.

The dread had wanted to start creeping in earlier today on Kai's boat, but I had managed to keep it at bay by repeatedly forcing myself not to think about it. I have no choice but to think about it now, though, because it's time to start packing my belongings into my suitcase—much as I don't want to.

Sitting in the dark by the pool, avoiding the chore of packing, I am slowly and methodically ripping the petals from the lovely flower that was previously tucked behind my ear. I don't know why I'm doing it, but I can't seem to stop myself.

"He loves you." Kai has snuck up behind me and he whispers the words near my ear. The sweet and wonderful words send a tingly chill up and down my spine, even though I know it's too soon for them to possibly be true.

He sits down with me, and I know that I need to tell him that I am leaving, but I just can't seem to formulate the words. He has to know it is coming soon. Maybe he even knows our checkout is scheduled for tomorrow.

Our impending departure is all I can think about, but I just can't find a way to utter the words. Eventually, I cop out by saying that I am tired and feigning a yawn before heading back to my room.

I'm such a ridiculous chicken, I decide as I neatly tuck items into my suitcase. Baggy and Ruthie both opted to spend the night with their boyfriends—that juvenile word doesn't seem accurate, but I'm not sure what else to call them. Those two don't seem at all concerned about packing or getting ready to leave. They'll probably both slide in here at the last minute tomorrow and start tossing their few belongings and purchases into my bag. They both spend every moment in the here and now. It likely hasn't even crossed their minds that we'll be leaving tomorrow. Tomorrow . . . sigh.

I sleep fitfully, but must eventually doze off because I'm startled awake when Baggy and Ruthie return to the room. There is a queasy ball in the pit of my stomach about having to tell Kai goodbye today. I don't want to say the words or do the leaving.

Ruthie and Baggy are chatting amiably as if this isn't the worst day ever. "You two are pretty chipper, considering we are leaving paradise today," I grumble at them.

They both look at me with wide eyes, like this is complete news to them. "Come on, you didn't think we were staying here forever? It's time to head home." They both give me blank stares. A thought pops into my head that makes my stomach drop even further. "You *did* book your return flights, right?" I don't think I could handle heading home, leaving the two of them to live it up in paradise without me until one or the other of them has enough sense to come back.

"Of course we did," Baggy informs me. "We booked the same return flight you are on." I heave a sigh of relief. It might be selfish, but if I can't stay, I don't want them to, either.

"We will fly with you to Atlanta and pick up Gary's car." I squint my eyes because I'd be shocked if Gary hadn't already tracked down his car and picked it up, but I don't mention that. We will deal with getting them a flight or rental car when the time comes. "You can either take your scheduled flight from Atlanta or ride back with us," Baggy says, sounding surprisingly practical. It's not like her to be so levelheaded or to think these types of things through in advance.

"I don't want to go home," Ruthie pouts, actually sticking her lip out and stomping one foot. It looks like she might be the one who throws the toddler tantrum that I considered last night.

Baggy looks at her for a long moment. "Let's just stay then," she decides.

Quick as a wink, Baggy's practical moment is gone. I take a deep breath, wondering why I am always stuck being the Debbie Downer voice of reason with these two. For once, it would be nice if I were the one throwing the fits and announcing that I'm staying on permanent vacation. Alas, it's not meant to be, I decide, before jumping in to state the obvious.

"We can't do that," I tell them matter-of-factly. "It's time for us to get back to the real world." Two blank stares gaze back at me, so I forge on. "Besides, they probably have our room rented out," I try.

"Maybe, but we could always stay with our men." Baggy waggles her eyebrows suggestively.

I don't allow myself to think about how awesome it would be to stay at Kai's beach house. The nonstop temptation to make love would probably kill us both. I turn to Ruthie. "We need to get back to work."

"I'll give Jesse a call at the bar," she says flippantly. "I'm sure he won't mind if I take a few more days off. One of the other girls will be glad to pick up my shifts." I doubt if either of those last two statements are true, but I'm also quite certain that Ruthie really wouldn't mind if she lost her job at the Thirsty Dog Saloon. She'd find something else. She always lands on her feet. I, on the other hand, have a job at an accounting firm where people will be very upset if I don't return on schedule. Unlike Ruthie, I care about inconveniencing others, and I try my best not to ever do it.

I can't believe we are even discussing staying. I have responsibilities and people who count on me, and I'm a grown-up—unlike these two, who apparently think they can stay on vacation forever. "It's kind of expensive here," I point out, but even as I say the words, I know it's a moot point because money is never a consideration for Baggy.

I'm not sure where her never-ending supply of hundred-dollar bills comes from, but she never seems to give a thought to the idea that they might one day run out. *Maybe she prints them in her basement*, I think crabbily before chastising myself. Baggy is wild and crazy and unpredictable, but she is also honest and loyal and faithful. She would never do something blatantly wrong like that—she's more of a "gray area" wrongdoer.

"Pish-posh." Baggy waves off the money issue like I had anticipated she would. "I'll pay for everything. Don't you worry about it, sweets." She pats my cheek. "I'll go down and see if our room is available for a bit longer." I can't help but wonder what she considers to be a "bit." I briefly consider calling my office and telling them I have some tropical-sounding illness, but I just don't have it in me. The idea of telling them the truth—that I'm having a wonderful time and want to stay here longer—is not a viable option.

I shake my head. I can't believe these two have me trying to work out scenarios of how to stay here. "No," I say vehemently. "I can't stay here. It's time to get back to the real world."

Ruthie looks concerned as her eyes swoop between the two of us. "I'll just go check how long the room is available," Baggy announces before sailing out the door.

26

*R*uthie beelines for the bathroom, presumably to get away from me angrily stuffing items into my suitcase. I'm not sure why I *always* have to be the responsible one with these two. You'd think for once—like maybe on *my* honeymoon—I'd get to be the carefree, spontaneous one.

I guess it just isn't meant to be. Apparently I don't have it in me. I shouldn't blame Baggy and Ruthie because I didn't inherit whatever loosey-goosey gene that allows them to not think about consequences or mundane things like jobs and bills. I wish I could do it, but I just can't. If the temptation of spending more time with Kai in Hawaii can't beat the sensibility out of me, I guess nothing ever will.

I try placing my paintings flat on top of my belongings in the suitcase, but I must not have packed as orderly as I did on the way here because the bag won't zip around them. Reluctantly, I decide to roll them up and place a soft ponytail holder around them. I'll carry them on board the plane by hand. It's not an ideal solution for my canvases, but it will have to do. At the last minute, I decide to leave one of them out of the scroll.

Once I'm packed, I flop down on the bed, already tired and frustrated. I look around the room and realize it won't take Baggy and Ruthie long to throw the meager belongings they have purchased here into a bag. Perhaps Baggy will come back with news that the resort is booked. Then it will be much easier to convince them to come home. The idea of leaving them here while I have to leave really irks me. It will be hard enough with the two of them in tow to leave Kai.

As if on cue, Baggy rushes through the door. "Oh good, I caught you," she says to me. "We get to stay!" She exclaims these words as if they are the answer to all of our problems. I guess she had expected me to jump for joy because when I don't, she continues, "Honey, there's no reason to be blue. I booked the room for a bit longer, so we don't have to leave today."

I just stand there looking at her. Ruthie emerges from the bathroom, evidently having decided, after hearing Baggy's voice, that it is once again safe. It is so tempting to stay, but I know it will just make it that much harder when we do have to leave.

"Didn't you hear me?" Baggy seems perplexed about my lack of enthusiasm. "Unpack your things. We are staying."

"I'm not," I say flatly. "I have a job and responsibilities to get back to. It was nice of my office to allow me to go ahead and take the time off for the honeymoon, even though there wasn't a wedding, but they need me to come back." I'm not completely sure if I'm trying to convince her or myself when I continue, "I'll already have piles of work to catch up on when I get back. If I stay longer, that will only get worse."

"Do as you wish," Baggy tells me, as if I would wish to leave this paradise and the man of my dreams.

Realizing that I will never be able to explain it so the two of them will understand, I heave my suitcase off the bed. "I'll see you whenever you decide to come home." I hug them both, managing to hold back the tears despite the giant ball of fire in my throat.

"I wish you'd stay with us," Baggy tries one more time and Ruthie nods her agreement.

I just shake my head for fear that the tears will start flowing if I attempt to speak. With that, I scurry out of the room, almost flipping my suitcase from its rollers in my haste. Once I have it righted, I leave without looking back.

Peeking around the corner, I am relieved that Kai is not yet tending bar. I'm certain that I won't have the strength to leave if I see him again. I leave the present on the counter for him, along with a quickly scrawled note, which reads, *To help you remember our time together. Always, Roxy.*

Using my cell phone, I look up and call an island taxi service. I know that I am being a coward, but I don't think I can face Kai, and I know I can't bear to tell him goodbye. It is all I can do to leave without seeing him one last time, but my sanity requires it. I walk around the outside of the open-air lobby and find a bench out front to wait for my cab. I'm sure that someone from the front desk would contact Kai about my leaving if I walked through there.

I really don't think I can handle seeing him. Besides, it's better to make a clean break. He'll probably have moved on to a hot new tourist before the dinner show and forgotten about me, but I know that I will never forget him.

At this point, the tears start flowing, and by the time my cab arrives, it's all I can do to blubber out that I'm going to the airport. The driver gives me the sad, slightly frightened look that men reserve for crying women—as if he's trying to determine if he should comfort me or keep his distance because I'm loony.

He puts my bag in the back, but when he tries to take my rolled-up canvases, I snap, "No!" a little more harshly than I intend to. He bugs his eyes out at me, but doesn't say anything. I climb into the back of the minivan and the rest of our ride is in silence, except for my occasional snuffling.

In a daze, I check my bag and board my flight. I must look like a crazy person because the flight attendants don't even ask me to stow the paintings I am clutching in both hands. I spend the entire, ridiculously long flight and the shorter one that follows it silently freaking out, afraid that I have just made the biggest mistake of my life.

By the time I give the local taxi driver my home address, I have resigned myself to my decision. I did the right thing. I can't just stay on permanent vacation. No one can. Eventually, even Ruthie and Baggy will have to come home.

If I had stayed, I'd have just become more and more attached to Kai, and I can't have him. He's amazing, gorgeous, sweet, intelligent, funny, kind, generous, honorable, and all of the things that any woman would want in a man. Why would I have thought that an average woman like me should be with such a catch? He deserves someone as wonderful as he is, and I'm sure he'll find her. I definitely don't want to be hanging around when that happens. *I made the right choice*, I tell myself for at least the 14,700th time since leaving. *Surely, one of these times I'll start to believe it, right?*

In the cab, I look at my cell phone, which I haven't turned back on after my flight. I am afraid that there will be a message from Kai, and I can't handle hearing his voice right now. I don't have the strength to resist him and stand by my plan. I want nothing more than to run back into his arms, even though I am almost certain that isn't the right answer for either of us.

If I'm completely honest with myself, I know the real reason I am refusing to turn on my phone is that I'm worried there won't be a message from Kai. I don't know if my fragile ego can handle it if he is indifferent over my leaving. The

ANN OMASTA

decision to leave was the hardest choice I have ever had to make. While I don't want to hurt Kai, it would shatter me to find out that he doesn't care.

In the end, I leave my phone off. When the taxi drops me off at home, I shove some money to the driver, drag my suitcase into the hall, and stumble to bed on autopilot. Once I am in bed, I realize that I have never before gone to bed without unpacking from a trip. The old me would have not been able to ignore the luggage in the foyer. The new, brokenhearted, post-Kai me can't drum up the energy to care.

27

"*H*ow could you leave without them?" I hold my home phone away from my ear so that my mother's screeching doesn't burst my eardrum. I should have known that this would all get turned around to be my fault. For some reason, despite the fact that I was sensible and came home when I was scheduled to, I am somehow responsible for Baggy and Ruthie not doing the same.

I resent the fact that they got to stay and I didn't. I especially resent the fact that I am inexplicably now being blamed for it. *How is this fair?* I want to scream at my mother, but I don't—of course.

As she prattles on about how I should have insisted that they come home with me, my mind wanders. For once, I'd like to be reckless and carefree. Maybe I should hop on a plane and go back to Hawaii. Wouldn't that shock everyone? Knowing my luck, Kai would already be with someone new, and I'd have to turn around and come home—*again*. I guess it just isn't meant to be for me to be wild and spontaneous.

After half a day of walking around my luggage in the foyer, I resign myself to unpacking and laundering my dirty clothes. I just don't have it in me to ignore it, but it seems so final to actually unload the contents from my suitcase. It is a depressing process, but it has to be done. Life must go on, I guess.

On Monday morning, I arrive at work a few minutes early—of course—going through the motions of being my "normal" self. Sadly, I watch my computer slowly boot up. It takes longer than normal because it has been off for so long. When my e-mail window shows on the bottom that it is downloading 1,348 messages, I feel like screaming in frustration.

Why on earth would I have so many messages?! This is ridiculous. Everyone knew that I was out. I had made arrangements with my coworkers for coverage on all of my open issues. I sigh deeply and start slogging through the onslaught of messages.

An hour later, I am staring off into space, daydreaming about sitting at Kai's beach bar. I can't focus on my work, and I don't want to. This morning has been the most unproductive hour I have probably ever spent at work. I run a hand through my hair in frustration then look toward the ceiling and have what I can only describe as an epiphany. I may not have all the answers, but I know that sitting here is not the right choice for me.

In what is no doubt the most spontaneous and adventurous moment of my life, I grab my purse, get up, and walk out of my office. My coworkers watch me leave in stunned silence. They must be wondering what I am up to because I usually don't even leave for lunch. I am like a robot at work —well, I used to be.

I am tempted to yell, "See ya, suckers!" over my shoulder, but at the last minute I chicken out. Feeling incredibly bold and wild, I drive to the airport. I don't have any luggage and it dawns on me that a same-day flight will probably cost a fortune.

Even though the practical side of me is demanding to go home to pack and perform an Internet search for flights later in the week, I don't. The newly discovered, crazy-in-love side of me says to jump on the first plane and run into the arms of my man. For once, I am listening to that wild, reckless voice that I have kept buried for so long.

On the plane, my nerves start to kick in. *What if he didn't miss me? What if he doesn't have real feelings for me? What if he has already moved on? What if he's angry about the way that I left?* A flood of anxious questions bombards my brain.

By the time we land, I am a jittery mess, and I have nearly convinced myself that Kai will not want to see me. It is tempting to turn around and head home to save myself the agony and embarrassment, but I need to see this through. Besides, those flights are way too long to turn around and do again so quickly.

I reach for my cell phone, deciding it is time to see if Kai has left me any messages, only to find that it is dead. I am so out of my usual routine that I failed to put my phone on the charger while I slept. I guess this visit is going to be a true leap of faith. I am returning to the island blindly—without knowing what Kai's reaction was to my departure. I can only hope that he'll be happy about my return.

One of the great things about not having any luggage is getting to bypass the baggage claim. I breeze through the airport and into a waiting taxi while my plane companions rally around the carousel, likely crossing their fingers and hoping their luggage made the trip.

When my driver pulls up at the resort, I toss some cash his direction and race inside. I am so anxious to see Kai that I am practically bursting with nervous energy and excitement.

I hope he is thrilled to see me—or at least not furious with me.

I see from a distance that a woman is tending the beach bar, so I check all of his other usual haunts. Much to my chagrin, Kai is nowhere to be found. When I bump into Leilani, I inquire about Kai's whereabouts. If she is surprised to see me at the resort, she gives no indication of it as she tells me that she hasn't seen Kai lately.

Seriously bummed about my anticlimactic return, I decide to find Baggy and Ruthie. At least I know they'll be pleasantly surprised to see me. I spot them at a table near the pool, papers spread out around them.

"Roxy, you're back," Baggy says to me, barely bothering to look up. Their reaction to my arrival is no more enthusiastic than if I had just returned from napping in the room.

"You're just in time to help plan the wedding," Ruthie tells me.

"What wedding?!" I demand, wondering exactly how long I've been gone.

"Howie and I are engaged," Baggy beams, looking up at me at last. She shows me her gnarled, bony ring finger, which is weighed down by a marble-size pink diamond. "I have some serious ice now," she brags enthusiastically.

I fawn appropriately over the ring, until my eyes are drawn to a specific word that stands out on the paperwork. "Tomorrow?" I ask, pointing at the word, almost afraid to hear the response. "What is happening tomorrow—a meeting with the wedding planner?" I inquire hopefully, already knowing in my gut that my guess is incorrect.

"No, silly!" Ruthie rolls her eyes at me. "The wedding is tomorrow. We have it all planned out." She indicates their scanty notes. "The ceremony is tomorrow, on the beach." She points proudly at her stick figure drawing of a beach wedding, as if it will magically transform itself into a grand celebration.

I decide that I will have to deal with their crazy ideas later. For now, all I want to do is see Kai. When I ask them where he is, they tell me they haven't seen him in a while. That seems to be the popular answer, I think to myself, wondering where he could be.

When Baggy lowers her voice and says that he was "quite upset" about my leaving, I feel an awful sense of relief (which I immediately feel guilty about) that he missed me. I head to the beach bar, hoping that he was just on break earlier, and am thrilled to find that the painting I left for him of the two of us ravaging each other behind the secluded waterfall is hanging over the cash register. It has been framed in a lovely aged teak wood, and it looks fantastic—if I do say so myself.

The painting has to be a good sign, right? He can't be too angry with me if he went to all the effort to frame it and hang it so prominently. I keep trying to fill my mind with these positive thoughts, but I would much rather find Kai to see for myself how he feels. The guilt over the way I left is starting to become overwhelming, and I want to apologize to him.

Honi relieves the bartender for her break and begins wiping down the counter with a wet cloth. He beams a chubby-cheeked smile at me when he sees me approaching, then his face falls into a look of concern. I try not to let my insecurities creep in as I ask him where I can find Kai.

"He went to see you," Honi informs me.

"But I went home." At Honi's serious look, realization dawns on me. "He followed me?" A secret thrill runs down my spine as I begin to dare to hope that Kai might be as serious about us as I am.

Honi seems to register what has happened. "And you came back here for him," he squeals in his overly high voice.

"It's so sweet." He claps his pudgy hands together in obvious delight.

I float back over to Ruthie and Baggy's table. "He followed me home," I inform them dreamily.

They both stop what they are doing. "That's amazing!" Ruthie finally exclaims.

Baggy nods in approval. "I told that boy he better not let you get away. He looked like a lovesick puppy after you left. I think that one's a keeper." She pats my hand sweetly. Seeing her giant ring brings me back to the dilemma at hand.

"If this wedding is tomorrow, we have some serious planning to do," I state in my all-business voice.

"It's all taken care of, sweetheart." Despite Baggy's confident reassurance, I doubt if they have thought of a tenth of the things that need to be taken care of.

"Who is officiating the ceremony?" I start in with my questions.

"Oh, Howie and I used all of our magic jelly. We couldn't find Kai to order more, so I walked to the address listed on the bottle." I wonder what any of this has to do with my question, but I let her talk without interruption. "Kai's crazy grandmother lives in a cottage on the property." I have to bite my tongue to keep from saying anything snarky about Baggy having the audacity to call anyone else crazy. Nana Lana must be pretty eccentric for Baggy to think she's quirky. "We really hit it off," Baggy continues, "and she gave me a big ol' tub of magic jelly." She holds her arm up for me to admire. "My skin practically glistens with vibrancy."

I nod, but since she has stopped digressing, I verbally nudge her again. "Who is officiating the wedding?"

"Nana Lana, of course. Didn't I just tell you that?" She shakes her head as if I am the exasperating one. "She's some kind of Hawaiian goddess or witch doctor voodoo queen or something. It's gonna be a hoot!"

"It *is* going to be a hoot," I agree, and with that simple statement, I let the worry go. Every detail of this wedding doesn't need to be planned. It is Baggy's day, and it should be her way—so I guess we will fly by the seat of our pants.

"Only one thing left to do," Baggy proclaims. Ruthie and I look at her in anticipation. Baggy sets her dated cell phone in the middle of the table. "Someone has to tell your mother."

We all lean back, staring at the phone as if it might bite us. Several long moments tick past. "Fine." I finally give in when I decide the standoff has gone on long enough. "You two owe me," I inform their now-smiling faces. They had both known that I would be the first one to cave.

I pick up the phone before I can chicken out. "Hello, Mother." My voice sounds shaky and a little squeaky. "I have something to tell you . . ."

I barely get the news of Baggy's impending wedding out before my mother starts her tirade. I hold the phone out away from my ear as she yells. Baggy and Ruthie stare wide-eyed, wincing periodically as she rants. I try to intervene a couple of times, but she won't stop long enough to listen. Eventually I set the phone back in the middle of the table. Baggy, Ruthie, and I get up and leave her squawking at the palm trees.

hen I go to our room, I immediately plug my cell phone in to the charger I find in the outlet. One of them must have been responsible enough to purchase a replacement after my departure. I am impressed that either of them thought of it. Maybe I haven't been giving the two of them enough credit.

I immediately nix that idea as I look around at the room. It is an absolute disaster zone—clothes are strewn everywhere (mostly on the floor), the beds are unmade, and wet towels are piled in the bathroom. It looks like they haven't picked up anything since I left, but good grief, I wasn't gone *that* long. They must have left the Do Not Disturb sign on the door the entire time because housekeeping obviously hasn't been here recently.

Absentmindedly, I begin picking up their mess. As I retrieve the clothes from the floor, I realize the two of them must have gone on one heck of a shopping spree. There are plenty of clothes for me to choose from, even without the luxury of luggage. The sundresses will be just a little shorter and skimpier on me, but they will work. Deciding to utilize the resort's laundry service, I bag the clothing to be washed. As I'm doing so, I wonder what they would have done if I hadn't returned—pick up dirty clothes from the floor to wear again or buy more? I'm fairly certain they would just go buy more, but Baggy's stack of hundred-dollar bills will have to run low at some point, right?

My dead phone has buzzed back to life, so I take a deep breath and enter the code to check my voice mail. Since I am the only one in the room, I push the speaker button, and Kai's voice immediately fills the air. On the first message his voice is perplexed as he asks where I am. There are several other messages where he begins to sound hurt, angry, and sad. I feel terrible for putting him through this. *What had I been thinking?*

The last message from Kai is simple and heartbreaking. "I love you, and I don't want to lose you. I'm on my way to find you."

His words fill me with joy. It feels too soon to be proclaiming our love for each other. It's not logical to feel this way after so short an amount of time together, but there is no other way to describe my feelings for Kai. *I love him*, I realize, finally allowing myself to think it. "I love Kai," I say aloud, letting the words roll off my tongue. "I love Kai!" I shout the words, twirling as giddy laughter bubbles out of me.

"And he loves me," I add quietly, wrapping my arms around my shoulders and letting this amazing knowledge and pure euphoria wash over me as I actually allow myself to accept it as truth.

I'm surprised that Kai didn't ask Baggy and Ruthie about how to find me, but maybe it was a spur-of-the-moment decision to follow me, just like mine was to return to him. It seems that spontaneity is in the air, I decide, thinking about Baggy's impending wedding.

I try calling Kai's cell phone, but he doesn't answer. I decide that this conversation is too important to have via voice mail, so I don't leave him a message. He and I will find each other, and when we do, it will be earth-shattering, but for now, I need to focus on Baggy's upcoming nuptials.

I decide to track down Baggy and Ruthie, so we can make arrangements for the food. We also need to decide on dresses and flowers and music and seating. The more I think about it, the more I start to sweat. We have lots of work to do—but fun work.

I want this day to be perfect for Baggy. I didn't get to go to her wedding to my late grandfather—it was way before my time. Although the rumor is that my mother attended in Baggy's belly, which was quite the scandal at the time. I am guessing circumstances made Baggy's first wedding stressful and less than ideal, so she deserves the wedding of her dreams this time around. I am just the person to make sure all of the details are covered for the big day.

It shouldn't be a huge surprise to find Baggy and Ruthie sunning themselves by the pool, but it shocks me nonetheless. "What are you doing?" I ask, my voice an octave higher than normal.

Baggy lowers her oversize black sunglasses to peer at me. "Getting some color so people can tell where my white dress ends and I begin," she tells me as if it should be obvious. I don't bother to point out to her that she has been in Hawaii for more than a week and her leathery skin is already a deep shade of brown or the fact that, since she is a grandmother, virginal white probably isn't the most appropriate dress color choice.

"Oh, good." I plop down in the empty reclining chair adjacent to them. "You already have the dress. I was afraid you hadn't taken care of that yet."

Baggy and Ruthie give each other a meaningful look before turning wide eyes on me. "We'll go pick one out this evening." Baggy waves me off as if finding the perfect wedding dress isn't her most pressing chore today.

"Isn't the rehearsal this evening?" I'm starting to feel a ball of nerves churn in the pit of my stomach.

"Rehearsal?" Baggy looks at me as if I've grown a second head. "What do we need to rehearse?" She asks the question like I have insulted her in some way. She leans her head toward me as if she is sharing a great secret. "We've both done this before, you know. All we need to do is swap rings, say 'I do,' and give each other some tongue." Ruthie and I both cringe a little at the mental image of them French kissing, but we try not to let it show.

I decide she probably does have a point about the rehearsal. Besides, if there's one thing I know about Baggy, she is a fly-by-the-seat-of-her-pants kind of lady. If we ran through a full rehearsal tonight, she would probably just use the time to come up with some kind of crazy stunt to pull at the ceremony.

I draw the line at waiting until the very last minute to find a dress, though. Knowing Baggy and Ruthie as well as I do, I appeal to their girly sides. "It's time for you to stop lounging around and get busy," I start, which earns me glares from both of them. "We need to go shopping!" These magical words get their attention and I bustle them back to the room.

Before long, we are standing in a boutique, and I am rolling my eyes at Baggy's dress selections. *It's her wedding.* I keep repeating this mantra to myself over and over as I scan the hot pink, neon green, and fire engine red ensembles Baggy has chosen to take to the dressing room. When Ruthie takes her a black mini-dress with white polka dots to try on, I resign myself to the inevitable uniqueness that is sure to surround every detail of these nuptials.

One thing is for sure. Like everything Baggy is involved in, this wedding is destined to be unforgettable.

29

*W*e stay busy the rest of the day, choosing outfits and flowers, getting mani-pedis, tasting cakes, and laughing. We laugh so much that my face hurts. Baggy is crazy, I decide as I watch her smear chocolate frosting all over her front tooth and smile at us with what looks to be a gaping hole in her teeth. The appalled look Victoria, the prim wedding cake lady, gives her only serves to make the whole situation funnier.

When Baggy says that she would like to have wedding cupcakes, the uptight woman splutters, "Cupcakes are not appropriate for such a solemn occasion." Baggy shows no sign of backing down, so the woman turns to me for backup. I must look like the most reasonable—or stuffy—one. When I steadily stare back at her, she adds, "This is a wedding, not a six-year-old's birthday party."

"It's Baggy's wedding." I state the obvious.

"Baggy?" the woman inquires, pursing her face as if she has just smelled something distasteful.

"Yes, it came from a shortening of Bad Grandma." Seeing

Victoria bug her eyes out, Ruthie lets her voice trail off without finishing her story.

"Mmmm," the woman responds noncommittally. Obviously she is not amused by our humor. I wonder if I seem like this much of a fuddy-duddy to my wild sister and grandmother.

Baggy has had enough of this standoffish, judgmental treatment and stands to leave. "Cupcakes or die!" she announces loudly to the room at large.

I can't help but snicker at her dramatics. She truly lives in the moment and enjoys every second of her life. It might be a struggle for me to ever whoop it up like she does, but she sets a great example of how to live happy. I am going to strive to do the same going forward—in my own way, of course.

I am shocked to see the bakery lady actually crack a smile at Baggy's antics. "Cupcakes it is then," she acquiesces, and from that moment on, we get along famously.

It seems that Baggy's quirky charm is irresistible to even the staunchest traditionalists. By the time we leave the bakery, we have a plan in place for red velvet cupcakes (gasp!) with cream cheese frosting, and Victoria (whom I have now dubbed in my mind the cupcake lady) actually admits that she might consider adding cupcakes to her wedding selection lineup.

"Thanks, Vicky!" Baggy yells over her shoulder as we bustle out the door. I turn just in time to see the shock register on Victoria's face before the door closes. We mellowed her out somewhat, but clearly she's not quite ready to hang-loose as Vicky.

30

$\mathcal{W}$e spend the evening telling stories and giggling in our room, just the three of us, and it is one of the most memorable and fun nights of my life. I don't want it to ever end, but eventually our eyelids begin to droop, and Ruthie announces that she is going to get some beauty sleep before Baggy's big day.

It seems like my head barely hits the pillow before sunlight is streaming through our window, and there is an incessant banging on our door. I sit up and look around. Baggy is snoring peacefully, apparently not hearing the rapping, which is getting louder by the moment. Ruthie has a pillow over her head, which tells me she hears the knocking but has no intention of answering the door.

"Here, let me get it," I say sarcastically as I shuffle over to see what all of the ruckus is about. I look through the peephole and see one of my mother's huge eyes staring back at me.

"Let me in," she demands. "I can see your shadow through the looking-glass, and I know you are in there."

I stand there for a moment, debating what to do. I really

don't want to deal with her before having my morning tea, but I don't see any viable option besides letting her in. If we ignore her, it will only be that much worse when we eventually have to face her.

Finally, I give in and unlock the door. Before I even have a chance to open it fully, my mother takes charge and barges into the room. It's all I can do to back out of the way to keep her from plowing right over me. She is definitely in a tizzy.

"Why are you still sleeping?" she demands. "It's a good thing I'm here." She shoves Ruthie's feet aside and plops down on the fold-out couch. "If this ridiculous wedding is going to happen, we have a lot to do."

Giving up on feigning sleep, Ruthie sits up. Her hair is poking out in impossible directions. "Hello, Mother."

Rather than answer her, our mother turns to me and says in a serious tone, "How can you let this happen? You know that Baggy is irresponsible and reckless. Do you really think this spur-of-the-moment wedding fiasco is wise?"

I am stunned by her accusatory tone and blame-Roxy-for-everything attitude. Although by this point in my life I should probably be used to it, it just doesn't make sense. *How can I be held responsible for what Baggy decides to do? I wasn't even here until yesterday.* My thoughts are whirling, and I feel like screaming.

For once, Ruthie jumps in. "It's not Roxy's fault. Besides, Howie is a wonderful man. He and Baggy are perfect for each other." Ruthie's sleepy face has taken on a dreamy expression.

Mother rolls her eyes in my direction as if to say Ruthie is an idealist whose opinions can't be trusted. "Let's try to stay focused on reality," she admonishes, her eyes focused on me. "How do we know this man isn't after Baggy's money? He could be trying to use her in some way." She is sitting primly on the sofa with her spine perfectly straight.

I wonder if she might be jealous of Baggy's spontaneity

and happiness. It's not like she and Daddy are madly in love. It's more like they tolerate each other. When I don't respond to her suspicions, she adds, "I don't trust this man." She spits out the words "this man" like they leave a foul flavor on her tongue.

"You don't even know him, Mother," I tell her calmly. Even as I say the words, I know that having her meet Howie with all of his delusional spy stories is not going to help the situation. That is not the point, though. He could be a totally sane, rational human being, but she still doesn't like him, sight unseen.

"None of you know him," she bursts out. "Not even her." She points a finger at her still-sleeping mother.

My eyes travel to Baggy. She is sleeping peacefully, letting out tiny whistling puffs of air with each exhalation. She looks so sweet and fragile. No one would guess by her sleeping form what a spitfire she is. Watching her, I am overwhelmed with love for this wildly irreverent, tiny woman. I want to protect her from my mother's harsh judgment. If she wants to have a rushed wedding with a crazy man who believes himself to be a spy, then I will do anything in my power to make sure her day is perfect—even stand up to my mother, which I have never really done before.

"Stop it." I hiss firmly. "Just stop it," I add for extra emphasis. She bugs her eyes out in surprise, but I can't stop now. "Baggy has every right to marry whoever she pleases, and she doesn't need your judgmental looks and comments about it."

I'm surprised that Mother hasn't interrupted me. Years of frustration over her hoity-toity attitude and condescending treatment of all three of us bubbles up inside me and demands to be released. "You need to let us live our own lives —even if that means we make mistakes along the way. A kind mother would be there to help us pick up the pieces when we do have errors in judgment, rather than admonishing us with an 'I told you so.'"

I pause and look at the others for the first time since my tirade started. Ruthie has her arms wrapped around her bent knees, looking at me with a mixture of shock and awe. Mother is looking at the floor with her lips stiffly pursed. Baggy is still sleeping soundly.

Mother stands up, stretching her long limbs to her full height in an attempt to look down her glasses at me. This intimidation tactic is very effective with most people, but since I am just a hair taller than her, it isn't as dramatic. "I'm surprised by you," Mother finally says. Although her voice isn't as stern as I would have expected, I sense that she is very disappointed in me.

I refuse to back down in the slightest. My back is rigid, and I keep my face a blank mask, refusing to allow the concern I have over her disappointment to show on my face. She has never before experienced me standing up to her, so the fact that she is surprised is not news to anyone. When she sees that her words haven't caused any type of reaction, she goes for the jugular. "I expected better from you, Roxy."

Her verbal darts miss their mark because rather than making me swing around to her way of thinking, they infuriate me. "Why? Why do you expect more from me than anyone else? I'm always held to some higher standard, but that standard is unachievable, Mother. I'm not perfect, and I never will be."

"I hold you to a higher standard because you are smart, rational, and you have your feet planted on solid ground— well, usually. I do expect more out of you," she admits, "but it's only because I know you are capable of so much more."

Her words surprise me because it is the first time she has ever openly admitted that she treats me differently. I look to

Ruthie to make sure Mother's comparative words haven't hurt her feelings, but she seems to be perfectly fine.

I'm too shocked by our mother's revelations to respond. I hadn't realized that she was aware of the disparities in the way she treats her daughters. On the one hand, I am flattered and relieved that she believes in me. On the other hand, I realize it's not fair to have placed me on a pedestal for all these years with higher expectations than I have any hope of ever achieving.

"Perhaps my faith in you was unfounded." With these cutting words, Mother whirls around and leaves our room, calmly closing the door behind her.

Once the door has clicked into place, Baggy, never opening her eyes, says, "Nice job standing up to her." She lets out another little puff snore for good measure, which makes us start giggling.

"You were faking being asleep?" I ask her disdainfully. When she gives me a shit-eating, toothless grin—her false teeth are still in the glass on the bedside table—I lob a throw pillow at her.

She sits up and looks at me proudly. "You handled yourself just fine, but I was going to do a surprise ninja attack if a brawl erupted."

I shake my head at her. Only Baggy would be faking sleep while plotting a surprise ninja attack on her daughter on her own wedding day.

"Guess I better get my old bones a movin'," Baggy announces, stretching loudly. "Hot diggity! I'm getting hitched today!"

31

We order fresh fruit, toast, bacon, and tea from room service, which we eat on our patio. Then we spend the rest of the morning in the room, just the three of us, getting ready for Baggy's big day. We don't hear from Mother again, and no one mars the perfection of our time together by bringing up the topic.

I am dying to go look for Kai, but I also know that this special pre-wedding bonding time with Baggy and Ruthie is a not-to-be-missed, once-in-a-lifetime opportunity. Hopefully, Kai and I will spend the rest of our lives together, so this slight delay won't make any difference. Although, if I'm completely honest with myself, I'm frightened to hear what he has to say. If he's furiously unforgiving about my abrupt departure, I'd rather keep the hope for a happy ending for us alive for a while longer.

It is almost like the three of us have created a bubble of happiness for ourselves in this bungalow, and we aren't quite ready to let it go. Eventually, I decide that it is time for me to head down to the beach to make sure that everything is set up for the ceremony.

I am pleasantly surprised as I walk along the sand to see white chairs with light pink ribbons tied on them. A pale pink silk aisle, which is held down by queen conch shells, separates the chairs. A giant arbor trellis has been set up overlooking the water.

The reception tent is lovely as well. Only a few tables are set up, but each has a bright pink hibiscus floral arrangement as a centerpiece. A makeshift stage, where the band will play, has been created at the front of the tent. Just outside the tent, a large pig is smoking, buried deep in a pit in the sand.

Someone has thought of every detail to make this wedding unforgettable, and I wonder who it could have been. I can't imagine that Baggy or Ruthie came up with all of this on their own, even though they kept telling me not to worry because everything was handled. Perhaps they had a wedding planner they didn't bother to tell me about? The only other explanation I can come up with is that Howie took care of the planning, but this seems like a storybook fairytale wedding scene, not one that he would have created.

In any case, I am thrilled for Baggy. Her wedding day is going to be perfect, and I am so grateful to be here for it.

If I'm completely honest with myself, I have to admit that I have been looking around for Kai the entire time I've been scoping out the wedding setting. If my parents had time to get here, shouldn't he have had time to return? I'm dying to speak with him, but I want it to be in person.

I sit down on one of the white folding chairs in the front row. As I'm working out in my mind how I can explain to Kai what happened, I feel someone sit down next to me. Only a tiny bit of disappointment courses through me when I look over and find my dad in the adjacent chair. After that initial letdown, I am thrilled to see him, and I hope that over-joyed emotion is the only one that shows on my face.

We chat about the gorgeous weather, the ridiculously

long flight to get here, the upcoming crazy nuptials, and just about everything under the sun—except for what I really want to know. Finally, I take a deep breath, deciding there is no time like the present. "Dad, did someone call or come by your house looking for me?"

"You mean Kai?" Just hearing his name come out of my father's mouth makes my heart beat faster. I nod quickly, wanting to see what else he has to say. "Yes, he stopped by."

Infuriatingly, my father doesn't seem to be inclined to continue. "And?" I nudge.

"Oh, well, he seems like a nice boy." I would hardly refer to burly Kai as a boy, but I don't point that out. We sit in silence for a few long moments. Dad has placed his arm around me and is gently rubbing his thumb over my shoulder. "He sure seems to love you," he adds, almost as an afterthought.

My head snaps around instantly. "He does? What did he say? Is he angry with me for leaving? Was he on your flight? Is he here?" The questions that have been floating around in my mind burst out in a flood.

"Whoa, whoa, one at a time, sweetheart," Dad says calmly, chuckling softly at my overly enthusiastic barrage of questions. "He should be on the next flight in. Our flight had only two seats left, and he wanted to make sure that your mother and I made it in plenty of time for Baggy's ceremony."

I feel an irrational swell of pride at Kai's gallantry. Although I didn't have anything to do with it, I'm glad my father was witness to such a selfless act from my quasi-boyfriend—soon to be full-on boyfriend, I hope. "That was sweet." I smile at my father, who nods in agreement.

"Yes, he seems like quite a nice fellow." This simple statement is glowing praise compared to anything my dad has ever said about any guy Ruthie or I have ever brought home. My heart feels full. Somehow, my father's blessing makes me even more certain that Kai is a keeper. I wouldn't have thought that I would be so concerned with my dad's approval, but since he's never before liked a guy whom I have dated, I didn't know how great it would feel to get his confirmation of my choice.

"You know, your mother wasn't going to come to this wedding." Dad drops this bombshell news as if it is no big deal. "Kai is the one who talked some sense into her. She wasn't listening to me, of course." He smiles sheepishly at this revelation. It's not like it is a secret that my parents don't exactly get along, but my father and I have never before discussed it, especially not so openly.

"How did he convince her?" I ask, truly curious.

"Oh, something about not missing out on the great moments of life and not having your parents around forever, that kind of mumbo jumbo," he teases. "It really wasn't anything earth-shatteringly different from what I said, but for some reason she paid attention to him. I think she really likes him."

My mouth falls open at this news. "Mother likes Kai?" I splutter. My mother has never approved of anyone I have dated, and she is very up front and outspoken about it—to the point of embarrassing me by vocalizing her distaste right in front of a couple of the poor chaps. Apparently Kai is so charming that even my straight-laced, judgmental mother can't resist him. The thought boggles my mind.

"Guess I better go get dressed for the ceremony and see if there's anything I'm supposed to be doing," Dad announces as he stands, and I suddenly wonder what time it is.

"Me, too." I give him a huge hug before running off to finish getting ready.

32

When I get back to the room, Baggy is the only one there. I take full advantage of this special opportunity for one-on-one time with her. She is wearing a short, silky robe and, surprisingly, is most of the way ready. I decide she has the right idea and don my robe until it's time to put on my dress.

I pull a chair over to the full-length mirror in the hall, so I can chat with Baggy while I borrow and apply some of Ruthie's makeup. Baggy brings a hairbrush and walks over to stand behind me. She is so tiny that with me sitting in the chair and her standing, we are roughly the same height.

I am so pleased when she starts easing the brush slowly through my tresses. Wonderful memories wash over me as she gently tends to my hair with long, smooth strokes. She used to brush my hair for hours when I was young. In fact, she was the only one who could detangle my long hair without hurting me. Mother would yank at the snarls until I was in tears before getting frustrated and telling me I needed to "get that mop cut off."

Baggy patiently pulls the brush through my hair until it glistens. From her slow, methodical movements, one would think she had all the time in the world and nothing else to do today. I enjoy the loving attention so much that I don't point out that we should probably start getting dressed.

When she finally sets the brush down, I am relaxed and feel completely pampered. The memory of her taking the time on her special day to do this for me is one that I will cherish forever.

Baggy retrieves a bright pink hibiscus from our tiny dorm-size refrigerator. She uses a bobby pin to secure it just behind my left ear before standing back to admire her handiwork. "You look beautiful." Her eyes look directly at mine in the mirror.

I can't help but smile. The way she is looking at me makes me feel beautiful. She is the only person in my family who has ever told me I am physically attractive. Ruthie is the pretty one. I am the smart one. Everyone knows that— everyone but Baggy. She refuses to see the world like everyone else does, and I am so thankful that she insists on being different.

As I look at my reflection, I say a silent prayer that Baggy was right about the placement of the flower in my hair. Does Kai still consider me to be taken? I sure hope so.

Realizing that I am being swept away by wayward thoughts, I ask Baggy where she and Howie are going on their honeymoon. When she says he hasn't told her, my first instinct is to balk. Shouldn't the bride get a say in where she would like to go? Baggy doesn't seem at all concerned about it, so I bite my tongue.

"Maybe we'll get called out on a secret spy mission," she says excitedly.

With that, my sweet, wonderful grandma is gone. She has

been replaced with my slightly crazy, always entertaining Baggy. I think about the fact that it's not "secret" or "spy" if you tell others about it. I also wonder if Howie is delusional and truly believes the tall tales he tells. In the end I decide that it's Baggy's day, and it should be Baggy's way, so I smile at her in the mirror and say, "Maybe."

33

*O*nce I'm dressed, I give Baggy a little time in the room alone, telling her it would be a great opportunity to mentally prepare for the wedding and reflect on this momentous occasion. I'm sure she'll probably ignore that advice and instead use the time to lube her entire body with magic jelly, but I prefer not to think about that.

The real reason I leave is to find Ruthie. I haven't seen her, and it's time for her to get dressed. If she has flitted away somewhere and ends up being late for Baggy's wedding, I'll be so angry with her. It wouldn't surprise me too much, though, because the attention isn't focused on her. Surely she wouldn't be so selfish as to ruin Baggy's big day. Would she?

I can't deny that I'm also looking for Kai in my search for Ruthie, but she's the one I'm really after right now. I find Howie talking animatedly to my father, but see no sign of Ruthie or Kai. When I pass near my father, he bugs his eyes out at me, and I can only imagine the tall tales he is hearing. I smile knowingly at him but breeze by without butting into the conversation, even though I'm sure Dad is hoping that I will rescue him.

When I get to the reception tent, I'm pleased to see that the cupcakes have arrived and are displayed beautifully. Victoria may not have initially deigned it appropriate to do wedding cupcakes, but once she came on board with the idea, she did them with class. They look almost too delicious to eat, but I'm sure I'll get over that when the time comes.

I wander around the entire resort in my light pink bridesmaid's dress and flip-flops, and no one gives me a second look. That's part of the beauty of Hawaii—anything goes, and there is a wedding in close proximity every fifteen minutes or so. After a short while, even tourists become used to the ceremonies. Other than a dreamy smile and friendly wave, most are numbed enough by the frequency of them to barely even take note of the near-constant wedding preparations and ceremonies.

"Roxy." I hear a voice quietly croak my name as I walk past the pool. I turn to find Ruthie wadded into the fetal position on a lounge chair. Immediately, I turn and run to her to see what is wrong.

When she sits up, I see long black mascara streaks on her cheeks as evidence that she has been crying. I sit beside her and pull her into a hug. "What happened?" I ask her. My voice is gentle, even though I am ready to pound whoever has upset her so much.

"He . . . he . . . he took that skank to his cottage," she splutters, before a giant sob erupts out of her.

My first thought is Kai, and ice immediately runs through my veins. Once the initial panic subsides, and I am able to form a coherent thought, I realize she can't be talking about Kai. His seaside retreat could no more be called a "cottage" than Kai himself could be called a "boy," as Dad had referred to him earlier today. Besides, Ruthie wouldn't be this upset if Kai had betrayed me. This must have to do with Curtis.

"You saw Curtis with someone else?" I ask her softly, trying to verify my assumption.

She confirms with a watery-eyed nod. I try to calm her and make sure she isn't jumping to the wrong conclusion. "Just because someone goes into his house doesn't mean anything is going on between them." She gives me a look like I might be the densest person on Earth, so I elaborate. "They could have gone in there for something totally innocent. Maybe she had to use the bathroom or he's showing her his surfboards or something." I know my possible scenarios sound lame, so I stop trying to come up with more.

"I know what happens when a lady goes into his cottage, and believe me, it is not innocent," she wails.

Deciding she is probably right, I change tactics. "Were the two of you seeing each other exclusively?"

"We hadn't talked about it," she admits. "I just assumed with all the fun we were having that he wouldn't have time for or want to be with anyone else."

I nod, opting not to point out that one should never assume in these types of situations.

"I mean, it's the best sex I've ever had," she confides, "and we were doing it all the time—*all* the time," she repeats for added emphasis. She's sharing a little more than I want to know, but I am her sister, and I want to be here for her— even if it means I have to suffer through hearing about her overly active sex life when mine is nonexistent.

"Now he's in there banging that prissy prude, Victoria." She spits out the name with venom.

I try to hide my shock at this revelation. Perhaps we really brought out the wild side in old Vicky. I wouldn't have thought she had it in her.

"What does he see in her? She's a Goody Two-shoes who probably just lies there the entire time waiting for it to be over," Ruthie sneers unkindly. I know that her words are just coming from a place of hurt and anger, although I'm uncertain why she would be lashing out toward Victoria, rather than Curtis. He's the one, not Victoria, who had a relationship with Ruthie. Victoria probably has no idea that Ruthie and Curtis had been seeing each other.

Instead of playing the rational older sister and pointing out the flaw in her logic, I nod and listen while she rants about what an ice queen Victoria is. All the while, I am secretly thinking that Vicky probably has an adventurous and dangerous side that bubbles just under the surface of her prim facade. If she has let her fiery red hair down, she might be completely rocking Curtis's world right now. I wisely keep that thought to myself.

My phone buzzes with a new text. Normally, I wouldn't take time away from such an important conversation to check my phone, but I really need to talk to Kai, and it might be him. Besides, Ruthie is so much in her own world that she probably won't even notice.

To my surprise, the text is from Lizzie, my lifelong best friend. The text reads, *"I'm sooooo sorry. Can you ever forgive me?"*

I smile at the words because I realize that I should be thanking her for stopping me from making the biggest mistake of my life. Although I didn't know at the time that marrying Gary would have been disastrous, I know it now. Without their betrayal, I would have met Kai as a newly married woman. Would I have still felt the instant attraction I had for him yet been unable to acknowledge it in any way? Would I have already figured out that marrying Gary was a huge blunder?

I decide not to completely let Lizzie off the hook. I mean, she did betray our friendship by having an affair with Gary. I type a quick response. *"Perhaps. I'll call you in a few days."* I'm sure I'll eventually forgive her—I might have already done that, but I won't be able to forget what happened. She has been a friend my entire life, and I don't want to cut her completely out of my life. I don't think things will ever be exactly the same between us, though. Some breaches of trust can never be entirely absolved.

When I tell Ruthie about the text exchange with Lizzie, she quickly turns the discussion back around to her current situation. "That traitor ruined your wedding day by cheating with *your* man, just like that awful redheaded puffed pastry is in there doing with Curtis right now." I nod, letting her vent.

Ruthie eventually tires of alternating between broken-hearted sobbing and belittling blustering about Victoria. I retrieve a couple of napkins from the bar. She loudly blows her nose on one, and I use the other to help wipe the tears from her cheeks. Once we have her relatively cleaned up, I put my arm around her and say that we need to get her ready for the wedding.

At first I think she might try to weasel out of going, but then she rallies. I can see the determination rising in her before she says, "I don't want either of them to see me looking like this. The next time Curtis sees me, I'm going to look so gorgeous it will knock his socks off, and he's going to beg me for forgiveness."

She pauses, and concern grows in me as I wonder if she would actually take him back after he slept with someone else. Even though they weren't officially exclusive, it still doesn't seem right. I don't have to worry too long. "Then I can tell him to bite me before I saunter off with the most handsome man around."

There's the Ruthie I know and love, I think to myself as I help her up. I smile at her spunk before adding, *It will have to be the second most handsome man around because Kai will be with me.*

34

"*Y*ou!" the tiny Hawaiian woman growls at me, while jabbing a short, brown finger into my belly. The top of her head barely reaches my chest, yet somehow I feel intimidated. "You hurt my sweet Kai."

Her words leave no doubt that she is Kai's Nana Lana. Seeing her glaring eyes peer up at me, I wonder if there might be some truth to Baggy's assessment that the woman is crazy. Her next venomous words leave little doubt. "You hurt my sweet boy. I put a hex on you."

"No, you don't understand," I stammer, suddenly concerned. "I didn't mean to hurt him." Her dark eyes look almost black as they squint at me in disbelief. "I came back here to be with Kai."

"You left him," she snarls at me.

"I did," I confess, "but I quickly realized what a mistake that was, and I came back for him." The woman seems to be all long, dark hair (except for the stark white streak in the front) and mean, beady eyes as she continues to glare at me. I wonder if she's putting a hex on me right now or if it requires a chant or a full moon to conjure. I've never been a big believer in magic, but there is no denying that there is something mystical about her. She is one of the few women I have ever met who would give Baggy a serious run for her money in the "nontraditional grandmother" category.

She keeps staring at me, and it is making me wildly uncomfortable. I am not sure what she is waiting for me to say or do. My nervousness makes me start rambling. "I was miserable at home. I should have never left Kai. It doesn't make any logical sense that in such a short time he has become so important to me, but it's true. I don't want to live my life without him." I pause, but then decide I might as well go all in—especially if she's getting ready to curse me anyway. "I love him, Nana Lana." It is the first time I have admitted it to anyone else.

"You do?" I don't know when Kai walked up behind me, but he must have heard my last statement. I turn to face him. He's even more impossibly gorgeous than my recollections. I nod my head, but it doesn't satisfy him. "You love me?" he asks again.

"Yes," I confirm, and I am rewarded with the most gorgeous, slightly gap-toothed smile I have ever seen.

"All right, then," Nana Lana says, giving me for the first time since our less-than-friendly introduction a hint of what might be a slightly friendly look. I can't help but notice that she has gorgeous, youthful skin, especially for a grand-mother. I make a mental note that I need to start slathering on the magic jelly. "It's time for the ceremony," she announces to the group at large, effectively cutting off my discussion with Kai. I suddenly go from being almost fearful of her, to wanting to flip the end of her nose. She had somehow managed to butt into and stall the single most important conversation of my life.

I have never wanted to hear what someone has to say

more, but I don't have a choice. It's time to line up for the wedding. Kai and I will have to finish this potentially life-altering discussion later.

Before I know it, I am whisked away and find myself standing near the altar beside Ruthie, watching my father attempt to wrangle Baggy down the aisle. Seeming to sense that Baggy is going to be easily distracted, he locks his elbow more firmly with hers and steers her toward us.

Deciding that my father has the matter well in hand, I chance a look at Howie. He is beaming from ear to ear, as if he has just won the lottery. He has the right idea, I decide. Getting to spend the rest of his life with Baggy is like winning a huge jackpot. I just hope he is up to the challenge.

Honi and Leilani have been standing off to the side of the altar in traditional Hawaiian attire. Not having been involved in much of the wedding planning, I am uncertain what their roles are in the ceremony. I am pleasantly surprised when Honi starts playing the ukulele and singing a haunting but beautiful love song. Leilani begins slowly swaying her hips to the music. Her graceful movements are mesmerizingly smooth and all eyes are on her—all except for Kai's.

I can feel his gaze on me. When I lock eyes with him, delicious warmth spreads over me. I like the way he is looking at me, and I don't want him to stop. At the same time, I am desperate to hear what he has to say about my proclamation of love for him and what ideas he has for our future—assuming he wants a future with me. From the unabashed desirous look of adoration that he is currently beaming at me, I'm guessing that's a safe bet.

When the lovely ballad ends, Nana Lana gives an extended blow into a conch shell. She then efficiently and authoritatively explains in her melodic voice that blowing into a shell or *pu* is a signal to the land, air, fire, and sea that something very special is about to happen. Howie tenderly kisses Baggy's cheek. I don't remember ever before seeing her look this lovely or happy.

The ceremony is a harmonious blend of native Hawaiian traditions and familiar nondenominational wedding customs. The bride and groom exchange platinum wedding bands and floral leis that they have woven for each other. When Nana Lana explains that these circles unite the bride, groom, and their loved ones in an eternal loop of aloha or love, I hear Ruthie sigh dreamily behind me.

My eyes travel from Kai to the nuptials, then, almost involuntarily, they travel back to Kai. He doesn't seem to be having the same issue. Every time I look at him, he is steadily and lovingly gazing back at me. My heart melts a little more each time.

Baggy and Howie call each other "Boris" and "Natasha" when they exchange their vows. I hear some tittering from my mother, but my father manages to calm her enough that she doesn't stop the ceremony. I'm sure her traditionalist views of how solemn and serious a wedding ceremony should be have been incredibly offended, though. Boris and Natasha don't seem to notice that anything is amiss as they blissfully promise to love each other until death parts them.

When it's time for the groom to kiss the bride, their lips and tongues linger beyond the nervous laughter of the crowd, beyond the uncomfortable shifting in the seats, and beyond the inevitable clearing of the throats. They kiss and kiss and kiss. I don't know why I'm surprised. I would expect nothing less from Baggy and the man lucky enough to snag her.

I chance a look at my mother while the public display of affection drags on. No surprises there: she is pinched and pursed like someone has broken wind and she has just gotten a big whiff of it. A bubble of laughter starts to burst out of me, but I am able to tone it down to a minor giggle. Ruthie hears me, and she starts chuckling, too. Soon, several others are laughing as well. The uncomfortable factor of watching these two have a full-on make-out session is too much to take—the nervous energy has to escape somehow.

Finally, they stop kissing. Our small group of wedding attendees immediately launches into applause. We all smile at one another, probably wondering the same thing: *Are we clapping because they just got married or because that extremely tongue-filled kiss finally ended?* Either way, it feels worthy of celebration.

We are all so busy clapping and grinning at one another that no one notices the bride and groom have turned their backs to us until Nana Lana blows the *pu* once more. The conch shell horn immediately silences us. Having gained our full attention, Nana Lana presents the happy couple to the group. They turn to greet us for the first time as husband and wife, and we all freeze in place when we see their faces.

They are beaming grotesque smiles at us, having evidently exchanged false teeth with each other when their backs were turned. Baggy is sporting Howie's teeth, which are much too large for her tiny mouth. They make her smile look like a toothy, creepy caricature. Howie's smile isn't much better; with Baggy's too small teeth in his mouth, his scary grin is almost all gums and lips.

Mother flinches and makes an odd, gurgly sound. I silently pray that Baggy's antics don't shock her into fainting or give her a heart attack. Looking at all of our surprised, appalled faces makes Baggy and Howie guffaw with laughter. They are obviously proud of themselves and their odd prank.

Once their laughter subsides enough for her to speak, Baggy clears her throat, obviously intending to make an announcement. "Well, I guess this is as good a time as any to fess up," she starts, making us all dread what might be coming. "Howie and I had to get married 'cause he knocked me up!"

Her announcement brings on a second round of loud laughter from the two of them. This time the rest of the group joins in with them—everyone except Ruthie, who says to me, "Baggy isn't really pregnant, is she?"

Her question is so ridiculous that I can't even answer her with a straight face. I shake my head even as I'm doubled over with laughter at the thought. When it dawns on Ruthie how silly the idea is, she begins laughing, too.

As I scan around for Kai, I see the resort photographer unobtrusively snapping photos of all the joyous, laughing faces. *These are going to make some wonderful pictures and memories*, I think to myself. Well, everyone except Mother, but she never looks overly thrilled. At least she looks only mildly annoyed right now. After all of Baggy's shenanigans during the ceremony, I would have thought she'd be fit to be tied.

As the photographer snaps some pictures of the bride and groom a passerby photo-bombs them. We are so stunned that no one says a word as he kisses Baggy's cheek and congratulates the happy couple before moseying on down the beach.

"Was that . . . ?" I finally say, but it seems so farfetched that I don't even bother to finish the question.

"It sure looked like him." Ruthie answers my unfinished question, confirming what I thought.

"That Jason Mammy fellow really does look like Kai," Baggy says to us, rubbing her cheek where he had just pressed his lips.

"Momoa," Ruthie and I say in unison.

"I do think he lives at least some of the time in Hawaii, but that couldn't have been him, could it?" Ruthie looks hopeful since Baggy even noticed the stranger's resemblance to the actor.

"Nah," I say, shaking my head and thinking that the chances of a super-famous person photo-bombing and kissing my grandmother on her wedding day are pretty slim. Although, if anyone's known for having surprising, almost unbelievable events happen to her, it's Baggy.

"There's a chance it is him, though." Ruthie is gazing wistfully in the direction he went. "I have to find out," she adds, already following in his footsteps.

"I think he's married," I yell after her, but she's already in hot pursuit. "I guess she's over the heartbreak of losing Curtis," I say aloud to no one in particular. Even though I'm shaking my head, I can't help but admire her resilience.

The music starts in the reception tent, so I head in that direction. Victoria, looking mildly rumpled, is serving the wedding cupcakes. From the change in her looks, I'd have to say that Ruthie was right about what was going on in Curtis's bungalow. Victoria's slightly sex-tousled hair and rosy cheeks are a definite improvement over her previous perfectly sleek look. She had looked like she needed to loosen up, and by the looks of things, she definitely has. It's amazing what a great roll in the sack can do for an uptight woman.

35

*M*y eyes search the white tent for Kai to no avail. I've never wanted to talk to someone so much in my entire life, and he's frustratingly absent.

I do see Honi and Leilani slow dancing in the sand in front of the small band. Leilani gets on her tippy toes to whisper something in Honi's ear before giving him a sweet kiss on the lips. I wonder if she shared the news of her pregnancy. After the kiss, he smiles from ear to ear, which I am thrilled to see. As far as I know, this is the first public acknowledgment either of them has made of their feelings for each other. I earnestly hope the two of them are able to make things work.

I'm also surprised to see my parents dancing with each other, which is a definite first. They normally find opposite corners to complain about each other to anyone who will listen. Mother even has her cheek resting on Dad's shoulder. She has to bend her head at an awkward angle to make it work, but they both look content. *Maybe there really is magic in the air here*, I think as I look at them. *That or Nana Lana slipped them some kind of love potion, which is also a distinct possibility*, I snigger to myself.

Suddenly, I feel him behind me. "Hi," he whispers near my ear. His closeness sends a shiver of delight up my spine.

"Hi," I respond turning my head. Our lips instantly find each other's as I lean back into him.

"Did I hear a rumor that you love me?" he asks when our lips finally part.

"Oh, it's no rumor." I turn to kiss him fully on the mouth. When the kiss ends, we keep our faces close together, our arms wrapped around each other. "I was miserable at home," I confess. "I don't know what I was thinking when I left here and left you." I look down when I say the last two words, still uncertain if he's angry with me for bailing the way I did. "I am going to be here with you for as long as you want me around." It's an incredibly bold statement for me. I don't usually wear my feelings on my sleeve.

I want to hear his reaction. I need to know if he wants me here. I have poured my heart out to him, and now it's time to find out if he feels the same way about me, or if I have been delusional.

Unfortunately, Baggy chooses this moment to grab the microphone from the singer to make an announcement. "I'd like to thank you all for coming and sharing in this joyous time," she says. Just when we start to think that she might make a coherent and rational speech, she adds, "Today, I've made a husband out of my best friend and spy partner." Seeming to realize that she has just shared something she shouldn't have, she adds, "Don't tell anyone about the spy thing. It's top-secret." Some amused chuckles escape from around the tent. No one seems to be certain if she is serious. My mother rolls her eyes dramatically.

"We have been called out on a mission, and we will need to head out soon," she stage whispers into the mike as if she's sharing a great secret with us. "We got lei'd during the cere-mony"—she holds up her flower necklace to clarify her meaning before continuing with a naughty twinkle in her eye—"but we're leaving now so we have time to really get . . ."

Thankfully, the rest of her sentence is drowned out by the whirring blades of a helicopter landing on the roof of the resort. We all know where she was going with that state-ment, and none of us want to think about that. She blows a huge kiss to the group before taking off with Howie toward the helicopter.

We cheer and wave them off. Kai and I exchange curious looks after the helicopter whisks them away. It's a much more dramatic departure than either of us had been expect-ing. "You don't suppose they really have some sort of legiti-mate mission, do you?" I ask him.

"Nah," we both say in unison.

"Baggy is much too outlandish and loud to be able to blend in like a wallflower and not be noticed," I point out.

"Which might just be the perfect disguise," Kai adds, making us both consider the idea again.

We give each other a long, pondering look before we both say once more, "Nah."

36

Kai takes my hand and leads me to the sandy dance floor. I watch my mother swaying to the music in my father's arms. Her sandals are dangling from her finger. She looks lovely and relaxed—more relaxed than I have ever before seen her.

The sand feels cool on my feet as Kai and I slow dance to the reggae tune the band is playing. I'm glad that Baggy insisted that Ruthie and I go with bare feet (like her) for the ceremony. The sand in my shoes would have been driving me crazy by now. As I look around, it's easy to see that pretty much everyone has given up on wearing shoes.

"My feet are going to be so soft. This sand is better than any loofah scrub."

He stops dancing and looks down at me with a look that I can only describe as pure adoration. I have never before had anyone gaze at me like this, and it makes my heart melt. I'm sure I am giving him the same sweet look. He stuns me by saying, "Marry me, Roxy."

My eyes immediately dart to my mother as if they are seeking her approval. I can't process what Kai has just said. I look back to him, assuming that he must be joking. He looks completely sincere. I can feel myself blinking way too frequently and my chest feels heavy like I can't quite take in enough air. His words don't make sense. We barely know each other. We can't promise to spend the rest of our lives together after such a short period of time—it's not logical.

It may not be logical, but the thought of spending the rest of my life with Kai is thrilling, and the idea makes my heart race with happiness. It would be a dream come true. He is sweet, kind, thoughtful, funny, beyond handsome, and his kisses make my knees quiver, but I can't marry a man I've known for such a short amount of time. My mind is warring with itself. The rational side of me says *no way*; but the recently found, whimsical, seize-the-moment, be happy, and live-life-to-the-fullest part of me says *go for it*.

"You want a wife with soft feet, huh?" I joke, trying to buy a little time and make light of the timing of his comment. Dodging the subject will give him a chance to think about what he is saying. I don't want him to rush into something he will regret later.

He gazes steadily at me, not accepting my implied offer to laugh off his proposal. My heart is slamming into my chest as I give him another out. "You just want to have sex," I accuse, smiling to let him know I am teasing him.

"That would be an amazing perk." He chuckles, leaning in to nibble on my ear. "But the truth is, I just don't want to waste another minute without you." His wonderful words tell me that he is not going to take me up on this second chance to laugh the topic off as a momentary lapse in judgment. When he continues, I can barely manage to breathe in and out. "I know that you are the one for me. If you feel the same way about me, let's throw caution to the wind and do what we know is right for our future."

Verifying that he is sincere, he gets down on one knee in

the sand. My mind is swirling as he begins speaking. "Roxy, you are the most amazing woman I have ever met. I love you and want to spend the rest of my life with you. I will do everything in my power to make sure that you are the happiest woman on Earth. Will you do me the extraordinary honor of becoming my wife?"

I am in shock and my mind feels sluggish—like my thoughts are wading through Jell-O—but I am coherent enough to know that this is exactly what I want and need. It may not make sense, but it makes me happy. What more could a lady ask for?

"Yes," I say to Kai, and he rewards me with an enormous, slightly gap-toothed, yet perfect smile. He stands and pulls me into his arms for a knee-bending, soul-shattering, and mind-numbing kiss.

When we finally break apart, I am practically incoherent with giddiness—until I look around at the attention we have drawn and see my mother's face. She is clearly not pleased. The other reception guests smile and give us a spontaneous round of applause. Honi appears at Kai's side and hands him a vibrantly colored lei to place around my neck.

As Kai tenderly eases the flower necklace over my head, I can't keep the flicker of thoughts about my previous engagement out of my head. It had featured an enormous diamond ring and a fancy restaurant. Gary had executed the ideal proposal perfectly—according to what societal customs dictate a wedding proposal should be. It should have been a dream come true, but if I'm completely honest with myself, I knew even that night that our whirlwind of an engagement wasn't right. It didn't feel at all like Kai's proposal feels. Kai didn't present me with a fancy ring or have a string quartet on standby to serenade us after my acceptance, but it is perfect—perfect for us. I know in my heart that this is right.

Several people give us congratulatory hugs. We smile and

say "Mahalo"—the Hawaiian version of thank you—to everyone. When Nana Lana approaches us, she shakes a bony finger at me. "You take good care of him," she warns me sternly, implying that I'll have her to deal with if I don't.

"I'll do my best," I reassure her.

When she reaches up to give Kai a hug, he stoops down to speak to her. I try not to eavesdrop, but I am secretly thrilled when I overhear him say the words, "the one I've been waiting for."

Just as I'm wondering if it's possible to actually burst with joy, I see my parents approaching us. Nana Lana floats away just before my mother's voice intrudes on our bubble of happiness. "Have you two thought this through at all?" she asks incredulously. "There are so many things to consider—like where do you plan to live?"

"Here," we both say in unison, then smile at each other.

"I can move if you would prefer it," Kai offers sweetly, "but I thought if we stayed here, we could set up an artist's studio for you right over here." He points to an unused corner of the resort. "It should get great light all day, and you can sell your masterpieces on the beach."

"Perfect," I tell him, and I mean it. I couldn't have conjured a better solution if I were to have a genie who would make all of my wildest dreams come true.

"What about your job?" Mother asks. "Your *real* job," she clarifies when she realizes that we have just decided on my vocation. She has never taken my art seriously, and her insinuation that it isn't "real" proves that she still feels like it is a silly hobby.

"I've never liked being an accountant, Mother," I inform her, although I'm pretty sure she already knew that. "Painting is my calling, and I'm good at it. For perhaps the first time, I'm going to listen to my inner voice and follow my intuition. This is how I want to spend my life."

Not to be deterred, Mother tries another angle. "You two barely know each other," she points out. "Have you even discussed any of the big decisions?" At our blank stare, she prompts, "How many children do you want to have?"

"Two," I say at the exact same time that Kai says, "Four."

We look at each other in surprise, before both of us say, "Three." We beam at each other.

Mother throws her hands up in the air as if we are completely doomed. "We'll figure it all out, Mother," I tell her. "We are committed to this, and we are going to make it work."

Her lips are still pursed, but she evidently decides that she won't be able to change my mind tonight because she says, "Well, as long as you have a nice, long engagement to truly get to know each other, I guess we can figure it out."

I'm certain that she's thinking she will be able to talk some sense into me once the euphoria of the evening settles. I know that I am meant to be with Kai, and she will never be able to change my mind about that, but I'll wait until a more appropriate time to inform her of these facts.

"About the length of our engagement," Kai says. "We couldn't ask for a more picturesque setting for our wedding, and all of our loved ones are here . . ." He smiles down at me, and I can tell where he is heading with this. "If you want more time to think it over, I'll understand, but tonight seems to me like the perfect time to get married."

"Perfect," I answer him, and I mean it.

My mother's glasses, which she always has perched on the tip of her nose, slide down her face. "What? Why? How?" she blusters. "You don't even have a marriage license," she finally tries.

"We'll take care of that later," Kai shoots that argument down. "We will tie ourselves to each other forever in our hearts in front of our family and friends this evening. The paperwork is just a formality. It can wait."

"You're rushing into this because you know it's a mistake." She glares at me.

I don't point out that her logic doesn't make any sense. Instead, I say, "I've never been more sure of anything in my life." Kai and I gaze at each other, and I know without a doubt that I am making the right decision.

"Your father and I do not support this marriage." Mother drops her trump card.

I suck in a breath, but it's my dad who speaks. "Stop it, Caroline." My quiet, reserved father steps in. I have rarely seen him stand up to my mother, and I am overflowing with joy that he still has it in him. "Roxy, you are our daughter, and we love you unconditionally. If you say this is right, then we are wholeheartedly behind you." My mother's mouth opens and closes a few times. She looks like a hooked guppy gulping for water, but she remains silent.

I hurl myself into my father's arms for a big hug. "Thank you, Daddy," I say, unsure why I reverted to calling him that. He squeezes me tight before kissing my cheek.

"I love you, sweetheart," he tells me before releasing me.

When I turn to my mother, I'm surprised to see an unshed tear glistening in her eye. Behind me, I can hear Kai and my dad shaking hands initially then deciding to hug it out. "I only want what's best for you," Mother informs me.

"I know," I tell her, and I mean it. Although she almost always tries to bully me into her way of thinking, I know that her intentions are pure. We stay there for a long moment. I have stood up to her and am now knowingly going against her wishes. The anticipation of waiting to see her final reaction is unnerving.

Finally, she huffs out a breath and says, "If you really think this is what you want, then I'll stand behind your decision." I exhale in relief before lunging myself at her for a hug. She can't seem to keep herself from adding in my ear, "Even if I do think it's a monumental mistake."

I refuse to let the snide comment bother me. I am getting ready to marry the man of my dreams. My life is absolutely perfect right now, and I won't let anything intrude on my happiness.

Baggy and Ruthie aren't here. The thought barges its way into my mind. Despite my wish not to let anything mar my perfect surprise wedding night, my absent sister and grandmother might be a dealbreaker. *Should I wait until they can be here to enjoy my big day? Will they be disappointed in me?* That last worrisome question is what convinces me. If there are two people on Earth who encourage me to be spontaneous, carefree, and maybe even a little reckless, it's Baggy and Ruthie.

I am confident that they will be delighted with my disregard for the rules and social norms by marrying Kai on a whim so soon after my planned marriage to another man. They will be convinced that they are turning me into a free spirit who lives her life as she pleases, by no one's rules, but her own. If I'm completely honest with myself, that doesn't sound like a bad way to live. It's time for me to step out of my comfort zone and enjoy the life that I am meant to have.

"Let's do this," I say to Kai, and the tent quickly erupts into a rambunctious roar of excitement. Even Mother is smiling.

37

Tiki torches light the path to the altar where Baggy just got married, which has now become the altar for my wedding. Our ceremony is remarkably similar to Baggy's, with the omission of the ornery shenanigans. Nana Lana blows into the *pu* before Kai and I exchange vows that are identical to the ones my grandmother and her new husband made earlier.

I love the way Kai looks at me as he promises to love, honor, and cherish me. When I say those same words to him, I mean them with my whole heart. We may not have known each other for as long as most couples who marry, but I know deep inside that this is right. For the first time in my entire life, I feel like I am exactly where I am supposed to be, with exactly who I should be with, doing exactly what I should be doing.

I feel confident in my decision and, maybe for the first time ever, utterly happy. I glance down at the pale pink bridesmaid's dress that Baggy chose for me, which has now become my wedding gown. Even though it is not at all what I would have pictured myself getting married in, it is somehow perfect. I don't know where the simple platinum wedding bands came from, but they are perfect too. Everything about this wedding is slightly quirky and not quite what I would have envisioned, yet perfect.

The ceremony goes by in a flash and before I know it, I am kissing Kai in front of most of our family and friends as his wife—his WIFE! Our first kiss as husband and wife is slow and luxurious and delicious, but not nearly as outlandishly long as Howie and Baggy's had been. When our lips break apart, our foreheads remain touching as we smile at each other. The small group breaks into spontaneous applause—likely relieved that we didn't make them endure the same type of lengthy tongue tangling we all witnessed earlier.

The evening is a blur of hugs and well wishes. Before I know it, Kai and I are once more slow dancing in the sand— in almost the exact location where he proposed to me earlier. "Are you ready to go fool around?" I ask him, figuring that he is probably more than ready to see what he's been missing all these years.

"I've been waiting a lifetime to be with you," he says sweetly. "A few more hours won't kill me. We can stay as long as you want and enjoy every moment of our wedding reception."

I appreciate his patience and willingness to continue to wait if it will make me happy, but I am ready. I want nothing more right now than to be with my husband. Since my new brave, carpe diem attitude has worked out quite well so far, I decide to embrace my new boldness. I get on my tiptoes to whisper huskily in Kai's ear, "I am ready to become one with you."

I tip back to my heels in time to see his eyes widen in surprise at my brazen comment, just before they darken with unbridled desire. He looks like he could eat me alive as he stares down at me, his chest rising and falling with each deep breath. He doesn't have to think about it long as he allows himself—probably for the first time in his adult life—to contemplate making love with a woman.

"You don't have to tell me twice," he proclaims as he grabs my hand, whisking me away.

I hear chuckles from the revelers in the tent as the two of us jog away hand in hand, leaving no doubt as to what we are about to do. At least we didn't announce it over the microphone, like Baggy would have if the helicopter hadn't drowned out her voice.

We decide to go to Kai's beach house, which is now our house. I can't even fathom that right now. *Whose marvelous life have I stolen, anyway?*

His house is too far from the resort to jog the entire way. We slow to a walk that is intermittently sprinkled with pauses to kiss and grope each other. It feels so amazing knowing that tonight, finally, we won't have to stop. As excited as I am, I can't imagine how much anticipation Kai must be feeling.

When we reach his property, I stop short, a sudden thought paralyzing me. "Kai," I start. "We aren't officially married. Should we wait until we have the license in order before we consummate the marriage?"

As long as he has waited, I don't want a simple matter of paperwork to make him feel guilty. I don't want to wait, but more than that, I want Kai to have a clear conscience when we make love.

He surprises me by looking up at the sky. "I believe my mom is smiling down on us right now." The idea makes me slightly uncomfortable, but I don't tell him that. "The intention of her request was to make sure that I didn't hurt someone the way my biological father hurt her. She wanted me to wait until I was ready to commit my life to someone before we shared our bodies with each other. Tonight, you and I declared our promises to live the rest of our lives together in front of some of the most important people to us. In my heart I am married to you, and that is what matters. I don't think some silly paperwork should stand in the way of that."

I nod in total agreement. "I just wanted to make sure."

His lips gently brush mine. "My heart and soul belong to you," he says intently. "Mom knows that." I nod again, seeking the heat of his lips with mine. When our lips separate slightly, he whispers, "It's time for my body to belong to you as well."

The anticipation of what is about to come is so heavy that I can barely breathe as we walk—hands locked—into his yard. *He's right*, I say to myself. *It's time.*

I must be channeling my inner Baggy because I break the significant tension of the moment with humor by repeating my exclamation from earlier in the evening. "Let's do this!" I shout, and we both bust out laughing.

"Let's do this," he agrees as he removes his shirt and tosses it aside.

EPILOGUE

To my surprise, we do not go inside the house. Instead, he leads me to the open-air hydrotherapy garden. I had seen the outdoor water circuit of various showers the day of my jellyfish attack, but I hadn't indulged in the tranquil, spalike experience.

"Since the day you were here," Kai reveals, "I have dreamed of taking you through the vitality showers as they are meant to be used."

I can't help but wonder what he means, but I am up for pretty much anything he has been dreaming about. After closing the small distance between us, I place my hands on his chest. He shivers as I graze my palms lightly over his bare skin.

We kiss each other hungrily. My fingers rake down his back. When he tilts his head back to hiss in air, I seize the opportunity to press light kisses down his neck and across his chest. I circle to his back to brush my lips across the red marks my fingers have just made. When I flick my tongue out to lick them, he lets out a deep, seductive growl, which spurs me on.

Moving back around to face him, I take a step back away from him. His eyes take on a slightly panicked look until he sees me seductively reach for the zipper of my seashell-pink wedding dress. With painstaking care and deliberate slowness, I undress for my husband.

He watches every move I make with a look that is a delicious mixture of awe and unadulterated lust. His gaze makes me feel beautiful and sexy, and I like it.

After I twirl my panties in the air from one finger and toss them away, he quickly shucks the rest of his clothes. I just want to stare at his body. It is absolutely magnificent—rock solid and sexier than I could have even imagined. Okay, I don't want to just stare at it. I want to touch it, too.

He walks to the entrance of the ring of showers and points out a rock that I hadn't noticed before. Etched into the stone is a stick figure drawing depicting a man and woman having missionary-style sex.

I can feel Kai's hand shaking slightly as we both lie down on the ground. I am pleasantly surprised to find the shower floor has soft, gel-like mats that provide a comfortable barrier from the concrete. This oasis was made for having sex. I wonder briefly who installed it. My best guess is Nana Lana, so I decide to immediately put that thought out of my head.

Our naked bodies are stretched out beside each other. He runs a hand lightly over my skin as we kiss. Deciding the foreplay has gone on long enough, I pull Kai on top of me. We look deep into each other's eyes as he presses into me. He stays there, deep inside me, enjoying the moment. He drops tender kisses onto my forehead, nose, cheeks, and lips, which makes me feel cherished.

He slowly slides in and out of me a few times. It feels glorious. Something with our movement sets off the sensor and warm water begins raining down on us. We laugh in surprise, then Kai shocks me by pulling out of me.

At my questioning look, he says, "We can't stay at any of the stations very long or we'll never make it around the circle tonight."

Understanding dawns on me. I'm dying to see what thrills the other stations hold, so I hop up and follow him to the next one.

The rock at this shower shows one figure sitting while the other kneels in front. "We can skip this one, if you want," Kai offers.

Is he actually blushing? For an answer, I gently shove him down to a seated position on the gel-covered rock slab before kneeling down on the gel pad at the ground in front of him. I kiss and lick my way along his chest and down the side of his firm abs. The water spray at this pleasure station starts, and I am tickled with a fine mist along my backside.

He tips his head back and moans in ecstasy when I take him inside my mouth. In an extreme and impressive show of willpower, he says, "We better move to the next shower right now, or I won't make it any farther this round."

I like the sound of "this round." The thought of perfecting our lovemaking technique at this circle of pleasure sends a thrill through my already excited body.

When we look at the next suggestive etching, it is my turn to blush. "We don't have to do this one, if you don't want to," I offer.

"Are you kidding me? It's payback time," he teases me. "I want to bring you so much pleasure that you can't think of anything but me for days," he growls near my ear. I'm quite sure that is already the case, but I don't tell him that.

After he eases me down into a sitting position on the mat, I reach a hand out to wrap my fingers around him. He inhales sharply before telling me to lie back and relax. I grab a fistful of his hair as he suckles each breast before making his way down my belly. When he nibbles on the inside of each of my thighs before gently placing my leg over his shoulder, I let out a little whimper of anticipation and delight.

He hesitates, and I wonder if I'm not what he expected. I am splayed before him, completely open and vulnerable.

My insecurities melt away when he looks up at me. His melted chocolate eyes are filled with a look of utter adoration. "You are so beautiful," he murmurs before lowering his mouth to me.

As if it somehow knows the perfect time, the water starts streaming down, pelting in glorious jets against my breasts. I cry out in pure bliss as he worships me with his magical lips and tongue.

The tremors of pleasure are still jolting through me when we make eye contact again. "I want you inside me NOW," I tell him.

We don't bother to move to the next shower as we sit up and scramble to meld out bodies together. I mount him and we both groan when I lower myself onto him, taking him all the way in. Riding him slowly, I enjoy the full feeling of having him deep inside me.

As I start to feel the pressure building again, I pick up the pace of my hip thrusts. "Let go with me," I order him.

"Yes, ma'am," he responds, likely relieved that I don't expect him to make it all the way around the circle on our initial spin.

The smell of fragrant flowers engulfs us as warm jets of water pelt down with delightful precision on all the right spots of our joined bodies. I pump harder over him. When he cries out in release, I again spiral into the vortex of pulsing ecstasy.

We are both breathing hard, spent. I rest my head against

his broad shoulder. The night is warm and clear. It seems like a bazillion stars are twinkling at us from above, and I have just had the most mind-blowing sex of my life.

"Wow." It's a simple statement, but it says so much.

"Wow." I agree and kiss his neck. The water has stopped; so when I shiver, he asks if I am cold. "No," I shake my head. "Just ridiculously happy."

After a while, he says, "I'm sorry I couldn't last for a full revolution around the circle."

I smile at him, wondering what other sensuous delights the circle has in store for us. "We can spend the rest of our lives practicing," I reassure him, grinning.

Judging by his reaction to my offer, I think he agrees wholeheartedly.

~

*R*ead on for a sneak peek of Ruthie's exciting story, *Cruising for Love*.

NANA LANA'S COCONUT OIL
BEAUTY TIPS

If you haven't yet discovered the luxurious, super-moisturizing benefits of coconut oil, Nana Lana suggests running (not walking) to get some right now—unless you have a coconut allergy. For skin and hair application, be sure to use unrefined, extra virgin coconut oil. Below are just a few uses for this magical hydrator.

- Slather it on as an extreme skin softener. Coconut oil is solid below 76 degrees, so either rub between your palms to warm it before applying or heat it in a wax warmer for a few minutes until it becomes liquid. (Don't forget to test the temperature to make sure it isn't too hot.) Putting it on immediately following a shower or right before bed will work wonders on parched skin. Be sure to put on old clothes or a robe for a few minutes after applying—until the oil has a chance to be absorbed —or stay naked!
- Apply with a cotton ball to use as a gentle makeup remover.

- Tap it gently around eyes (not too close), on the backs of hands, or on the neck to utilize it as an antiwrinkle cream.
- Tame frizzy hair with a tiny dab. Bonus: it also adds shine. Be careful not to use too much on hair —less is definitely more on your locks.
- Alleviate allergy symptoms by applying inside nostrils.
- Increase sun tolerance—equivalent to SPF 4.
- Shave with it for an ultra-moisturizing shaving cream.
- Rub into cuticles to use as a cuticle softener.
- Swirl a dab in your palm along with your favorite face cream. The added moisture will give your skin a velvety texture without the greasy feeling of undiluted oil.
- Massage it into wet hair for a super-hydrating leave-in hair conditioner.
- Steam up your romantic time by using it as an all-natural personal lubricant. It works better than most of the store-bought versions, without the harsh chemicals.
- Add salt or sugar to make a softening body scrub. Experiment by mixing in your favorite essential oil or pure vanilla extract.

The list of coconut oil's potential uses and benefits goes on and on. Best of all—the light, coconut odor leaves you smelling like a relaxing Pina Colada on the beach!

CRUISING FOR LOVE SNEAK PEEK

"*H*itting the cow in the road was *not* my fault!" I inform the others, making them burst into laughter yet again.

"Whose fault was it...the COW's???" This incredulous question comes from my best friend, Macy. She looks especially cute tonight because she has set her sights on her new co-worker, Kyle. When Kyle mentioned wanting to try the new Mexican restaurant in town, Macy had quickly thrown together this small group outing to ease her path into getting to know him better. I see them make eye contact, beaming at each other, and realize that my ridiculous hot mess of stories is serving as the ideal ice-breaker for them, which is likely exactly what Macy had intended when she brought up my less-than-stellar driving record.

"Well, yeah. I mean, what was it doing in the middle of the road?" It makes perfect sense to me, but they are still laughing at me. I chuckle, even though the hilarity is at my expense. I know it sounds crazy, but these odd situations just somehow seem to find me.

ANN OMASTA

"Is the cow okay?" This concerned question comes as the first words of the evening from our suddenly quiet friend, Jasmine. Jas is one of the most outlandishly fun people I know, but it takes her a while to warm up to strangers. Having the new faces from Macy's law office join us for dinner has evidently caused her shyness to flare up.

"The cow is fine," I reassure her. "My car on the other hand..." I let the sentence dangle, allowing the group to draw their own conclusions about my car's fate after tangling with a bovine. "I still go visit the cow occasionally," I add, "but I don't think she likes me."

"You're probably not her favorite person," Kyle confirms, earning a flirty eyelash flutter from Macy.

When the waiter drops off our second pitcher of frozen margaritas, Macy stands to pour refills of the slushy, lime deliciousness into everyone's glasses. She manages to give Kyle a lengthy peek at her ample cleavage as she bends to pour his drink. I can't help but chuckle as I watch his eyes nearly pop out of his head. If her intention with that maneuver had been to get his attention, she definitely succeeded.

"Tell them about your wreck with the Dr. Pepper truck, Ruthie." She encourages me to move on to the next car disaster story as she sits down and digs into the fresh basket of chips and salsa that have unobtrusively appeared at the table.

"Okay, but that one really wasn't my fault," I start, making them all laugh in anticipation of another of my ridiculous-but-true vehicle stories.

"They never are." Macy shakes her head at me.

As I proceed to tell them about the Dr. Pepper truck fiasco, which ended with my convertible being filled with exploding cans of hissing Dr. Pepper, I know we are being much too loud in the crowded restaurant. We are having fun, though, and I don't want to try to hold down the volume on our merriment.

Just then, one of the only people who could ruin my great mood walks in. She is already seated by the time she sees me, or I'm certain she would have slunk out of the restaurant like the man-stealing traitor that she is. My sister's ex-best-friend, Lizzie, and I make eye contact for the first time since she shattered Roxy's wedding day by stealing the groom. I narrow my eyes into a cool glare until she looks away.

I note that she isn't with Gary, the prick who had the audacity to dump Roxy by text message on their wedding day. Rumor has it that the man-stealer and the cheating jerk have broken up. *Karma can be a bitch,* I think to myself. Even though Roxy is giddily happy with her Hawaiian hunk, Kai, whom she met on her would-be honeymoon, I'm not quite ready to forgive and forget what Lizzie and Gary did to her. I might never be.

Lizzie's mother joins her, and I force my attention back to our table. The topic of conversation has now moved from my accident-prone driving skills to the plethora of jobs that I somehow manage to get fired from. *Great, now they all know that I'm vehicle AND job-challenged,* I think to myself. "She's always coming in late or not showing up at all," Macy tells the table. "Once she dropped an entire tray loaded with food. It's *never* her fault, though."

"It's not," I affirm, making the group laugh again as Macy pats my arm in a slightly condescending (but somehow still loving) way. I don't get offended by her teasing. It is all true, after all. My life is a series of complete disasters.

"She lost one job because she couldn't stand to leave Hawaii to come back to work," Macy shares with the group.

"It was HAWAII." I smile at them, lifting my shoulders as

if that explains it all. *I might as well own it,* I decide. "Besides, it was totally worth losing that cocktail waitressing job to stay in paradise a bit longer. I was able to attend Baggy's wedding while I was there. Baggy is my crazy grandmother," I clarify for Macy's co-workers. Deciding to go all in, I confide, "I missed my sister's wedding that same night, though, because I thought I saw Jason Momoa, and I went chasing after him."

Most of the others are shaking their heads in bewilderment, as if my life is the biggest train wreck they have ever encountered. "It wasn't him, but it *really* looked like him. I just *had* to follow him and find out."

It is quiet for a bit, so I add, "I guess I'm truly a jump-in-with-both-feet kind of gal...none of that dipping a toe in to test the water stuff for me." I smile at them, and most of them smile back.

As if the universe heard my bold declaration, a tall, well-dressed (if slightly slick looking) gentleman appears at our table. He hands me a business card, which I peer at warily. The card is made of thick black stock that feels surprisingly heavy in my hand. The gold block lettering says simply, "T.J. Stone, Producer."

I crane my neck up at him with a questioning look. Checking him out more closely, I find that he's wearing a tailored, dark suit. He is tan and has on more jewelry than any of the men from this area in the Midwestern section of the country would normally wear. I quickly decide he must be from California or New York City.

Speaking for the first time, he looks down at me and informs us, "I couldn't help overhearing your stories." I wonder if he expects an apology for our rowdiness. *He's not getting one,* I think to myself. *We were just having fun.* Instead of chastising us, he floors me by saying, "How would you like to be the world's next big reality television star?"

~

Get *Cruising for Love* now to continue reading Ruthie's exciting story.

REVIEWS ~ BEST. GIFT. EVER.

Now is the time to help other readers. Many people rely on reviews to make the decision about whether or not to get a book. You can help them make that decision by leaving your thoughts on what you found enjoyable about this book.

<u>If you liked this book, please consider leaving a positive review</u>. Even if it's just a few words, your input makes a difference and will be received with much gratitude.

ABOUT THE AUTHOR ~ ANN OMASTA

Ann Omasta is a USA Today bestselling author.

Ann's Top Ten list of likes, dislikes, and oddities:

1. I despise whipped cream. There, I admitted it in writing. Let the ridiculing begin.

2. Even though I have lived as far south as Key Largo, Florida, and as far north as Maine, I landed in the middle.

3. If I don't make a conscious effort not to, I will drink nothing but tea morning, noon, and night. Hot tea, sweet tea, green tea––I love it all.

4. There doesn't seem to be much in life that is better than coming home to a couple of big dogs who are overjoyed to see me. My other family members usually show significantly less enthusiasm about my return.

5. Singing in my bestest, loudest voice does not make my family put on their happy faces. This includes the big, loving dogs referenced above.

6. Yes, I am aware that bestest is not a word.

7. Dorothy was right. There's no place like home.

8. All of the numerous bottles in my shower must be lined up with their labels facing out. It makes me feel a little like Julia Roberts' mean husband from the movie *Sleeping with the Enemy*, but I can't seem to control this particular quirk.

9. I love, love, love finding a great bargain!

10. Did I mention that I hate whipped cream? It makes my stomach churn to look at it, touch it, smell it, or even think about it. Great––now I'm thinking about it. Ick!

On a serious note, I hope that you enjoy reading my contemporary romance novels as much as I love writing them!

LET'S STAY IN TOUCH!

Join Ann Omasta's Reader Group:

Get VIP access. Be the first to know about new releases, sales, freebies, and exclusive giveaways. We value your privacy and will not send spam.

Join at: annomasta.com

Connect with Ann Omasta on social media

LIKE Ann's Facebook page:
facebook.com/annomasta

FOLLOW Ann on Twitter, Goodreads, and Bookbub:
twitter.com/annomasta
goodreads.com/annomasta
bookbub.com/authors/ann-omasta

EMAIL Ann to be added to her mailing list:
author@annomasta.com

VISIT Ann's website:
annomasta.com

Are you a SUPER FAN of Ann's? Do you LOVE Ann's books? Do you READ all of Ann's books and leave REVIEWS? Do you like SHARING great books with your friends? If so, send an email message to <u>Ann</u> at author@anno masta.com to see if there is a slot available in her group: **ANN's CLAN.**

What's in it for you? You'll get Advance Review Copies (ARCs) of Ann's hot new releases, insider info, special give-aways, personal interaction with one of your favorite authors, and tons of other fun stuff. As a member of Ann's Clan, you might get to name a character in one of Ann's books, help choose a title, or vote on a book's cover. The possibilities are endless! Email now to see if there is an opening in **Ann's Clan**.